TIME OF JUSTICE

A Mara Brent Legal Thriller

ROBIN JAMES

He called it God's Brew. Here, the water churned to a frothy white then belched out brown and gold as it made its way over the rocks and dropped down the three-foot falls. At the base of it, the smaller baitfish would spill. Stunned for a moment, they made an easy meal for the larger panfish. Walleye, smallmouth, sometimes even catfish. Here, Tucker Welling told me he could catch a fish on nearly every cast. His grandfather taught him how to bait a hook in this very spot for the first time when he was three years old. Tucker had done the same with his son. He would have done the same with his grandson, but now he could never go back. The place gave him nightmares.

I stood at the side of the road staring down at Tucker Welling's God's Brew. There were a handful of other fishermen there now. I wondered if they had a clue about what Tucker found here two decades ago. Though it haunted his dreams, it had been nothing short of a miracle.

If it weren't for those three-foot falls and those stunned minnows, Tucker might have tried his luck upstream. Or maybe he wouldn't have come out that day at all. But he did. He was here. In this spot with the sun shining directly in his eyes. It made him lose his footing and he fell face-first into the soft embankment.

That's when he saw her. Though, at the time, he couldn't tell if it was a man or woman. She was caked with blood, her face battered and bruised. Tucker didn't need to be a doctor to know this poor person would never get up on her own again even if she were still alive. Her legs were at wrong angles. As he pulled himself out of the dirt and went to her, he saw the ropes around her wrists and two more around her legs. At the end of one of her feet, Tucker saw the block of cement tied to the other end of the rope. It was then she opened one swollen, blood-caked eye and managed to mouth the word "help."

The fishermen spotted me standing on the berm. I got a friendly wave from one and a curious, cock-eyed smile. I didn't belong here. Anyone could see. In my three-inch heels and tailored blue suit, I clearly hadn't come for the fish.

To be honest, I don't know why I came here that day. Actually, I did it once or twice a year. Ever since I heard about Tucker Welling and the broken woman he found dying by the side of the Maumee River.

The wind kicked up and I took it as a sign it was time to go. I don't know. This bend in the river was a place where a miracle could happen and sometimes I needed that reminder. As I turned toward my car, I wondered if this might just be the last time I ever came here. When I did, I found myself praying for her. Praying I could give her the one thing she asked me for. I smiled as I tucked a hair back into place and slipped behind the wheel.

God had been here that day, watching over Denise Silvers as she lay broken and dying. And He'd guided Tucker Welling to her. I could only wonder what plan He had for me in all of this.

I drove the winding road along the river until it split off toward town. Waynetown, Ohio, population 28,813, was tucked into the valley. We were a sleepy little town without the crime rate of neighboring Toledo. Eight hundred miles from the affluent New Hampshire town where I was born. It was never in the cards for me to end up here. Except, like Tucker Welling on that fateful April day twenty years ago, I now knew it was exactly where I was supposed to be.

I was due back at the office within the hour. I could have done this by phone, but it was important for me to deliver the news in person.

I turned down Gaylord Street. It was quiet here, abutting the woods. Most of the homes here were built near the turn of the last century. They had fallen into disrepair by the 1970s. Over the last twenty years though, the area had gone through gentrification, the houses restored.

Denise Silvers lived in an adorable craftsman style home painted white with yellow trim. The long wooden ramp leading to the back door was decorated with flower boxes. Pink and purple geraniums quivered in the breeze, almost as if they were waving to me. I parked in the side lot and turned off my engine.

I left my briefcase in the car as I walked up the ramp, my heels knocking loudly beneath me. I peered in the front door.

"Denise?" I called out. "It's Mara. You have time for a visit?"

"Let yourself in," she said, her voice cheery and bright. I opened the screen door and walked into Denise's living room.

She sat in the corner, stick-thin legs poking out beneath a black-and-red Afghan I knew she'd knitted herself. Her hands worked at a furious pace, her knitting needles a blur as she produced another. This one made of yellow, white, and purple yarn.

"It's for a baby shower," Denise said. "Just got the order a week ago. Special client. It would have to be cuz I don't like working this fast."

"It'll be gorgeous," I said. "They always are."

"Sit down," Denise said. "You have that look on your face. Something's wrong."

I smiled. I met Denise Silvers the first week after I got hired as a Maumee County assistant prosecutor. I took the job against the protest of my mother, Natalie Roth Montleroy, the king-maker of New Hampshire politics. I had my reasons. I'd been warned about Denise from day one. Actually, my boss, Philip Halsey, had mentioned her almost as an afterthought.

"Oh," he'd said. "Denise will be at your doorstep soon enough. She can smell fresh blood a mile away. She knows she's a hopeless cause. She just wants to make sure nobody in this office ever forgets her."

I don't know how anyone could. Denise had a kind face, deep-set green eyes. Her once blonde hair had gone almost white even though she was just forty-one years old. Her hands were gnarled like a much older woman's as well, with deep purple veins webbing over her knuckles.

I'd seen pictures of her as a younger woman. High school

4

yearbook photos. She'd been a popular, vivacious girl with a knock-out figure and ready smile. Captain of the cheerleading squad. Homecoming queen.

She wanted to be a nurse like her mother before her. There was still plenty left of that wonderful girl. But Denise's eyes had dulled from the horrors she'd experienced.

Other photographs I'd seen of her often came to the forefront of my mind. I saw her in a hospital bed, her face swollen and beaten beyond recognition. The bones around her left eye had been crushed, her lips torn.

Deep, cruel ligature marks cut through her wrists. Each injury had been carefully documented and filed away. Her attacker had taken her from behind, covering her mouth with a cloth as she kicked and screamed.

She remembered waking up in a moving vehicle, her hands and feet bound with rope. She knew she'd already been raped once. She could still feel it. She couldn't see her captor as he'd put duct tape over her eyes, her mouth. Later, she would scar from its removal.

But Denise Silvers still had fight left in her that day. And there were miracles yet to come.

Her captor had stopped the vehicle. He dragged her out by her feet. She tried to kick, scream, wriggle away.

He dropped her. That's how the bones of her face broke. He hummed as he dragged her from the rough pavement to the softer grass. He sang "Oh Susanna" as he tightened the rope around her ankles. She felt the weight of the cement and knew it might be her day to die.

It wasn't though. Something made her monster stop. She

remembered his voice, going from that sing-song quality to something dark and sinister.

She felt the headlights cut through the duct tape covering her eyes as another car approached. Headlights. It was night or early morning. She didn't know which. Only that she'd suffered hours of torture. Denise found the strength to kick out. She had no way of knowing how close she was to an embankment leading straight down to the river.

Down and down she tumbled. Her spine cracked at the base along the way. She didn't feel it though. She told me she never felt it. She only felt cold and alone.

"Denise," I said. I reached for her. She stilled her knitting needles.

"How long have we known each other?" I asked.

"Eight years," she said. "And you're the only one left who will put up with me."

That got a laugh out of me. "Well, I mean. You can be a lot."

She waved me off. "I've only ever gotten up to a five with you, Mara. I save eight through ten for Phil."

Oh, I'd seen Denise at a ten. Once, she'd rammed her wheel-chair into Phil's shins right as he was about to field questions from the press.

After Denise's attack, she'd formed a victims' advocacy group called The Silver Angels. They acted as liaisons for victims of sexual violence between the prosecutor's office and law enforcement. They provided support during trials and parole hearings. Denise and her volunteers would often stand at the hospital bedsides of new victims, providing a steady hand and a friendly face while rape kits were administered.

Denise herself held the dubious honor of having the coldest rape case in Maumee County history. The moment I was assigned my first sex crime case, Denise was at my door.

"Well," I said. "I think Phil deserves it most of the time. Keeps him humble. Though I'll never admit I said that. We clear?"

Denise smirked. "Oh, we're clear. You're one of the good ones, Mara. Though *I'll* never admit that. We clear?"

I held out my hand to shake Denise's. Her grip was firm.

"So," she said. "Tell me the bad news. I can already guess. I had a call from Kimberly Marks late last night. Phil won't go to bat for her. Is that it?"

Kimberly Marks had been one of our more problematic cases of late. She alleged a date rape against a friend of her brother's. Unfortunately, two witnesses—friends of his—provided him with a solid alibi. Kimberly said they were all lying. I believed her. But right now there was no good way to prove it.

"They're going to drop the charges," I said. "I'm sorry."

Denise waved me off. "Right. Your hands are tied."

"Denise," I said, shifting in my chair. "I didn't actually come here to talk to you about Kimberly's case. I came to talk about yours."

Denise went still. She folded her hands in her lap and painted on an unnatural smile.

"Denise," I said. I moved closer to her. "Look at me."

She did. She blinked rapidly. I'd known her for over eight years now. She trusted me. As much as she hated what happened with the Kimberlys of the world, she knew I was forever on her side.

"Denise," I said, swallowing hard. I'd played this moment in my mind a million times over the years. I made her promises we both knew I shouldn't. I did it anyway.

"Don't," she said, her voice breaking.

"We got him," I said. Then I repeated it, my voice even harder. "We *got* him. Are you hearing me?"

She shook her head no.

"Yes," I said. "His name is Neil Shumway. I told you I submitted the DNA from your rape kit to a genealogy site over a year ago. Well, we got a hit. He had a daughter he didn't even know about. Through her, we were able to trace him. Do you hear what I'm telling you? There's no doubt. It's a match, Denise. He's been arrested and charged. It's happening."

Silent tears fell down her face. "Neil Shumway?" she asked.

I nodded. "And I'm going to nail his ass to the wall for you."

Denise exhaled. I had the sense it was a breath she'd been holding in for twenty years.

She reached for me, gripping my shoulders. Though she could never move her legs again, Denise's hands were mighty.

"Promise me," she whispered. "Swear it to God."

"I swear," I said. "He's being extradited from Michigan as we speak. I've had some help from a lawyer there his daughter hired to help find her birth parents. We're gonna get him, Denise. He's going to pay for what he did to you."

Finally, she let her shoulders drop and nodded.

"I knew you'd be the one," she whispered. "From the second I met you. I just knew. So go do it. Let's nail that bastard to the wall."

I hugged Denise. Tucker Welling had delivered the first miracle when he found her by the side of the Maumee River and saved her life. Now, it was up to me to deliver the second and make her monster pay for what he'd done.

Chapter 2

"He doesn't look like a rapist."

I froze, squeezing the ballpoint pen in my hand so hard I'm surprised the ink didn't spill.

"What?" I said. I turned to the young kid sitting at the desk beside me. Scott Farmer. He was new. A twenty-one-year-old summer intern fresh from the paralegal program in one of the nearby community colleges. He was on his way to law school this fall.

Scott shrugged. He kept his voice mercifully low so no one but me could hear him. "He looks like ... I don't know ... Lance Armstrong or something."

I looked across the room. Neil Shumway sat at the defense table calmly pushing on his cuticles. Though I wanted to smack him, Scott Farmer was right about the Lance Armstrong resemblance.

Shumway was sixty-four years old but from a distance could easily pass for twenty or thirty years younger. Tall, lanky, with a runner's build and coarse blond hair that went gray only at the temples. He wore a black suit with a light-blue tie. Twice, he caught my eye and shot me a bright smile.

"What is a rapist supposed to look like, Scott?" I said dryly through gritted teeth.

"Uh, sorry," Scott said, realizing the idiocy of his remark.

I had no more time to school this kid on this particular point before Judge Rita DeCamp took the stand. She was just about as fresh as the Farmer kid, only having been appointed by the governor three months ago.

Her job here was easy. She read Shumway's indictment into the record. The grand jury bought everything I presented. Shumway was on the hook for rape, kidnapping, attempted murder, and the lesser charge of aggravated assault. If convicted, he'd never see the light of day again. If Denise Silvers hadn't had her miracle through Tucker Welling and died, this would be a death penalty case.

"How do you plead, Mr. Shumway?" Judge DeCamp asked, barely looking up from her notes.

Shumway leaned toward his attorney, Matt Orville. Matt was well known throughout the state as a top-notch criminal defense lawyer. He'd crossed paths with my office a half a dozen times. Though I'd never personally tried a case against him, his record against Maumee County prosecutors was perfect. Matt had scored acquittals on four murder cases and two drug cases.

"Absolutely not guilty, Your Honor," Shumway spoke into the microphone. His voice had an almost southern lilt to it. That made a certain degree of sense. My research told me he'd been raised a few miles south of Cincinnati before winding up in mid-Michigan. He'd made his money as a pharmaceutical sales rep serving clients in Michigan, Ohio, Indiana, and parts of Wisconsin. We had a task force working on tracking his movements over the last thirty years to try and connect him to the dozens of other unsolved sexual assaults and two murders.

"Your Honor," I said. "The State objects to bail in this case for the reasons set forth in our memorandum."

"Your Honor," Matt spoke up. "I'll be honest, I've never seen anything as egregious as the State's memo on this. There is no basis in the law that allows a criminal defendant to be penalized for crimes he's not even close to being charged with committing. I mean, I wouldn't be surprised if Ms. Brent and her colleagues march in here accusing my client of being Jack the Ripper. It's ludicrous."

"Judge," I said. "Mr. Shumway is a person of interest in no less than a dozen cases covering four states. He has significant resources and ties to those four states. He poses a substantial flight risk and as we've presented, the law is clear. The court is free to take these factors into consideration under the circumstances. We do not believe bail is appropriate in this case."

"I agree." Judge DeCamp said it so abruptly I had to clamp my mouth shut to keep from arguing something I'd already won.

Matt Orville didn't shut his mouth. He yammered on for a full minute about the travesty this court was about to perpetuate. Judge DeCamp sat calmly and listened. When Matt paused to draw a breath, she banged her gavel.

"Bail is denied. Mr. Shumway will be remanded to the

Maumee County jail for the time being. You'll have a sched-
uling order from my office by the end of the week. That is all."

For his part, Shumway stayed remarkably calm. He even had
a polite smile for the two deputies who came forward to cuff
him and lead him through a side door. Though Neil
Shumway would likely escape media attention today, I knew I
would not. Matt Orville would eat it up and thump his chest
about how sure he was his client would be vindicated. As a
prosecutor, I could not participate. The reporters outside the
courtroom would get nothing but a terse no comment
from me.

I collected my files, ignored the icy smile from Neil Shumway
as I passed within a foot of him, and headed out the doors
with Scott Farmer sprinting to keep up.

"HE's IN THE THRONE ROOM," Caroline Flowers said as I
walked into the office. Caro had the dubious honor of being
the longest-serving county employee. She started out as a file
clerk in probate court back when it was housed in the bowels
of the old City-County building. Twenty years ago, Waynetown and Maumee County offices finally got their own space
and Caro moved to the prosecuting attorney's office. She
pretty much ran the place. Elected prosecutors would come
and go but Caro kept the engine running.

"He's ready for me?" I asked.

Caro nodded. She got along reasonably well with my boss,
Philip Halsey. There were those who thought he simply
inherited the job. There had been a Halsey serving in some
facet of the county government for something like sixty years.

Phil's father had been a common pleas judge. His grandfather had also been the prosecutor. It was a rough reputation to shake, and for many, Philip never would. For me, I empathized with him. Though I was a New Hampshire transplant, I too came from a long line of public servants. Plus, Phil had hired me one year out of law school when I had no track record to speak of. He'd been a fair boss and worthy mentor.

But Philip Halsey wasn't without his affectations. I walked into his corner office and found him leaning far back in his leather chair with his shoeless feet up on the desk and his hands tucked behind his head.

He straightened when I crossed his threshold and spit out the unlit cigar he liked to chew on. He quickly shoved it into his "secret drawer" where he also kept a decanter of bourbon he liked to bust out on Friday afternoons. "What happened?" he asked.

"No bail," I said, smiling.

Phil had just turned sixty. He had a thick head of salt-and-pepper hair and a well-groomed mustache that turned up at the corners.

"Fantastic," he said, beaming. "Mara, that's excellent news. How was Matt Orville?"

"Strutting around like a peacock," I answered. "I didn't stick around to hear his soliloquy to the local media. The Farmer kid was going to take notes for me."

"Good, good," he said. "And that was some great work you did before the grand jury. This case is going to get national attention. You know that, right?"

Phil's voice took on a certain tone that sent my stomach dropping to the floor. I closed my eyes for a moment to steady myself. I felt my temper rising. Phil gestured toward the chair on the opposite side of his desk.

"Sit down, Lady Montleroy," he said. It was an affectionate nickname he used, playing on my mouthful of a maiden name.

I did. I crossed my legs and folded my hands. "What's going on, Phil? I know that look. You've got something to tell me and you don't think I'm going to like it."

"Mara," he said. "You've done incredible work on this case so far. If it weren't for you, Neil Shumway wouldn't even be on anyone's radar. It was your idea to submit the DNA sample from the Silvers's crime scene to that genealogy site. And you're the one who kept following up with that. How long has it been?"

"Almost five years," I said. "That sample has been sitting in the Tree of Life database for almost five years. It was sheer luck that Shumway ended up getting one of his victim's pregnant. And it was a miracle she chose to have that child and she submitted her own DNA to that site."

"And you tracked it all down," he said. "That had to have come as a hell of a shock to his daughter. Man. I can't even imagine."

"What's this about?" I asked. "You're acting like this story is news to you. I know you. You're buttering me up for something. Just come out with it."

Phil's face fell. I knew that look in his eyes and felt a cold chill down my spine.

"I'm getting some pressure," he said. "Orville's reputation in this county has a few people scared."

"Well," I said. "He's never faced *me* in court."

My comment had a little more teeth than warranted, but my gut told me something else. I didn't say the obvious next sentence. Five of Matt Orville's victories were against Phil himself.

"Mara," Phil said. "I don't think you realize how much attention this case is going to bring. Shumway's DNA matched what, four other rapes? And there's that girl in Kalamazoo they like for her murder?"

"None of that is on my radar right now," I said. "I mean it is, but we have one case. One very solid case against him for what happened to Denise Silvers. That's my focus."

"The Silver Angels," he said. "That's another thing. Look, Mara. You're a star. I don't have to tell you that. It's just, I don't think it's a good idea to have you in the center of this thing when it goes to trial."

My lungs burned. Rage boiled within me. He was bumping me?

"What are you talking about? Phil, this is my case. Nobody knows the ins and outs of the Silvers matter like I do. I've profiled this guy. You just said if it weren't for me he wouldn't ..."

"Mara," Phil cut me off. "People are worried about your baggage."

"My baggage?"

"If this thing catches fire like we think it will, it'll be on the trial cable channels. *Dateline*. *Fox News*. All of it. And we've got an election coming up. You can't want that kind of a spot-light on you right now."

I couldn't breathe.

"So this isn't about my skill in the courtroom at all. You think my personal life will interfere with me doing my job? Phil. You know me. You know what I can do. And you know I'm the only one who can make sure Neil Shumway goes down for this."

"And it's not all the way up to me," he said. "Mara, Matt Orville is a predator. A shark."

"So am I," I said, my voice dropping low.

"I know. But he's going to go after you. He'll air your dirty laundry. And if that happens, it's not just bad for the case."

My heart dropped. Phil kept dancing around it, but I read the truth in his eyes.

"Say it," I said.

"Mara."

"No, I mean it. I need to hear you actually say it."

He pounded a fist to his desk. "Dammit, Mara. Don't you get it? I'm trying to help you! Are you going to sit there and tell me you want someone like Matt Orville poking around in your personal life? Because he will. You can be sure of it. And when he does, he won't just ruin your life and muddy the waters on this case."

"Jason's people?" I said, my breath coming quick. "Are you telling me my husband's campaign is behind this?"

Phil didn't answer. His silence spoke volumes.

"Never mind," I said, rising. "I'm going to need you to grow a pair and tell them all to shove it. Because I'm not letting go. Not for you, not for Jason, and certainly not for Orville. The only way you're going to get me off this case is if you fire me."

Phil sat slack-jawed as I stormed out of his office and slammed the door.

Chapter 3

SEVEN YEARS AGO, this had been the house of my dreams. A rarity for Waynetown, it sat on a ten-acre, wooded lot with a small pond where Jason could teach Will how to fish. I drove up our long driveway, framed with tall oak and pine trees. The house itself was built in 1908, a two-story federalist style that we had restored.

It was supposed to be our forever home. I always knew Jason's political ambitions might take us to Columbus or even D.C. at times, but we'd always return to the house on Hyatt Road.

Sometimes, dreams become nightmares.

I parked my Lincoln in the detached garage and made my way up to the house. It was dark now. The lights were only on in the kitchen and Will's playroom.

I found Kat waiting for me at the white quartz kitchen island I just had to have. She'd already poured me a glass of white wine.

"Bless you," I exhaled.

Kat sipped from her own glass and gave me that knowing look she had. "He won't come down from his room," she said. "He's working on the Carpathian."

"Ah," I said, taking a quick sip of wine.

I headed to the top of the stairs and stood leaning against the doorframe. My son, Will, had his back to me; hunched over, he sifted through a cedar chest full of Lego pieces. To me it looked like a needle in a haystack. But he always emerged with the perfect shape to add to his growing sculpture.

"Wow," I said. This morning, I'd left him in a pile of black bricks. Now they began to form into a one-hundred-year-old ocean liner. In one corner of the room, Will had built a four-foot-long replica of the *Titanic*. In another corner, he'd molded the beginnings of a copy of that same ill-fated ship as it appeared now, broken in half at the bottom of the Atlantic.

I went to him. Will didn't acknowledge me. He seldom did when his mind was at work like this. But he didn't move away or stiffen as I leaned in and kissed him in my favorite spot, that little patch of skin on his neck behind his left ear.

"Buddy, that's truly amazing," I said.

It was. My nine-year-old son was a master sculptor in Lego. Two years ago, Jason and I had taken him to Legoland on a Florida Disney trip. He'd been a goner ever since. I'd probably spent a few grand buying new kits for him every month.

"It had a capacity of seventeen hundred," he said. "Took them over three hours to get to the *Titanic* survivors in their lifeboats."

I knelt beside my son, watching his mind at work.

"Is that what you're going to build next?" I asked. "The lifeboats?"

He nodded. "People say it was a mistake not to fill them to capacity."

"Well," I said. "I mean, more people would have been saved, right?"

He shrugged. He looked so much like Jason when he was lost in concentration like this. They had the same line right between their eyes. The same dark lashes and gray eyes.

"They did the best they could," he said. "The ship was listing badly. They weren't so easy to launch. You can't imagine the stress."

"No," I said. "I can't. How was school today?"

Will shook his head from side to side. I knew he saw something in his imagination. Some tiny detail about the ship he was building wasn't right.

"Will," I said. "It's time to walk away for the day. You know what will happen if you start dismantling this thing now. I can't have you up all night. It'll all be here for you tomorrow. Give it a snap, okay?"

He sat back on his heel. He had a red rubber band around his left wrist. He did as I asked and snapped it once. Then the line on his forehead settled. I felt myself relax right along with him. That one was easy. They weren't always.

"Did you eat dinner?" I asked.

"Aunt Kat made spaghetti," he answered. "With the tube noodles."

He meant penne. They were his favorite. "Aunt Kat's spaghetti is the best. I'll have to dig into some leftovers later. You want to come down and watch some television with me later?"

"I'll take a bath," he said.

I smiled. "Okay. I'll meet you in the family room in an hour, okay?"

"Eight o'clock," Will said.

"Eight o'clock." I leaned in again. Will went stiff, but he didn't pull away as I kissed the top of his head. My little man was having a very good day today indeed. It helped make my own that much better.

He got up and headed into my bedroom. Will liked to take baths in my Jacuzzi tub with the jets. He had his own bathroom attached to his bedroom but he liked mine better. Jason hated that I encouraged him. But these days, he was the last person I'd take a lecture from on boundaries.

I slipped off my heels and headed down the hall as I heard the water running in my tub. I stopped at the study Jason had finished for me. It had a keypad lock. Anything else, Will could pick and open. I pressed the code and opened the door. I flicked on the light and stared at the far wall. We'd covered it with corkboard. Now, it was papered over with a giant U.S. map. Colored pushpins marked crime scenes. Each pushpin was connected to red yarn that led to a photograph of a different young woman.

Rape victims. Twenty-two in total. And then there were the two who hadn't survived.

I ran my hands along the map. I'd memorized the women's names by heart. I said them every night as a prayer.

The adjoining wall was covered with newspaper clippings from local papers highlighting the crimes. The timeline spanned over twenty years.

I picked up one clipping. It was a front-page feature from the *Toledo Blade*, our largest neighboring paper, published one year after Denise's attack. An update on the status of the case. A single photograph caught my eye. His haunted eyes stared back at me. This was Detective Ken Leeds, the lead detective assigned to the case from the Maumee County Sheriff's Department. I never got to know him. Ken died six years after this article's publication of a heart attack. Those still in the department considered Ken to be one of Neil Shumway's victims too. The case ate at him, much as it did me.

Above the map, I'd pinned my most recent photograph. Neil Shumway's mugshot stared down at me. He smiled in it as if it were a yearbook photo.

Scott Farmer's words echoed in my mind. *He doesn't look like a rapist.*

I prayed a jury could see past that charming smile. My hand settled on Denise Silvers's photo. It was taken a few months before her attack. So young. So vibrant. And because of the monster at the top of the wall, she'd never walk again.

This was my case. No matter what, I couldn't let Halsey take it from me. I knew the ins and outs of it like no one else. Jason said I'd become obsessed. Just like Will was with the *Titanic* disaster or presidential assassinations. He meant it as a criticism, but I knew it was my strength. And I also knew in my heart I would win. If Halsey would just give me a chance.

"HE HAD A GOOD DAY?" I asked Kat. I was on my second glass of wine now. She sipped hers and nodded.

"So did you, I hear," she said. "Shumway's arraignment was all over the internet. Will hasn't seen any of it. Don't worry."

"It's okay," I said. "It's going to continue to get a lot of press. He's bound to hear about it somewhere."

"Do you really think that bastard committed as many as thirty rapes?"

"Yes," I said. "I do. And I'm going to see to it he never sees the light of day again. The judge's bail denial was a big deal. Shumway's hired a hotshot lawyer who isn't used to that kind of loss."

Kat smiled. "Well, then he's not used to coming up against Mara Friggin' Brent." She raised her glass to clink mine. I didn't feel like telling her about the wrench my boss had just put into that plan.

I checked my phone. It was seven-thirty. I'd have just enough time to make the call I'd been dreading since I stormed out of Phil Halsey's office. But it had to be done.

"Can you keep an ear out for Will?" I asked. "I promised him we'd watch something at eight."

"On it," Kat answered. I was so lucky to have her. She was one of only five people Will felt wholly comfortable and unguarded around. When Kat agreed to move with Jason and me out to what she had to consider this little nowhere town, it meant the world to me. With everything that had happened over the last three months, I would have understood if she'd wanted to leave. It could have been awkward. Kat was Jason's family, not mine. But her loyalty was with Will. Whatever problems we had between us just didn't register for her. I loved Kat to the depths of my soul.

"He's called twice," Kat said, her expression grim. She'd answered the question I had yet to ask. "Mainly, I think he just wants to know if you're okay."

I pulled up the contacts on my phone. My thumb hovered over Jason's number. Was I okay? Would I ever be okay again where Jason was concerned?

As his contact picture popped up, I felt ripped in two. I believed I would forever have those warring emotions where he was concerned. I missed his solid strength, the warmth of his body, how he could comfort me like no one else. Then I replayed that single phone call from a stranger that changed our lives forever.

"I'll go check on Will," Kat said. "Be down in a few. Try not to kill my brother while I'm gone."

She shot me a wink to take the sting out of her words. It didn't help.

I walked into the family room and sat on the couch. I pulled the yellow-and-blue Afghan Denise made me around my shoulders. She'd knitted the University of Michigan block "M" at the center of it. My law school alma mater. The place that brought Jason into my life.

He answered on the first ring, breathless.

"Mara," he said. "I've been trying to reach you all day."

I thought I knew what I'd say to him. I always thought that.

Anger and grief rolled through me, making my heart pound. I took another sip of wine.

"Halsey's trying to pull me from the case," I said, knowing how flat my tone must have sounded.

Silence.

"This was you," I said. It was a statement, not a question. "Your people."

"Mara ..."

"Jason, this case is too important. Neil Shumway is mine. Nobody else will stand a ghost of a chance nailing him to the wall like I can."

"I know," he said. Jason's voice sounded defeated. "And no, this wasn't me. I didn't reach out to Phil Halsey."

"But your campaign manager did. Tell me the truth. Was this Len?" Len Grantham had helped elect the last two governors from Jason's party. He'd also worked on a winning presidential campaign. He handpicked Jason to serve in his current role as Ohio's Assistant Attorney General. A stepping stone to far greater things. As far as the party leadership was concerned, he was the best of the best. His job now was to make my husband the next U.S. Representative from Ohio's 5th congressional district. It had been the main reason why I agreed to move to Jason's tiny little hometown after we married. Beyond that, Jason's ambitions had no limit.

"I haven't talked to Len," he said. It was a classic cop-out. The grief in my heart flipped over to pure rage.

"Jason, I'm not walking away from this one. Not for you. Not for anyone. If Len's worried about it shining some spotlight on me or our marriage, then it's you who needs to step down. Pull out of the race. I don't care."

"I'll talk to Len," he said. "If he put pressure on Halsey to take you off this case, I'll undo it. I promise. But Mara ... we can't keep doing this. If Len or Phil are worried about problems with your personal life, the best way to fight that is to show them there are none."

"Don't," I said.

"Mara, I want to come home. I miss you. I miss Will. He misses me. We can be a family again. This doesn't have to ruin everything."

Tears welled in my eyes. No. I wouldn't do it. I would not cry. No more.

"I'm not what ruined us, Jason. That was all you. You and your new girlfriend."

He sighed into the phone.

"She's not ... God. Mara. I'll regret it for the rest of my life. I'll do whatever it takes. I'm not giving up on us. Not ever."

I shook my head and pulled the phone away from my ear.

"Save your air," I said. "I've said all I need to say for one day."

"Mara, I'll fix this. I swear. I'll deal with Phil and Len. Just let me come home."

My pulse skipped. "Is that an ultimatum? My God. Is that it? You throw a bomb into my career. Then you offer to defuse it if I let you move back into my house? Sleep in my bed?"

"No!" he shouted. "That's not what I'm doing."

Maybe it wasn't. The truth was, I believed Jason that he had no personal involvement in Phil Halsey's machinations today. But I knew in my heart his people did.

"Mara, I'll fix it. I swear to God. You'll have your case. The county can't afford to lose this trial and I know you're the one to win it. It's just ... are you sure? Because Halsey's right. Matt Orville will find out what's going on with us. Bet on it. And I know it's my fault. All of it. I'm so damn sorry, baby. I'll take whatever heat they throw at me and I'll deserve it. But it'll hit you too and I can't stop it. So ... are you sure?"

I lifted my chin. I took a steadying breath. "Jason, I don't have a choice. You may not have been able to keep your vows to me, but I will keep mine to Denise Silvers and the rest of those girls."

I didn't wait for his response. I ended the call. I found a smile as Will came downstairs hand in hand with Kat. She knew something was up by the look on my face but she never asked.

Will curled up beside me and my broken heart melted. At the same time, I knew this might be one of the last peaceful, almost normal days we had. My life was about to blow up all over again.

Chapter 4

WE WERE a small shop at the Maumee County Prosecutor's office. Though Phil was the public face, he didn't personally try many cases anymore. As the only one of us duly elected, he spent most of his time handling the political side of his job. He was a good boss on most days. A good manager. He hired the best people he could and then got out of our way to let us do our jobs.

That's why blocking me from the Shumway trial made no sense from a practical standpoint. Besides me, there were only two other full-time litigators in the office. Howard Jordan handled most of the white-collar crimes and criminal appeals. Kenya Spaulding and I split the felony docket with me taking almost all sex crimes exclusively. Misdemeanor cases rarely went to trial so Hojo, Kenya, and I rotated.

Four days after Shumway's arraignment, Phil still hadn't made a final decision on who would try the case. I busied myself on a few other pending matters and tried to keep my head down. I was doing just that when I felt a prickling along my spine that told me I was being watched.

Kenya stood in my doorway, her arms folded in front of her. She was a striking beauty with high cheekbones that looked like they'd been carved from granite. She stood over six feet tall in heels and had a mass of stunning braids she typically wore wrapped into a bun at the base of her neck. Kenya was a shrewd trial lawyer. Well-liked by most of the local bar and a mystery to most as she rarely socialized outside the office.

"This wasn't my doing," she said. Kenya often started conversations in what seemed like the middle of them. Some people found it rude. I'd learned over the years that Kenya's brain just seemed to operate on a faster frequency than most people's. She expected you to keep up. I'd like to believe I was one of the few people who could.

I put my pen down and folded my own arms in front of me. "I didn't think it was," I answered.

"I know ... everybody knows ... there wouldn't be a trial or an indictment or any of it if you didn't fight so hard."

My heart flipped. Kenya was talking like she knew something I didn't. Had Phil made the final call on who would spearhead this prosecution without giving me the courtesy of a heads up?

"Sit down," I said. Kenya looked behind her. She closed the door to my office and did as I asked. She wore ruby-red acrylic nails and clasped her hands over her knee.

"What's going on?" she asked. "Why is Phil even considering pulling you from this case?"

Her question struck me like a blow to the chest. As much as Kenya liked to keep her personal life to herself, she offered the same courtesy to everyone else in the office. For her to even be asking me this now meant she'd heard all sorts of rumors already.

"Mara," she said. "I'd like to think of us as part of a team. And maybe I don't share everything, but when I do, you know it's the truth. I've never bullshitted you."

"No," I said. "You haven't."

"Okay. So I won't start now. I *want* this case."

I let out a bitter laugh. "So was that whole speech about the work I've done just you handling me?"

"No," she said. "It's an acknowledgment. It's respect. You know you have that from me and you also know I don't hand it out frequently. But ... this is one of the most important cases to ever pass through this county. I've got the briefings from the task force too. They're thinking this monster's responsible for assaulting upwards of thirty victims. This case ... Maumee County ... it's the best of the lot in terms of the proof. If we don't nail him to the wall ... there's a chance nobody else will be able to either. That's not something I can live with."

"I can't live with it either," I said. "That's why I've put so much into building this case. I know more than the task force does about it. And Denise trusts me."

"And that's why you might be too close to this one," she said.

I felt my blood start to heat. "We're on the same team, remember?" I said, my voice taking a hard edge.

"We are," she said. "But if Halsey thinks there's a reason you shouldn't take point, it's got to be a good one. He's not talking."

"But other people are," I said. "Is that it?"

33

"Matt Orville plays dirty," she said.

"Of course he does," I answered. "He's a defense lawyer. He doesn't care whether Shumway did what they said he did. He took the case because he knows it'll keep him in the headlines."

"Yes," Kenya said. "People are starting to talk. About you."

I gritted my teeth. "You planning to enlighten me as to what they've been saying?" I hated that I asked. I hated that I cared.

Kenya stared me down, her brown eyes flashing. I didn't blink.

"I don't make friends, Mara," she said. "At least, not easily. But I meant what I said. I'm on your team. I will fight like hell for you against anyone or anything. I know you. But that doesn't mean I won't give it to you straight when it's warranted. Now, I don't like gossip. That said, in this instance … it's a distraction we don't need."

"Tell me what you heard, Kenya."

She took a breath. "I was approached," she said. "They were slick, but it didn't take much for me to figure out it was Evan Simpson's people."

Evan Simpson was my husband's opponent in his congressional race.

"Opposition research," I said. "Standard practice." I tried to wave it off, but Kenya was too sharp for that.

"Mara, they have something on Jason or on you. Something they think is big."

"What did you tell them?" I asked.

"Nothing," she insisted. "And you know you don't even have to ask me that. But I can admit to you that I did a little digging of my own. I wasn't trying to hurt you or even pry into your business. But these people reached out to me asking all sorts of questions about your personal life. And I'm not an idiot. Whatever this is has Phil thinking twice about putting you out in front of the Shumway case. If Evan Simpson's people have it, he's got to know Matt Orville will have it too. And it's likely he'll sell it to him."

"Does it matter?" I asked. "Did you come in here to tell me you want this case but you're too honorable to take it from me because of some dirty political dealing in my personal life?"

Kenya blinked. She bit her bottom lip. "No," she finally said. "If Halsey gives me this case, I'm going to take it either way."

A beat passed. Then I couldn't help myself. I barked out a laugh. Though part of me wanted to strangle her, more of me respected that Kenya Spaulding was one of the few people I could count on to give me unabashed honesty. I considered whether I would feel the same in her shoes. As Kenya kept that laser-focus on me, I knew she knew the answer to that question as well as I did. We were both very good at what we did. And we were equally ambitious.

It took a moment, but then the corners of Kenya's mouth lifted into a smile.

"Thanks," I said. "I actually do appreciate brutal honesty."

"Good," she said. There was something in her expression though. My throat ran dry as I realized what it was. As quickly as she'd figured out Evan Simpson's people were the ones to approach her about me, she clearly already knew at least the character of what they had on Jason and me.

I sat back in my chair, letting my shoulders drop. I took a breath. Kenya shook her head.

"That son of a bitch," she said. "He cheated on you."

I looked out the window. I had a view of the courthouse from here. The pear trees lining Cleveland Street had reached peak bloom. They swayed in the breeze.

"Yes," I finally answered.

"You think it was a set-up?" Kenya asked. "Or do you think he really had a thing for this chick?"

I shrugged. I felt my body go rigid. My shields were up, but somehow, I knew Kenya Spaulding was precisely the person I could trust with this secret. And it had been killing me for three months to bottle it up. She was right. We weren't friends, exactly, but she *was* on my team.

"I can't speak to his side of it," I said. "He says all the standard things you'd expect of a man in his position. But ... for her part, I found out by text. Picture texts, to be exact."

My stomach churned even thinking about those images that popped up in rapid succession on my phone. It had taken a few seconds for my brain to catch up with what my eyes had seen. Jason. My Jason. Those familiar curves of his body. The sleepy look in his eyes as he lay stretched out on a bed in a room I didn't recognize.

Then, there was her. Blonde. Thin. Cosmetically perfect.

"The bitch sent you pictures?" Kenya gasped. "She apparently missed a day in blackmail school."

"She tried it with Jason first," I said. "Or so he claimed. When he wouldn't bite, she figured I'd do just about anything to keep that stuff off the internet."

"Did you?" Kenya asked. "Pay her, I mean. Oh, crap. Is that what Simpson's people have? No. He didn't use campaign funds."

"No," I said. I realized it wasn't a full answer. Kenya, to her credit, didn't ask a follow-up.

"And Halsey knows enough about it he's afraid it'll distract from the Shumway trial if you're the face of it."

"Something like that," I said.

"Mara, I'm sorry. I mean it. Jason's an idiot. And it's all so ... ugh ... it's so inevitable. How the hell did he think he was going to keep a lid on this?"

I put a hand up. Kenya understood. I wasn't in the mood to dissect my husband's motives. Or mine for that matter.

"Thank you for telling me," she said. "I meant what I said. Any way that I can, I'll fight this off for you."

I smiled, believing her. "But you're still not going to let it stop you from taking the Shumway case from me if it comes to that."

Kenya rose. She had an odd smile on her face that gave me my answer. Once again, I had those twin urges to strangle her and shake her hand for at least coming at me head-on.

I rose to shake her hand. "Game on, then," I said, feeling the fire in my own eyes.

Kenya shook my hand and matched my grip.

Chapter 5

I MET attorney Cass Leary in the parking lot outside the Maumee County Public Safety building. She'd driven an hour to get here at my request. She was the lawyer I'd reached out to representing Neil Shumway's daughter, the one he never knew he had until now. The one whose DNA had finally broken this case. When Neil figured out who she was, he'd gotten close to Cass, lying about who he was. In the end, he tried to make Cass one of his victims. He had assault charges pending in Delphi, Michigan over it.

She was his type. Thin. Blonde. Pretty. Thank God she'd been able to do the thing so many of his other victims couldn't. Cass had fought back hard. She stood before me, eyes shining. She greeted me with a warm smile and held out her hand to shake mine.

"Thanks for coming," I said.

"Wouldn't miss it," Cass said. "Whatever I can do to help put that asshole away forever."

"How's Alicia handling all of this?" I asked. Alicia was Shumway's biological daughter.

Cass carried a large leather messenger bag. The thing reminded me more of something Indiana Jones would carry rather than a proper briefcase. She adjusted it on her shoulder. "She's good. She's eager to see Shumway brought to justice."

"The task force just wants a quick briefing on what happened to you," I said as we turned and started walking toward the building. "I can't use it in the Silvers trial, unfortunately. But I think they're looking at similarities to the other crimes he's suspected of committing. And you're the only one who's ever really had a chance to talk to the man to know what he's like. They're interested in your insights."

"Shumway's a chameleon," Cass said. "He was one thing to me. All charm and lies. I hear he's hired Matt Orville. You know he's gonna fight you tooth and nail to keep even the slightest mention of any prior or subsequent bad acts out of this."

"Oh, I expect mistrial motions aplenty," I said. "I'll be ready."

Cass smiled. "Good."

We went up the elevator together. The conference room was already full. I quickly introduced Cass and took a seat beside her.

"This meeting is a courtesy," Phil opened with. I gritted my teeth. Kenya sat on the other side of me and I saw her eyes flicker at Phil's statement as well. Something was up. Phil was agitated.

Around the table sat the men and women of multiple state

and federal law enforcement agencies all tasked with the same objective. Make sure Neil Shumway never sees the light of day again.

"Phil." Maumee County Detective Sam Cruz rose from his seat at the end of the table. Handsome, with dark eyes and a head of thick black hair, graying at the sides. I'd known Sam since my first day as an assistant county prosecutor. He'd been the first responding officer on a drug-related murder on the north end of town. Since then, I always breathed a sigh of relief whenever I saw Sam's name attached to a case. He was level-headed, thorough, and exceedingly good at what he did.

Today, what he was doing was saving Phil Halsey from himself. "We all have the same objective here. Mara, Kenya? You probably see some new faces at the table. Ms. Leary? Thanks so much for joining us. We've also brought in Emily Shultz, she's a detective with Kalamazoo."

Detective Shultz sat at Sam's left. She was a pale contrast to Sam's ruddy, rugged complexion. I pegged her in her late forties, with hair bleached so light it looked like cotton candy. She gave me a pleasant smile and peered up at Sam.

"You know Detective Ritter," Sam continued. Gus Ritter was one of the most senior detectives with Maumee County. When I saw *his* name attached to a case, I usually braced myself. He put together solid evidence, but fit every stereotype of a gruff, jaded cop and had little use for lawyers of any kind. He barely looked up at Sam. Long ago, when the case first crossed their desks, Gus had been a junior detective tagging along with the more seasoned Ken Leeds.

"You know our friend at the A.G.'s office. And Special Agents Josie Nowicki and Pat Doyle came up from the FBI's Cleveland Field Office." Rounding out our group were two officers from the Ohio Bureau of Criminal Investigation.

Nowicki cleared her throat. "We're working from the theory that Shumway crossed state lines with several of his victims," she said, politely directing her words to Cass, the newbie at the table. I'd worked with Josie maybe a half a dozen times over the last five or so years. Nearing retirement, she'd outlasted twenty years of shake-ups in the Bureau and had seen everything. I knew she'd be a great asset if I needed her.

"Cass came down from Delphi," I said. "Do you mind if we let her give you the brief rundown of her dealings with Shumway?"

Cass sat with her hands folded. She spoke in a clear voice. "Well, I know you all have the statement I gave to Delphi law enforcement. So you know the broad strokes. Shumway was married to my client's aunt. He victimized her mother and that's how my client was conceived."

Cass explained how Shumway strung her along by phone for weeks, pretending to want to help in Alicia Romaine's search for her birth mother. All the while, he knew exactly how she'd been conceived.

"What can you tell us about his demeanor?" Sam asked.

Cass took a breath. "He makes you think he's harmless. For me, he was fatherly. Kind of hokey, actually. Liked to call me darlin' over the phone. I fell for all of it, thinking he was just some bored old guy who'd stumbled into an interesting little caper. But the day he tried to assault me, I saw a different man. Cold. Cunning. Calculating. He's got a plan in all of this. I'm sure of it. I firmly believe he thinks he's going to walk."

"What's the status of your assault case with him in Delphi?" Schultz asked.

"The prosecutor is waiting for things to shake out here," she said. "Fortunately, he didn't get very far with me. He's only looking at a third-degree felony. He's got no priors as of right now so even if everything breaks our way, he'd be out in months at best. It's something. But it's not enough. You guys have to take him down for something much bigger."

"Can we cut to it?" Ritter asked. If there was one thing Gus Ritter hated, it was meetings. "Give me the odds on us nailing this asshole here in Maumee County."

Sam shot me a look. He had a pair of dark brown eyes that could cut right through you. Phil was still standing, slightly slack-jawed that Sam and Cass had wrested control of the meeting from him so easily.

"The case is solid," I said. Screw it. I knew this thing inside and out. Better than Kenya. Certainly better than Phil. And yet, he still hadn't made a decision on who would try this case. I didn't suppose the out-of-county people or the FBI agents picked up on that, but Ritter and Cruz knew it for sure. Cass was shrewd. I could tell she sensed some politics at play. She gave me a sideways glance.

"The DNA is dispositive," I said. "Blood, semen, the whole kit. We need to shore up any claims Shumway makes about an alibi," I said.

Sam nodded. "You'll have it."

Special Agent Nowicki rose and went to the whiteboard at the back of the room. She nodded to Sam. He flicked the light switch and turned on the projector. A map displayed on the screen and Nowicki picked up the wireless mouse from the table.

"We've got partial records from Blaine Pharmaceuticals. Shumway's sales territory overlaps with unsolved assault and kidnapping cases in three states." She clicked her pointer and Shumway's sales territory popped up as a shaded, gray area covering parts of Michigan, Ohio, and Indiana. Josie clicked her pointer again and red dots appeared representing the cities where the assaults took place.

"Can you confirm whether he made sales calls in those areas on the specific dates these women were victimized?" Cass asked.

Kenya sat with her pen poised over a notepad. I saw her sit up straighter and knew she didn't like feeling like a spectator. Sam's words about all being on the same team still echoed, but right now I felt pretty territorial.

"We're working on that," Detective Shultz from Kalamazoo said. Her victim, Jennifer Lyons, was one of the two times we believed Neil Shumway had actually killed. In my heart, I knew there may be more.

"He serviced seven doctors' offices within no more than a six-mile radius from where Jennifer Lyons's body was found," Schultz said. She traced a big circle around Asylum Lake. Jennifer's body had been found dumped there, weighed down by the same kind of cement blocks Denise had been tied to. The general resemblance between the two of them fit what we believed to be Shumway's profile. Blonde or light-brown hair, blue eyes, thin, pretty, young.

Cass squirmed in her seat. Shumway's type was sitting right next to me. So close. She'd come so close.

"Do you think you can keep the Lyons family under control?" I asked. News of Shumway's arrest had understandably rattled them. A few of them had come to Waynetown carrying picket signs.

"I was going to ask you the same question?" She directed her words at Ritter and Sam Cruz. Before they could answer, Pat Doyle, the other FBI agent, spoke up.

"Look," he said. "What I'm about to tell you can't leave this room. I mean it. No leaks. But we have reason to believe there's another cold case Neil Shumway could be connected to. Amelia Garner. Another dead girl in Toledo from 2006."

"Dead," Kenya said. "So we're looking at three murders."

"Possibly," Shultz answered. "She's in the right area for Shumway's radius. Other aspects fit his MO. We're waiting on DNA. This one's a tougher sell. The body was never found. Only her car was. There was some physical evidence and signs of a struggle."

"This is why I'm asking." Ritter rose from his seat. He rested his fists on the table. "Do you have your shit together, Halsey?"

His tone was far more adversarial than I liked. But that was Ritter more than half the time.

Phil took the bait. He leaned in and squared off with Gus Ritter. "That's the question I should be asking you. You know Matt Orville's filed an appearance on Shumway's behalf. He's rung your bell more than once on the witness stand. That can't happen."

Ritter slammed his fist to the table. "I'm not your problem. Your office is the problem."

Ritter pulled out his phone. He swiped the screen and slid it across the table. "This hit my newsfeed just before I walked in here."

From my position at the table, I had the same view of Ritter's phone as Phil did. Cass tilted her head and read along with me. My heart stopped cold. It was an article from the online version of our own little *Waynetown News*. Ritter had it open to an editorial essay.

"Justice for Denise Silvers in Jeopardy With Prosecutor's Office in Turmoil."

Before Phil could I grabbed the phone. I speed-read the article. It claimed insider knowledge of a key player on the prosecution's team facing possible criminal charges for election fraud. Though my name was never mentioned, there was no question it was me they were talking about.

"This is complete crap," I said, sliding the phone back to Ritter. But it had me rattled. The article hinted at an upcoming investigation into the campaign finances of someone close to the Shumway prosecution. It went on to imply that scandal was the reason the case had yet to be assigned even though the trial was looming.

Someone talked. Someone inside the office. My eyes went straight to Kenya. She had her own phone open and her eyes darted over the screen as she read the same article.

"This wasn't me," she said, meeting my hard stare.

"Not now," Phil said. He was right on that. I didn't want to have any of this out in front of the task force.

"This is Orville," Phil said. "Trying to stir stuff up. Muddy the waters. Rattle my people. Everyone here knows his tactics. Especially you, Ritter."

Phil was right. In Ritter's last head-to-head with Matt Orville, he'd kicked up dust about an old murder case Ritter was involved in. One of the very few the detective had ever lost. It was a dirty trick and somehow, Orville knew it was a sore spot for Ritter and he exploited it.

"This guy's a shitheel," Ritter said. "The question is, Halsey, are you?"

"What are you saying?" Phil said through clenched teeth.

"I'm saying, you better grow a pair."

Sam Cruz put a hand on Ritter and pulled him back down to his chair. Angry as I was, I took his lead and did the same with Phil.

Then Cruz took a breath and leveled a withering look at Phil Halsey. "Listen," he said. "Everyone in this room knows who should be trying this case. It would ease a lot of minds if you shut this crap down."

I couldn't breathe. Sam looked at me. My heart started beating again. Trapped butterfly wings. I didn't know whether to cry or kiss Sam Cruz and Gus Ritter. I had no idea how much sway they had with Phil. But it touched me and put me off guard that they'd stick their necks out for me like this.

"We're all on the same team," Phil said. "And last time I checked the Maumee County Sheriff's Department isn't in charge of personnel decisions in my office."

"Was this you?" Ritter asked, pointing to his phone again. "Did you leak this?"

"Go to hell, Ritter," Phil said. Even I knew Phil would never do something like that. Image meant everything to him. That's why there was even a question about my role in this case.

"What are you going to do about it?" Ritter persisted.

"Tomorrow," Phil said. I swear I could hear steam coming out of his ears. "Nine o'clock. I'll assign the case and issue a press release."

Before I could even react, Phil picked up his briefcase and stormed out of the room. Kenya quietly rose to follow him. She held the door for me. Cass was right on my heels. She stopped me with a gentle hand on my arm as Kenya and Phil hurried down the hall.

She kept her voice low. "Geez. Is there something else I should know?"

I bit my lip. "We'll talk later," I said. "And no. I've got everything under control."

"Listen," she said. "Those detectives have it right. This is pure bull. This is *your* case, Mara. They can't really be thinking of pulling it out from under you. Is there anything I can do?"

Even as she said it, we both knew the answer. She had no pull here. Still, her confidence in me mattered. In our brief association, I'd known her to be smart, capable, and downright superhuman in the courtroom.

"Thanks," I said. "I'll be in touch. I'm sorry. I was hoping we could grab lunch or something after this. Right now ..."

Cass put up a hand. "Don't worry about it. You've got your

hands full with these knuckleheads. Give 'em hell, Mara. And please, don't hesitate to reach out even if it's just if you need a sounding board. You know you can trust me. And I know how good you are."

She shook my hand. It was good to have her on my side. Then Cass heaved her monstrosity of a messenger bag over her shoulder and headed out of the room.

My heart still racing, I turned to join my colleagues. Before I did, I mouthed a thank you to both Sam Cruz and Gus Ritter who'd just come out of the conference room. Ritter gave me an uncharacteristic wink and a smile that only I saw.

Chapter 6

Two DAYS LATER, Phil called me into his office. As I opened the door, ice went through my veins. Kenya was already seated in front of Phil's desk. I caught them in mid-conversation and Kenya's half of it stopped me.

"You know you can count on me for this," she said.

"Lady M!" Phil said, his tone bright.

Kenya's eyes darted to the floor. She plastered on a quick smile as I came into the room and shut the door behind me.

"You wanted to see me," I said.

"Sit down," Phil said.

"I'll get out of your hair," Kenya said.

"No, stay," Phil told her.

I didn't want to sit. I stood behind the second chair with my hands folded. Phil's smile dropped a millimeter. His chair creaked as he sat back.

"Okay," he said. "So I'll get right to it. I don't have to tell you how much pressure this office has received on Shumway. It's coming from all quarters and it's only going to get worse. We have to win, Mara. Emily Shultz is nowhere near where she needs to be proof-wise on the Jennifer Lyons murder. We need to get him. You know this case was hand-picked by the Attorney General's office. And that's been the problem all along."

"Jason has nothing to do with this," I said. "There's absolutely no conflict and even if there was, they've put up a Chinese Wall. He's on leave campaigning ..."

Phil put up a hand. "We don't need to rehash any of that. I trust you, Mara. And I trust that in the end, you'll always do what's right for the team."

I saw red. Kenya, to her credit, kept her eyes straight ahead. By the looks of her, she wanted to be anywhere else but here.

"Phil, you need me. Denise Silvers needs me. Kenya, you're brilliant. But this case is mine. I practically sweat it from my pores. There's nothing Matt Orville can throw at me that I won't be able to handle with one hand tied behind my back. I'm ready for it. There wasn't a person at that task force meeting who doesn't want me leading this ..."

"Mara, stop," Phil said. "You need to listen to me."

"No," I said. "I'm not going down without a fight on this one."

"There's nothing to fight," Kenya said, her lips drawn tight. "The case is yours."

I took a breath, ready to launch into the rest of my speech. I'd rehearsed it a dozen times or more. I had to literally shake my head to clear it.

"What?"

Phil rolled his eyes. "Mara, I called you in here to tell you I've made my decision. You're trying the Shumway case. It's yours."

Slowly, I sank into the seat beside Kenya.

"Okay," I said.

"But I want Kenya involved," Phil went on. "It'll be your call how much or in what way. But you're lead prosecutor on this. I'll admit. I'm worried about you. Not about your skill in the courtroom or your command of this case. That was never in doubt. But you know this is going to get ugly. It's going to get personal. Matt Orville's going to use whatever's out there to try and throw you off your game. I know you think I was unfair, but I'm trying to protect you."

I nodded. "I respect that. But you know I can take care of myself."

"I hope so," he said.

"Just put me to work," Kenya said, her tone and expression earnest. That was the thing about Kenya Spaulding. Though she made no secret of her ambitions, in the end I knew she cared about serving justice above all else. She was a righteous warrior and I was glad to have her on my side.

"Thank you," I said.

"If you're done with me," Kenya said, turning to Phil, "I'll let you two talk."

She didn't wait for Phil to dismiss her. She got up and left the room, closing the door behind her. I turned back to him.

"I appreciate your concern. Truly, I do."

"Mara," he said. "I have no idea whether this is appropriate to say in this day and age. But dammit, I'm going to say it anyway. You know sometimes I think of you like the daughter I never had. At least, if I did have a daughter, I'd want her to be like you."

"Thank you." His sentiment caught me a little off guard. It made me think of my own father. Ford Montleroy passed away from lung cancer five years ago. It occurred to me, I could have used his strength and support right now on so many things. On the other hand, I didn't regret he wasn't around to know what happened with Jason. There was a good chance my father might have tried to kill him.

"Just ..." Phil said. "Don't let the bastards get you down on this one. And know you've got the whole office behind you. And apparently some pretty tough allies in the sheriff's department. You have any idea how many angry calls and lectures I've had to field from Cruz and Ritter?"

I smiled. "If you're looking for me to apologize for them, I won't."

Phil shook his head. "Just get outta here. Go win me a conviction on Shumway. I've got my own election to win in a year and need to take full credit for your work."

This got a laugh out of me. "Will do, boss."

I left him there still shaking his head. A weight lifted from my heart. The case was mine. And I would do it well. I would nail Neil Shumway to the wall if it was the last thing I did.

I was greeted to a round of applause as I made my way to the outer offices.

54

"Stop!" I said, smiling. "We haven't won yet. Save it. Because I'm going to need help from each and every one of you before this one's all over."

"And you've got it," Caroline said. "We've gotta get this guy."

"We will," I smiled. "God help us all, we will."

"Great stuff." Howard Jordan came over to me and squeezed my shoulder. Hojo was a man of few words but a tough-as-nails prosecutor. He'd been here the longest, predating even Phil.

"I mean it," I told him. "I want you watching over my shoulder every step of this. If you see something I need to be called on, do it."

"Guaranteed," he said. He looked over his own shoulder. "How'd she take it?"

He pointed toward Kenya's office. She hadn't emerged since she left Phil's. She and I were going to have to talk this out and soon. If she harbored even the slightest of hard feelings about Phil's decision, I wanted it hammered out now. The trial was only a few weeks away.

"You'll have to ask her that," I said, taking the diplomatic approach. Hojo pursed his lips and nodded.

"Mara?" Caro called out. She held the office landline to her ear. "It's Denise already."

"That was fast," I said. "Phil hasn't even sent his official press release."

"She's just calling to check in," Caro said. "You can break the good news to her yourself. I think she'd appreciate hearing it firsthand anyway."

"She would," I agreed. "I'll take it in my office."

I thanked the office for their support once again and headed down the hall. Line one blinked at me as I sat in my chair. I lifted the receiver.

"Denise," I said. "How are you holding up?"

"I'm anxious," she said. "Everyone's saying that defense lawyer Shumway lined up is some kind of rock star."

"I can handle Matt Orville," I said.

There was a pause at the other end of the line. Then Denise broke into a chuckle.

"Halsey's done the right thing?"

It was a loaded question. I sidestepped it. "I'll be trying the case against Shumway for the State. The whole team is gearing up for you, Denise. This is happening."

Her chuckle turned into a choked sob. I wished I was there with her to comfort her. I couldn't imagine how she must be feeling. Only, I knew this was going to get far harder before it got better.

"You have to win, Mara,' she whispered.

"One day at a time, Denise. That's how you've made it this far. But I'd like to set up a day next week. I said I can handle Matt Orville, but you have to handle him too. His cross-examination won't be gentle. He'll temper it for the jury. If he comes at you too hard ..."

"I'll be ready," Denise said, all emotion leaving her voice.

Though her back was broken, it was still made of steel. For a moment, I was just as scared for Matt Orville as I was for Denise.

"I know," I said. "I'm going to put you back on with Caroline. You tell her some good times next week. We'll go over your testimony."

"Mara," she said. "Thank you. I know you can offer me promises about what happens next. I've been involved in victims' advocacy most of my life now. I've seen all the crazy things that can happen with juries. But ... no matter what ... you've never quit on me or this case. I love you for that. And there's no one I'd rather have on my side."

It was my turn to get a little choked up and I knew I couldn't afford to. Not yet.

"Back at ya, Denise," I said. "Now get some rest. We have a lot of work to do. I'll put you on hold and Caro will pick up."

"Yes, boss," she teased. I said a final goodbye.

I finished a few things on some other pending cases of mine. That would be something else I'd have to discuss with Phil. My immediate future would now be wholly consumed with the Shumway trial. Hojo and Kenya would have to pick up the slack on the rest of my caseload. I knew Kenya wouldn't be thrilled. It was one more reason I needed to take her out to lunch and soon.

I left my desk and shut off the lights. As I made my way to the outer offices, they were all but empty. It was almost seven now. I'd lost track of time.

Thankfully, Will had a robotics meeting after school. Kat would be there with him until close to eight o'clock. She would have taken him out for subs at his favorite sandwich shop. Once again, I didn't know what I'd do without her.

Downtown Waynetown was a virtual ghost town this time of day. The parking lot had emptied a good hour before. It was just a ten-minute drive home. I'd have only enough time for a hot bath before Kat and Will got back.

As I made the last turn down my road, at first I thought I'd come upon an accident. Then I realized I was looking at three news trucks parked at the end of my winding drive.

Reporters approached as I slowed to make the turn.

"Mrs. Brent?" one of them said. I tried to get my bearings. This wasn't just the local news. One of the trucks bore the logo of one of the national cable stations.

I rolled down my window. "What are you doing here? This is my private home."

"Mrs. Brent," she continued. "Can you comment on Abigail Morgan's allegations?"

I felt numb. No. Not now. Not this.

"I have no comment," I said, not taking the bait. But they could see I was shocked. They wanted me to ask what allegations.

"Mrs. Brent," another of the reporters said. "What do you have to say about the claim your husband has violated federal election laws? He paid off his mistress using campaign funds to the tune of half a million dollars? Were you aware?"

I couldn't think. I could barely breathe. Headlights glared in my rearview mirror. I closed my window. The reporter got her microphone out of the way just in time.

I put my foot on the gas and barreled up the driveway. I expected the reporters to chase after me. God. Would they actually come up to the house? I grabbed my phone, ready to call Sam Cruz for an assist. The road was one thing; if they set foot on my property it would be trespassing.

It turned out I didn't have to bother. The headlights in my rearview mirror dimmed and I recognized the vehicle behind me. It came to a stop and Jason stepped out from behind the wheel. He looked so sharp and handsome in his tailored black suit, his hair perfectly styled. He straightened his tie and stepped up to the microphone.

Gritting my teeth, I slammed on the accelerator and left a trail of mud behind me as I roared up the drive.

Chapter 7

My FINGERS SHOOK as I gripped the service door and pushed it open into the kitchen. The house was dark and quiet. My heels echoed loudly across the kitchen tile floor. I felt sweat break out on my upper lip and I tossed my briefcase on the counter.

I couldn't think straight. I paced with fury from the kitchen to the front foyer as I waited for the security system to alert me to another vehicle heading up the drive.

It took ten minutes but the chime went off. Adrenaline coursed through me. Fight or flight. I felt frozen from it.

Then the service door opened and Jason walked in. I whirled around to face him.

I was angry. Quaking with it. And yet, old instincts stirred deep within me. I hadn't been in the same room with him in almost two months. He'd gotten a haircut. His rich brown hair was combed to the side, his part looked as if it had been made with a ruler. His cheeks were flushed. I knew some of the same adrenaline flowed through him. He wore the new Hugo

Boss suit I'd gotten him for Christmas. And he still wore his wedding ring.

"Mara," he said.

"You can't just show up here," I said. "We had an agreement. If you don't respect my boundaries ..."

"Mara, listen. Please. I'm sorry about that. I just found out things were about to ... hit the fan as I was driving in for something else. I wasn't planning on stopping here without your permission. But I wanted to get to you before they did." He gestured toward the front door.

They.

I hadn't been able to bring myself to turn on the news or pull up an internet browser.

"What's going on?" I asked.

Jason let out a sigh. He was tall, broad-shouldered with all-American good looks. He rubbed his thumb over the palm of his opposite hand. It was a gesture he made when he was nervous. His tell. Over the years I'd helped him control it so his courtroom opponents wouldn't pick up on it like I did. "Abigail's trying to sell a story," he said.

Ice went through my veins. Even the utterance of her name felt like a new betrayal. It humanized her. He thought of her as Abigail. Not "that woman." Not the person who'd tried to hurt his wife and rip our family apart.

"The reporter out there said something about an investigation into your campaign finances."

"It's all theater," he said. "I've told you the truth since day one, Mara. I made you that promise."

I bit the inside of my cheek. I wanted to lash out and remind him of the other fundamental promise he'd broken to me. But we'd done all of that before. I'd screamed. I'd cried. I'd thrown things at him. I thought I'd moved beyond that primal rage. Seeing him here like this, it tore the scab all over again and left me vulnerable and bleeding.

"There's nothing to it," he said. "This is Evan Simpson trying to throw me off course. And he's teamed up with Matt Orville. I'm sorry about that but we both knew it was the substantial risk about you taking the Shumway case."

"I *am* the Shumway case," I said." It's what I'm built for. And you know it's not just some ordinary trial for me, Jason."

I leveled a brutal stare at him. There was a challenge in my statement. If he'd come here to get me to fade into the background to further his ambitions, he was wasting his time.

"I know that," he said. "And you have the full support of the A.G.'s office. Leslie told me how the task force meeting went. I wish I could have been there. I know you're going to hate me for saying this, but I'm just so damn proud of you."

"I need you to manage this," I said, making my own gesture toward the front of the house. I had no doubt the reporters were still there waiting to see whether Jason left or stayed the night. Either choice would make for a good tabloid headline. And now, I knew his presence here backed me into a different kind of corner.

"What are you going to do?" I asked. "What's Len Grantham's advice?"

Jason's shoulders slumped. He took a seat on one of the bar stools at the kitchen island.

"He thinks we can weather this," he answered.

"We? You mean you and me or your campaign?" My voice dripped with sarcasm.

Jason met my gaze. "The campaign. Mara, there's nothing to her allegations. I never paid her a dime. Not from our personal accounts. Not from any campaign sources. Nothing. There's not a shred of evidence she can produce."

"Do you really think that's going to matter?" I asked. "Just the implication is going to be enough to keep you off message for at least the rest of the summer."

"No," he said. "This stops with me. I'm taking this to the media. I'm going to get ahead of it. That's what I wanted to talk to you about."

"Get ahead of it? Jason, it's out. You saw what's at the end of my driveway. They came here. To our house. You're not ahead of it. It's too late for that. It's about to flatten you. There's one thing left you can do."

My words hung in the air for a moment. Then they seemed to fall against him as if they had weight.

"No,' he said, his voice so low it was almost a growl.

"No?"

He slammed his fist to the table. "I have to pay for my sins. I'm trying to. You may not believe me, you may not want to hear it. But I love you. I will regret what I've done until the day I die and beyond if that's what's in store for me. I'll never stop trying to make it up to you. Though I don't accept it yet, I still want to fight for us, I know I may have done something you can never forgive. That's your choice."

"My choice? Believe me, Jason, there's not a single thing about this I choose."

He exhaled. "I deserve to lose you. I know that. But I don't deserve to lose the career I've built. Not over this. What I've done is a personal failing, not a career one."

I let out a bitter laugh. "You're a politician, Jason. There's no difference anymore."

He raised his eyes. I knew that look. Stubborn, hard, determined. Jason and I didn't come from the same backgrounds. I came from privilege. A political dynasty. He'd come from the worst part of Waynetown and spent most of his childhood in abject poverty. He'd even spent two years in foster care, separated from his sister until an aunt finally got them out.

Jason Brent was a fighter. A survivor. It's what drew me to him in the first place when I got beyond his striking looks. He was smart, cunning, shrewd.

I took a step back, coming to lean against the wall.

"You're not serious," I said. "Jason, you'll be chewed up through every news cycle on an endless loop. Our lives. Our family."

His nostrils flared. "I'm good for this country, even if you think I'm no longer good for you."

I wanted to argue with him. Tell him he was crazy. That he was wrong. The thing was, as much as I hated him for betraying me, I'd hated that he'd put all the work we'd done in jeopardy too. He *was* good for this country. Jason Brent was that rare man whose ideas and negotiating skills really could cut across both sides of the aisle. I still believed in his vision, even if I wasn't sure I could ever believe in the man.

"I'm not doing it," I said. "If you think I'm going to sit beside you on some interview couch and ..."

"No," he said. "No. I would never ask you that. I made this mess all by myself. I'll clean it up all by myself. Len's done some polling. We think ..."

"Polling? My God, Jason, stop talking. I don't want to hear how you've focus-grouped our marriage."

He hung his head. "I'm sorry. I'll always be sorry. If I lose this election because of all of this, then so be it. But I won't quit because of it. Not on my career. And not ... on you."

I raised a hand as if I could ward off the rest of his words. I'd heard enough for one day.

"What about my career? You said yourself you think Matt Orville is partially behind this leak. Denise Silvers is counting on me. Jennifer Lyons and countless other victims are counting on me. That's what really matters. Not your election. Not even our marriage, Jason. What if justice for Denise is another casualty of your actions?"

He didn't answer. He didn't have to. It was clear from his eyes that it was a chance he was willing to take.

I had more to say and nothing to say. For now, I was just tired.

Then the alarm system sent off another alert. Kat was home with Will. My jaw dropped as I locked eyes with Jason.

Once again, I felt trapped. No matter how much I wanted to throw him back out of the house, I couldn't do that to our son. At least, not for tonight.

Jason sat frozen as Will walked in through the service door.

His face broke into a smile as he saw his father sitting on that bar stool.

My breath left me in a whoosh as Will ran straight into Jason's arms. Jason reacted just in time to catch him. Kat came in, carrying Will's backpack. She let out a gasp as she saw the scene unfold.

Will hugged his father. We could count on one hand the times he'd done that on his own.

Jason's eyes flickered as he fought back tears.

"Come on!" Will said. "The Carpathian's all done. You have to see the wreck. The bow's done. The stern's going to be a real challenge."

He tugged Jason by the arm. The color had drained from my husband's face as he passed me.

Will was animated, excited. My heart was both broken and filled at the same time. The pair of them disappeared up the stairs.

"Wow," Kat said. "That's ..."

"I know," I said. "Were the reporters still in the road when you came in?"

"Uh ... no," she answered. "But I got an alert in my newsfeed while I was waiting for Will's practice to let out. Is he really going to do it? He's giving an interview?"

I let my gaze travel up the stairs. I could still hear Will talking a mile a minute. Jason was calm, patient, there for him.

"He says so," I said.

Kat came to me. I knew she felt torn apart in a very different way. She loved her brother but she loved Will and me too.

"Well," she said. "You two sure make things interesting around here. And congratulations. I got an alert about the Shumway case too. Big day, huh?"

I couldn't help it, Kat's words worked on me just as she knew they would. I couldn't stand to cry anymore so I laughed as Kat threw her arms around me.

Chapter 8

For all the pregame jockeying she did, Kenya Spaulding soon became my greatest ally as we prepared to go to trial on Neil Shumway. I'd had two meetings with Denise solo, but wanted Kenya's read on her. We drove out to her place together.

Denise greeted us seated in her kitchen. She looked Kenya up and down. Of course, they already knew each other reasonably well. Denise's Silver Angels had worked on behalf of plenty of the victims of crimes Kenya ended up trying. Denise had never said an unkind thing to me about her. Denise was an excellent judge of character and I knew she deeply respected Kenya.

"How hard do you really think Matt Orville's going to come at her?" Denise's older sister Betsy sat at the kitchen table with us. She was the last living member of Denise's immediate family. There are hidden crime victims. Denise's father had been one of them. Knowing what happened to the baby of their family ate at him, turning into stomach cancer by the time he was fifty. He fought brave and hard for almost a decade, but succumbed right after the tenth anniversary of Denise's assault. She lost her mother just last year.

"Orville's good," Kenya said. "He's as good as any trial lawyer I've ever seen. He'll be gentle on the surface, but don't mistake that for softness."

"What possible defense does he think his client has?" Betsy asked. She had a gruff, gravelly voice after years as a heavy smoker. She'd given it up not long ago. Betsy was beautiful once. You could still see it in her warm smile. But the years hadn't always been kind to her. I'd prosecuted her husband for domestic assault against her more than once. She hadn't suffered the same physical injuries as her sister, but Betsy Silvers's victimization was written in the deep lines of her face.

"The DNA is their one great hurdle," I said. "I fully expect they'll attack the science. I'm ready for that. Failing that, they'll try to give the jury an alternative explanation for why Shumway's DNA would have been present in the first place. A non-criminal explanation."

Denise looked at her hands They were gnarled and worn from her years of knitting. She wore her mother's wedding ring now, a two-carat round diamond in a princess setting.

"He's going to try and say I consented to having sex with him," Denise said, her voice flat, emotionless.

Betsy barked out a laugh. "That's rich. And did you also consent to have your head bashed in and your legs weighted down with concrete blocks?"

"Well," Kenya offered. "If it were me, I'd try to separate the two events. I mean, that you had an encounter with

Shumway, and then were abducted and attacked by someone else."

"The timeline can work in our favor," I said. "There's footage of your vehicle coming into the parking garage that morning. And your time card punching you out. But your car never leaves. Shumway's does."

"But you wouldn't see me in his car," she said. "I woke up in the back of it."

I didn't like the vibe I was getting between Denise and Betsy. Every other time we'd met since Shumway was arrested, Denise had been angry, defiant, confident. Right now, she looked like she was keeping a secret.

"Denise," I said. "Have you had a chance to look at that photo I sent you of Neil Shumway when he was much younger? Do you recognize him?"

Matt Orville had refused to provide one. But Cass Leary had gotten her hands on a family photo album with Shumway's picture when he was in his thirties.

"Deenie," Betsy said. "You've got to tell them. It'll be worse if it comes out as some surprise."

Kenya and I exchanged a glance.

"Tell me what?" I asked, my own voice sharpening.

"I didn't," Denise said. "Recognize him, I mean. Not the mugshot you originally sent over. But that older photo, he looked familiar. I do think I met him. But I didn't know him as Neil Shumway."

"Denise," I said, my pulse quickening. "How did you know him?"

"You already know I was working as a receptionist for that car insurance place. We were two floors down from the medical floor. But Shumway ... though I knew him by a different name. He called himself Newt. He'd stop by and chat up the support staff. I think I might have talked to him a few times. He was good-looking. A flirt. And I can't even tell you when or how long or what we talked about. But I think that's the guy I knew as Newt. You said he was a drug rep. That's what jarred my memory along with the photo."

"Okay," I said, breathing a sigh of relief. "Denise, that's not a problem. That's just the truth. It's how he profiled you. Is there anything else to it? Something you're not telling me?"

She shook her head. "No. I don't remember a lot about him. Just that he'd stop by my window every once in a while. And he'd give us some of the free stuff he passed out. Pens. Notepads. Candy. I sort of remember some kind of squishy stress ball. Those were popular."

"It's okay, Denise," Kenya said, reaching for her hand. "It's even okay if you remember liking him. It's actually helpful. Shumway can't deny knowing you."

Denise looked at me. I nodded, confirming what Kenya told her. "I just need you to be ready for it," I said. "If that's all Shumway has, to try to claim you were with him consensually, then I like our chances even more. I will do everything I can to protect you up there. Try not to let the man rattle you, no matter what he tries to imply."

"I've survived worse than Matt Orville," Denise said.

I took her hand. "You have. And the jury will see that."

"He's gonna try to paint Denise as some kind of a whore,"

Betsy said. Her tone was so flat I flinched.

"Maybe," Kenya answered for me. "But he's gotta walk a fine line with that. There's nobody in their right mind who isn't going to understand your sister was the victim of a brutal crime. The harder he goes, the more he risks them hating him. And like Mara said, she'll be there to protect you. And I'll be there to have her back."

My phone started to buzz from inside my briefcase. I did a quick check to make sure it wasn't Kat or Will's school. It was Phil Halsey. I flipped the screen so Kenya could read it. He knew where we were. It was odd for him to call. She narrowed her eyes and took out her own phone. I let Phil's call go to voicemail.

"Do you think he'll testify? Shumway?" Denise asked.

"I'm not sure," I said. "If Orville wants to double down on some inference that you and Neil had consensual sex, I don't know how he plans to get it in except through Shumway's lying mouth. And I'll destroy him. It's a huge risk and Matt Orville, at least in my experience, is too good a lawyer to take it. He knows how good I am."

Kenya was still looking at her phone and I didn't like the angry expression on her face. She covered quickly, smiled, and slipped her phone back in her purse. Something was most definitely up.

"We'll get together at least one more time," I said. "You'll have someone with you in the courtroom? Betsy, you know you probably won't be able to. I may have to call you to help estab-lish the timeline as you were the last person to talk to Denise before the attack. Orville will have a valid objection to you being in the courtroom hearing all the other testimony."

"I'll have Silver Angels with me," Denise said. "They'll be in that courtroom every second of every day."

"Good," I said. "But no disruptions. I don't want to give Orville ammunition to request they be removed."

"We know what to do," Betsy answered.

"Okay then," I said. "I think that's enough for today. If you have any questions, you give me a call."

Denise was still holding my hand. She squeezed it. I couldn't imagine how hard this all was for her. It had been the thing she'd most wished for twenty years. Now it was here.

Kenya jerked her chin at me. Whatever she'd seen on her phone and Halsey's missed call was connected. I had no doubt.

We wrapped up with Denise and Betsy Silvers and left the house. Kenya had driven. I climbed into the passenger seat of her Audi and waited for her to come around the other side.

She slammed the door and pressed the ignition. "We've got a problem," she said.

I braced myself. "Jason?"

She shook her head. "No. But we have a leak. The AP is running a story about Neil Shumway being connected to several other rapes. The Jennifer Lyons case has even been mentioned."

My heart dropped. "How?"

Kenya shrugged. "We're dealing with half a dozen different law enforcement agencies on that task force. It's a huge circle of people who know and expanding."

Anger boiled through me. We were days away from jury selection. The bigger this story got, the higher the chance Orville could successfully argue we had a tainted jury pool.

"As long as it wasn't any of our people," I said. "Or anyone from Maumee County. Lord. You don't think this came from our side?"

"We may never find that out," Kenya said. "We just have to keep our eye on the ball."

After a few minutes, Kenya pulled into a parking spot on Tipton Street, one block from the City-County building. I got out and went to the corner to press the walk light button as she fed her meter.

"Was this you?" A shout drew my attention. Matt Orville himself charged straight for me. He had his phone out opened to the Shumway headline.

I straightened my back and faced him. "Was what me?"

He shoved the phone in my face. "I'm on the way to talk to your boss. You people think you can't win your case on the merits, huh? This is bullshit, Brent."

I slapped the phone away. "This wasn't me. I want a fair trial, Matt. That's a lot more than I can say for you. You want to talk about leaks to the press, huh? Okay. So let's."

He narrowed his eyes. "The hell are you implying?"

"How many meetings have you had with Evan Simpson? Did he call you or did you call him? I know what you did, Matt. I know you play dirty, but coming after my family is low even for you."

"You're crazy," he said. "Whatever mess your husband's

gotten himself into is on him."

"Oh, I think you're scared," I said. "I think you know your client is guilty. And you know how strong the case is so you've got no other option than to try to come after me personally."

His face fell a fraction of an inch. For a second, he actually looked stunned by my words.

"I'm going to have fun proving you wrong," he said. "And I'm going to have fun proving it was your office who's trying to destroy my client's right to a fair trial. You won't have to worry about your husband destroying your life and your career. I'll enjoy watching you do it all by yourself."

I stood my ground. It occurred to me for the first time that Matt Orville was scared. Terrified, maybe. A smile grew on my face. Matt's face went white.

He shook his head then waved his finger at me. But he had absolutely nothing more to say. He stormed off, heading in the opposite direction of the City-County building. So much for taking things up with my boss.

"Well," Kenya said. "That was interesting."

I turned to her. "Where were you?"

She smiled. "Enjoying the show. You've got him scared to death. I've never seen Matt Orville give up the last word to anyone. Ever. Come on. Let's go talk Phil off his ledge."

"Right," I said. I turned and walked beside her.

"I know one thing," she said. "I'm glad to be on your side instead of his."

The feeling was mutual as we walked inside together.

Chapter 9

SAM CRUZ and Gus Ritter came to my office Friday at four. Jury selection in the Shumway trial was set for Monday morning at eight o'clock sharp.

I had my key trial exhibits laid out on two tables we'd brought in for that exact purpose. At the moment, I held on to Shumway's wedding photo.

"You're certain there are no surprises?" I asked. "Denise is tough. She knows what to expect. Orville's convinced someone from your office or mine leaked the task force's inquiry into the other crimes."

"It didn't come from us," Gus assured me. He kept that dour expression on his face. Come to think of it, I wasn't sure I'd ever seen the man smile. Cruz, as always, was the diplomat in their partnership.

"You know we're the last people who would want any hiccups with this thing. Denise means as much to us as she does to you."

I believed him.

"And I can't use any of it," I said. "Any hint of Shumway being suspected of committing these other crimes cannot come out at this trial. If it does, Orville will move for an immediate mistrial and he'll get it."

"Understood," Cruz said.

"Good. I'm counting on you, Gus," I said, leveling a stare at him. "You have got to keep your cool on the witness stand. Orville's going to try every trick in the book. He wants to get under your skin. You can't let him. Are we clear?"

Gus answered with a grunt that didn't exactly put my mind at ease.

"Gus," I said. "We've got him. I don't want to jinx this case with overconfidence, but we have a mountain of evidence against this bastard. Ken Leeds was thorough. He didn't have the DNA, but his case file is solid. He found the bread-crumbs. He just couldn't see the trail. We can. Let's do this for Denise. But let's do it for Ken too. This is the home stretch. Let's not give Matt Orville any ammunition. You keep your cool. If he steps out of line, you need to trust me to handle it. Okay?"

I tilted my head, trying to get Gus to meet my eyes. Sam had a slight smirk on his face. He shot me an almost imperceptible nod which told me yes, Gus understood.

"But the same goes for you," Gus said, finally picking up his head.

I held my breath, bracing for what I knew he'd say next. Sam and Gus passed a distressed look. I had the impression they'd flipped a coin to determine which one of them would bring up the elephant in the room on my personal life.

"I'm ready," I said. "For all of it. I'll keep my head. You keep yours. Together let's fry this asshole."

"Phil's a chump for not seeking the death penalty on this one," Gus said.

"She's alive," I said. "Thank God for that. Denise is still with us."

"He knew," Sam said. "That's our working theory anyway. Shumway's choices were deliberate. He killed Jennifer Lyons because he knew Michigan doesn't have the death penalty. It's a pattern. The two murders we can connect to him took place in non-death states."

"Except this new one, from Toledo?" I asked.

Ritter shrugged. "I don't know. He escalated. But then, as far as we know, he stopped."

A shudder went through me. I found myself saying a silent prayer Gus was right. That the girl from Toledo was the last victim. That he'd stopped. I almost couldn't let my mind go any farther. I had enough pressure on me as it was.

"You're probably right. But let's just focus on nailing him for life with what we have."

"If we don't ..." Gus started. Sam put a hand on his arm. I knew what he was going to say. If we don't get Neil Shumway, we ran the very real risk that no one else could.

"I wanted to thank you guys for burning the midnight oil on this. Sorting through all that parking lot security footage after all this time ... I mean ... keeping it safe. It's just as important as the DNA."

"It was just there," Sam said. "In the property room all this time. An old clunky VHS tape, of all things. I thought Orville was going to piss his pants when he viewed it with us. That bastard knows his client's guilty. I don't know how he can sleep at night."

"Fitfully, I hope," I said. "Very fitfully."

"Denise is lucky to have you," Sam said, his voice dropping low.

His statement caught me a little off guard. As soon as he said it, Gus's phone rang. He pulled it out of his pocket and his frown deepened as he looked at the screen.

"I gotta take this," he said.

"Go," Sam said. When Gus looked at me, I nodded. He put the phone to his ear as he got up and headed out of my office.

"Thank you," I turned to Sam. "And I don't just mean your work on this case ... or, uh ... you being the Gus Whisperer."

Sam smiled. He ran a hand along his jaw. Sam's thick, dark hair grew so fast I was pretty sure the poor guy had to shave twice a day to keep the stubble at bay.

"He's really a softie at heart, don't let him fool you."

"I'll take your word for it," I smiled. "And Sam, there's something else I wanted to thank you for. You and Gus, but I trust you'll relay it for me. I know you went to bat for me with Phil and the rest of the task force. It means a lot to me."

Sam waved me off. His face reddened just a bit and I think my words embarrassed him a little.

"We just want what's right. And what's best for this case. That's you, Mara. Everybody knows it. And it's nothing against Kenya. She's great at what she does too. But this case? You were born for it. We all know that."

It was my turn to feel a blush creep into my cheeks. "Thanks," I said.

"And don't let the bastard get ya down," Sam said.

I knew who he meant and in spite of it all, I felt an odd protectiveness over Jason. Lord. It was all so complicated.

"I appreciate that," I said. "And I also meant what I said. There's nothing—*nothing*—that's going to throw me off my game during this case. That's a promise. I know the stakes."

Sam nodded. "Well, for what it's worth. I think Jason's crazy. To even think of ..."

"Thanks, Sam," I cut him off. I felt myself blinking rapidly. It was almost as if I couldn't hear his words of kindness. Not then. I had armor in place but it didn't mean it couldn't crack.

"Well," he said, rising. "Anyway. Gus is ready. And he's dealt with people like Matt Orville before."

I bit my tongue. Sam was right. He had. But Gus's legendary temper had also been his downfall on the witness stand more than once. If I knew that, Matt Orville did too.

There was an awkward moment between us. I think Sam might have wanted to hug me. I think I might have welcomed it. Instead, he shook my hand and left to go join his partner.

THERE WAS nothing left to do. I had my opening statement written. My witnesses lined up. My plan clear. Will spent the weekend with Jason on our property in southern Ohio. Twenty-five acres with an Amish-built log cabin. Someday, Jason had promised to build us a second home there. Now those dreams were no more solid than smoke.

I was alone in the quiet. I sipped a glass of wine at the empty kitchen table, the steady click of the grandfather clock in the hallway the only sound.

When it chimed at eight, Jason came up the drive. From the window, I watched Will tumble out of the car, his arms filled with a new box of Lego. He was getting ready to build one of the Titanic's sister ships.

He looked happy and it squeezed my heart. For a brief, unguarded moment, Jason looked happy too. I held my breath. Then I closed my eyes. If I could wish the last six months away ... if I could summon some kind of magic and change every one of Jason's bad choices ...

I opened my eyes. Will came tumbling through the front door, out of breath.

"One thousand and one pieces!" he yelled. "Forty-three percent off!"

"Forty-three?" I asked. Will rattled off the math for me including price markup and sales tax issues that rendered the store's claimed fifty percent off to be technically inaccurate.

Then, still breathless, he ran straight up the stairs, headed for his room.

"Bath first!" I yelled up. He mumbled something down and a moment later, I heard the water running.

Jason stood in the doorway, his hands stuffed into the pocket of his jeans. It occurred to me I hadn't seen him like that recently. Dressed casually, his hair ruffled, rough stubble darkening his jaw. I'd only seen official Jason Brent these days.

"You can come in," I said. "Unless you've turned into a vampire along with everything else."

I wished I hadn't said it. I was tired. Sparring with Jason was the last thing I needed. For the next two weeks, until the Shumway trial was over, I had room for Will, work, and nothing else.

Jason knew me well. He mercifully didn't take the bait. He just stepped into the foyer and closed the door.

I heard the water running upstairs. I could almost set a timer to it. Will would be done in exactly eighteen minutes. Twenty-one until he brushed his teeth and waited for me to tuck him in.

"We had a good weekend," Jason said. "He had fun."

"I'm glad," I said.

"You know," Jason said. "I can take him with me during the trial. Kat can come down to Columbus. He likes it at the house down there too. It would take something off your plate while ..."

"I don't want my son off my plate," I said. "It's not a good idea to disrupt his routine. We'll be fine. When's your press conference, or your mea culpa interview?"

Jason's face fell. "Two weeks."

"Ah," I said. "Shrewd. Wait until after my trial."

"Mara ..."

I held up a hand in surrender. "It's okay, Jason. For today, it's just okay."

Jason knew me well enough to leave it there. Sadness came into his eyes as he pursed his lips and turned to leave.

I finished the last of my wine then walked upstairs to tuck Will in for the night. I found him already in bed, his hair slicked back, still wet from the shower. He looked so much like Jason my heart tripped. The box of new Lego sat on the floor beside his bed.

"No dice, mister," I said, picking the box up. "I know your tricks. You can dig in tomorrow after you do your chores. I'm going to check up on you."

Will frowned. "You'll be at work."

"I have my ways," I said. "Spies ... everywhere." I made circular jazz hands.

I climbed into the bed with Will. He settled back against his pillow, staring up at me.

"Dad said you had fun."

"He's pacing a lot," Will said. "And he talks on the phone."

I resisted the urge to ask with whom.

"He's got a lot going on at work," I said. "It'll get better once the election's over."

"Will he move back here then?" Will asked. "Or will we move to Washington D.C. if he wins?"

He'd asked that regularly, even before Will and I separated. I still didn't have a good answer for him.

"This is our home no matter what," I reassured him. "We'll make it work just like when Dad got the job in Columbus."

"But he wasn't moved out then," Will said.

My heart turned to ice. He knew. We'd been careful not to make it seem like there was anything more going on than Jason needed to spend more time in Columbus during the campaign. But dammit, he knew. Of course he did.

"I know," I said. There was no point in trying to make up some lie. "Did you ask your dad the same question?"

"Yeah," Will said. "He said sometimes husbands and wives don't live together but that I shouldn't worry. I'm still his main dude."

I smoothed his hair back. Will had the same cowlick in the back that Jason had. "He's right. That goes for me too."

"He could live here," Will said. "You don't have to be married. But he could live here. Like roommates. Maybe even build another house right next door. There's enough land. You'd need a variance from the township. I have the application paperwork."

I sat upright. "You do? Wow. You've been thinking about it a lot."

Sometimes it was a blessing my son struggled with showing emotion. But this alone told me he'd been feeling it. It gutted me. I'd missed it.

"Will," I said. "I know things are different right now. Change is hard for everyone. But we *will* make it okay. I promise you that."

"How?" he asked.

My nine-year-old son had me speechless. He looked up at me with trusting eyes. I gave him the only truth I could.

"I don't know. I just know we will. Because Dad and I love you and that matters more than everything else. Okay?"

He considered me for a moment. Then I saw his shoulders relax. "Okay," he said.

Then he closed his eyes. For as much as Will's brain could go a hundred miles an hour during the day, he had the same uncanny ability as his father to shut it off on a dime. In another minute, he was snoring.

I watched him for a few minutes, knowing he was the best part of both of us. Then I quietly left the room.

Chapter 10

Judge Vivian Saul had deeper political roots in Maumee County than Phil Halsey did. The longest-serving member of the bench, she still faced the perception that her family name and second X chromosome were the only reasons she had the privilege of wearing the robe. Those of us who practiced in front of her knew better. She was quick-minded and direct. She suffered no fool. That didn't mean she was immune to crazy rulings from time to time. It could be frustrating if you were on the short end of it. Sometimes Judge Saul acted like a parent who just wanted quiet rather than fairness.

"Your arguments are misplaced, Mr. Orville," Judge Saul said. We would address her as Your Honor, but I often thought Your Serene Highness might better suit her. Because she was. I'd never seen Judge Saul lose her temper. Never heard her so much as raise her voice. Though many believed she'd felt entitled to the role, I knew it was her calling.

"Your Honor," Matt said. "Voir dire is complete. Five out of the seven empaneled jurors have admitted to hearing about this case and the additional ... unfounded accusations against my client. We've shown bias."

"You haven't," Judge Saul said. She sat with her hands folded, her sapphire ring glinting under the lights. She dyed her thick hair brown and wore it tightly shaped so it curved around her jaw.

"All five jurors in question were adamant that what they've heard will *not* prejudice their ability to judge fairly and keep an open mind. We can't ask for more than that. Your motion for a mistrial is denied. Your ill-timed motion for transfer of venue ... is denied. Now, as soon as I have the bailiff bring our jurors back in, are you ready to deliver your opening statement, Ms. Brent?"

"I am, Your Honor," I said. Kenya sat behind me. I'd put her on witness wrangling today. We were already past the lunch hour after four grueling hours of voir dire. I doubted I'd get to put my first witness on until morning. That was my one beef about Judge Saul. She ended court at three far too often.

"Terrific," she said. "Get ready, Mr. Orville. It's full steam ahead after a five-minute recess."

She banged the gavel and stood so quickly her bailiff barely had time to ask the rest of us to. Then Judge Saul disappeared through the door behind her, leading to her chambers. Her robe spun a bit, giving her a caped crusader vibe.

"How's Denise?" I said to Kenya as soon as Judge Saul disappeared. Denise sat in the back with a few of her Silver Angels. I hadn't had a chance to talk to her myself today.

"Sharp," Kenya said. "And I like what we got."

So did I. Our jury was evenly split. Six men. Six women. We

had a good mix of boomers and gen Xers, and two millennials. Their socioeconomic groups ran the gamut as well. Despite Matt Orville's bluster, even I didn't think he really believed there was much risk of bias based on the news leaks.

Neil Shumway was another matter. He sat rod straight with his hands folded the whole day. His suit didn't quite fit. It was too big through the shoulders and gave him a gaunt appearance, which was new. He looked ... non-threatening. He looked old. And I knew every inch of that had been orchestrated.

"Make sure she knows I probably won't call her today," I said.

"She'll be ready no matter when you call her," Kenya said. "Are you?"

I could feel two sets of eyes on me. Kenya shot a nervous glance over my shoulder. I wasn't about to let Orville or his monster of a client rattle me.

"Bet your ass I am," I said.

A moment later, the judge retook the bench. I stood with Kenya at my side as the bailiff led our jurors back in. Only one stole a glance at Neil Shumway. I couldn't quite read her expression. I'd rely on Kenya for things like that. During trial, it was always critical to have at least one other person reading non-verbal cues from the jury. It helped to have a sense of what they were responding to so I could change course if necessary.

"You may begin, Ms. Brent," Judge Saul instructed me.

I rebuttoned my blazer and stepped up to the lectern.

"Good afternoon, ladies and gentlemen," I said. "I had a

chance to introduce myself a little earlier this morning. I'd like to reiterate my gratitude for you being here. It's a hard thing we ask. Sitting on a jury. Spending time away from your jobs, your families. The things you hear and see during this particular trial won't be easy. Because what happened to Denise Silvers on April 14th, 2000 might be one of your worst nightmares.

"Something was stolen from Denise that day. She was taken against her will. Beaten. Raped. Left for dead. It's only by the thinnest of chances—a miracle—that she's alive today.

"But Denise did get that miracle the same day she lived through her worst nightmare. She will tell you about the pain, the terror she lived through that day twenty years ago and every day since.

"You'll hear the truth through her words. And they will shock you. Break your heart. But you'll also hear the truth ... the indisputable truth from the story Denise can't tell you herself.

"You'll hear the painstaking care in which the first responders, the caregivers, the detectives took to preserve the evidence in this case. Evidence that held the key to identifying a monster. This monster."

I paused and pointed to Neil Shumway. He kept his shoulders slumped. His head down. But he saved a flicker in his eyes just for me. The jury didn't see. I turned my body so I faced him.

"You'll hear about the nightmares that still plague Denise Silvers today. They'll never go away and she'll have to live with that. She's lived in fear for twenty years, knowing the man who brutalized, broke her, left her tied to cement on the banks of the Maumee River was out there somewhere. He knew who she was but she couldn't know who he was.

"But now ... we know. We will prove to you beyond a reasonable doubt that the defendant, Neil Shumway, is that monster. Though it will be hard ... sometimes almost unbearable to hear what this man did to Denise Silvers. When you have all the facts. When you understand the evidence, you'll find your job is easy. Neil Shumway is guilty. And you'll finally be able to deliver justice for Denise Silvers and help her quiet her nightmares once and for all."

I paused for a moment, letting my words sink in. I chanced just enough of a look at the jury. Half of them were staring hard at Neil Shumway. The other looked to the back of the courtroom at Denise. There were tears in her eyes but she sat as straight as her broken body would let her.

I thanked the jury again and took my seat.

"Mr. Orville?" Judge Saul said.

Matt Orville cleared his threat. He squeezed Shumway's shoulder in solidarity as he passed him and made his way to the lectern.

"Ladies and gentlemen of the jury, despite what the prosecution would have you believe, this case is not easy. Your job is not easy.

"There is only one thing we can agree on. Ms. Brent and me. What happened to Denise Silvers is horrifying. Tragic. Miraculous too, because she *is* here to tell you about it. No one is more grateful for that than me."

I bristled. Beside me, Kenya wrote a note echoing my thoughts at that moment too. No. Denise was more grateful, asshole.

"Because I want to hear what she has to say. We need to hear what she has to say. She deserves to have us all bear witness to the horror she suffered. I want justice for her too. I have daughters. Like many of you. I have sisters. I have a mother. The thought that Denise Silvers's monster could still be out there somewhere, well, that's enough to sicken anyone. I want him caught. I want him to pay. If I had five minutes in a room alone with him ... well ... then maybe it would be me sitting here accused of a crime.

"But Neil Shumway is innocent. We cannot let the State's desperate need to win a conviction—to close the oldest cold case on their books as Ms. Brent's boss faces an election next year—cloud the truth."

I clenched my fists.

"This case has been an embarrassment for the Maumee County Sheriff's Department. For the prosecutor's office. Why, Phil Halsey campaigned on it years ago. Desperation. That's what has fueled this case, these charges. They're willing to pin this case on an innocent man if it will clear it off their books and make them look good to the voters."

"Your Honor!" I said. It wasn't usual for me to object during opening statements, but Matt Orville was dancing too close to the line. He needed to know I'd fight back at every turn.

"Save it for your closing, Mr. Orville," Judge Saul admonished. "If you can show evidence for it."

"Answers," Matt said, not missing a beat as he turned back to the jury. "Explanations. That's what the prosecution owes you. What they owe Denise Silvers and Neil Shumway, the accused. I put this to you ... the so-called answers the State plans to show aren't what they seem.

"They want you to ... no ... they need you to think they're ready to deliver a slam dunk for Denise Silvers. But what you'll walk away with is far more questions.

"There isn't a single piece of purported evidence the prosecution has against Mr. Shumway that doesn't have an explanation. An explanation that will help you understand that he's innocent.

"Reasonable doubt. That's your charge. It's the highest standard of proof we have in the legal system and rightly so. Because it's what will keep an innocent man from being wrongfully convicted of a crime he didn't commit.

"When the State is finished with their case, you'll see you'll have far more than reasonable doubt. You'll have absolute doubt. And you'll know the prosecution has wasted your time. Thank you."

Matt Orville unbuttoned his jacket and walked back to Neil Shumway's side. Shumway stayed stoic. The jury seemed uncomfortable already.

"Ms. Brent?" Judge Saul said, surprising me. I fully expected her to adjourn for the day. "Are you ready to call your first witness?"

I rose. "I am, Your Honor."

Chapter 11

"THE STATE CALLS Tucker Welling to the stand."

I had just one note card at the lectern. Tucker shuffled up
from the back of the courtroom wearing his Sunday best, a
charcoal-gray suit and a yellow tie with bluebirds on it. His
granddaughters got it for him last Christmas, he'd told me.
Tucker's shoes squeaked when he walked and he'd just come
from the corner barber.

He had a bad knee and hesitated a beat after the bailiff had
sworn him in. When offered a helping hand, Tucker waved it
off and hoisted himself into the witness box.

"Good morning," I said. "Mr. Welling, can you state your
name for the record?"

Tucker leaned closer to the microphone. "Tucker Elias
Welling. I live at 4154 Canterbury Road in Waynetown. One
street over from Scottsdale Park."

"Thank you," I said. "Mr. Welling, how long have you lived at
that address?"

"I was born there," he said. "I'm seventy-two. Lived there with my folks and my sister. She moved off to Phoenix. I stayed. Took care of my parents when they got on. Then they willed it to me after they died. That was, oh, fifteen years ago now the house has been mine."

"Mr. Welling, I'd like to direct your attention to the morning of April 15th, 2000. Do you remember that day?"

"I do," he said, sitting straighter. "I'll never forget it."

"Can you tell me what you remember about it?"

Tucker started to pull at his tie. "It was pretty warm that day. It was a Saturday morning. I came home from work and I'd just gotten into it with my father. My mom was having mental issues then. Dementia, you know. Anyway, I left the house about five in the morning to head down to the river to do some fishing. My dad was mad because he wanted to go with me but I just needed a break. I don't regret a second I had with either one of them, but if anybody knows what it's like caring for ailing parents ... well ... anyway. I just needed to clear my head for a while."

"Of course," I said.

Tucker cleared his throat. "Well, anyway. I have a spot. Kind of a secret spot where I know the fishing's best. I suppose it won't be much of a secret now that that lady's typing down everything I say. It's okay though."

Tucker's words got a little laughter from the jury box. He was charming them, as I knew he would.

"About maybe a mile south of the Bennett Street overpass. It's kind of wild down there. There's an embankment going up to Salter Road. People drive by there all the time and probably don't know what's right down there. There's like a little catch. The river drops off ... a little waterfall. Lots of rocks. That's why people don't go down that river much past Bennett. It's rocky and rough. Can't take a boat down there. But it's where you find the best fishing."

"I understand," I said.

"And back then, there were maybe two or three other guys who even knew about that spot. Like I said, it's pretty much off the beaten path. The way the hill is ... the embankment ... you can't see the edge of the river from the road."

"I see," I said. "So what happened that day?"

"Well, I left the house I'd say about five a.m. It's about a ten-minute walk from the house to my fishing spot."

"You didn't drive?" I asked.

"No, ma'am. There's no good place to park. It was warm enough that day for just a light jacket. I took a fishing pole and off I went."

"So approximately what time did you arrive at the falls near Salter Road?"

Tucker took a breath. "I'd say it was maybe five twenty in the morning."

"Did you fish?"

Tucker looked down. "No, ma'am. I never got to."

"What happened?"

"Well, I came down from the Bennett overpass. It's dicey. And it had rained the night before so it was extra muddy. I started walking south. I'd say it took me fifteen minutes to get to God's Brew ... er ... that's what we call that particular fishing spot."

"And you say this spot is roughly a mile south of the overpass?"

"Yes, ma'am," he said. "Anyway, I was just about to cast when I heard something to the left of me. I was facing west, you see. You gotta be on the west bank that time of day, that time of year or the sun'll darn near blind you."

"Anyway, first I thought it was a dog. Like whimpering, you know. So I turned toward the sound. Didn't see it ... um ... her ... right at first. Like I said. It was real muddy. *Real* muddy. My shoes were sticking in. I remember cursing myself that I hadn't worn my rain boots. I had on a pair of hiking boots just. I was thinking about how much trouble it was going to be cleaning them out."

"Then what happened?" I asked.

"Well, I kept walking. I heard the whimpering again. Kind of a moaning. At that point, I kind of knew it wasn't a dog. But I couldn't believe it. Then I saw her."

"What did you see, Tucker?"

He paused. His bottom lip quivered. "I saw Miss Silvers. I didn't know that's who she was at the time of course. That came later. But she was lying there in the mud. She had one leg kind of bent behind her, half in the river. She was face down. Her other leg was bent up, kind of like the number four. Almost like maybe she was trying to crawl. At least I thought that at first. But her legs weren't moving."

"Can you describe what she was wearing?" I asked.

Tucker's nostrils flared. He looked straight at the jury. "She had nothin' on the bottom. She had a bra on but it was ripped, like one strap was gone. But that was it. And she had ... there were ropes around her wrists, holding her arms behind her. And on her legs. The rope around one of her ankles was tied to a cinder block, like somebody tried to weigh her down."

I waited a moment so Tucker Welling's words would sink in.

"Was she hurt that you could see?"

He nodded.

"Mr. Welling?"

"Yes," he said. "She was ... there was a lot of mud. But she was bleeding. From the mouth. And there was ... blood on her legs. In between. And her face. She was ... she was all bruised. Swollen. Her eyes were both swollen shut. Her whole head was misshapen. Someone beat that girl. Badly."

"Objection," Matt said, but there was no emotion in his tone. "Calls for speculation."

"Sustained. Mr. Welling, you can answer with what you actually observed."

"I understand," Tucker said. "She had bruises, cuts, swelling ... all over her face. The one side looked like raw hamburger when I got up close."

"But Ms. Silvers was conscious?" I asked.

"Yes, ma'am. In and out though. She said help. Just that one word."

"What did you do?"

"I ... I was afraid to touch her. To move her. I took a first aid class. You're not supposed to move them in case there's a head injury. I mean ... there was ... but I didn't know. So I ... I took my jacket off. I covered her with it. I told her I was gonna go run for help. That got her upset. She was crying. She said no, like she didn't want me to leave her. But I had to."

"What did you do next?"

"I promised her I'd be back with help just as soon as I could. I told her she'd be all right. I told her she was safe. I was real worried though. Her legs weren't moving. Her fingers a little. And she was making noise. But ... I just had a feeling. I pulled the cement block up out of the water. I mean ... I didn't think she could move but just in case. I didn't want to risk her sliding into that water. Then I yelled for all I was worth. I climbed up the hill and went on to Salter Road. It took a few minutes. I kept going over to the railing and yelling down to her. Just telling her I was still there. It was still gonna be okay. She kind of answered, you know, cried out a couple of times. Then, nothing. I think she passed out."

"Then what happened?"

"I don't know how long I was on the road. Probably no more than five minutes. But it seemed like forever. I thought about running back to the house to call 911 but that would have taken at least fifteen minutes. And I didn't want to let her out of my sight. I promised. Anyway, finally a car came and slowed down. That was Gordon Cobb. I didn't know him before that. But thank God he slowed down. I had to have looked like a crazy person. But he did stop. He was on his way to work I found out later. Company car and all. He had a car phone in it. One of those clunky ones they used to make that is mounted to the floor. He called 911 from there. I think it was maybe five or ten minutes before the cops and the ambulance came. Gordon stayed on the phone until they got there. I went back down to Ms. Silvers. I waited with her. She was mostly out of it, but I wanted to try to keep her calm. I wanted her to know she wasn't alone."

"Thank you, Mr. Welling," I said. "Thank you."

A moment later, Matt Orville stepped up to the lectern.

"Good morning, Mr. Welling," he said. "I, uh ... you're ... well, you're a real hero. I mean, for being in the right place at the right time. I can't imagine what that must have been like for you."

I shot Kenya a look. Tucker Welling handled Orville's opening perfectly though.

"Are you asking me a question? Do I think I'm a hero?"

He looked at the judge then back at Matt.

"Mr. Orville?" Judge Saul said.

Matt appeared not to hear her. I knew that was all an act. He furrowed his brow and rifled through his notes.

"I just have a few things to ask you. Mr. Welling, you say that particular spot, along the river. You say it's tough to see from the road."

"Yes," Tucker said. "It's one of the reasons it's been such a good spot for walleye. There are parts of the Maumee River I won't even go near. Every yucko in town trying to catch fish or see what you're doing. Like it's some secret."

"Right. So you've driven by that area quite a bit."

"Yes," he said. "It's just a couple of miles from my house. My grandfather's actually the one who named it God's Brew. That's just a family secret."

"Of course," Orville said. "So that really is remarkable. If you hadn't been in that exact spot at that exact time, no one would have ever known Denise Silvers was down there."

"Probably not," he said.

"Uh-huh," Orville said. "And you ... you didn't see anyone else around that morning."

"No, sir."

"And likewise, nobody else saw you at that particular spot on the river, correct?"

"As far as I know."

"And Mr. Cobb. The driver you say you flagged down. He was the only other soul in the area?"

"At the time I tried looking, yeah."

"Your Honor," Matt said. "The prosecution and I have stipulated to the authenticity of a number of written statements in this matter. One of them being an affidavit prepared by Mr. Gordon Cobb. I'd like to mark it for identification now."

"Go on," Judge Saul said.

"Mr. Welling," Matt said. "You're aware that Gordon Cobb passed away some years ago. He ... unfortunately can't participate in these proceedings."

"I heard he passed, yes," Tucker said.

"And you say you actually had to come into the road to flag Mr. Cobb down, is that correct?"

"That's correct."

"So if Mr. Cobb told the police he saw you ... near the river ... well before you came into the road, would he have been lying?"

"Objection," I said. "This calls for hearsay and speculation. Mr. Cobb's statement, if properly admitted, speaks for itself."

"I'll withdraw," Matt said. "Just one last thing: do you know whether Gordon Cobb got a good look at Ms. Silvers that morning?"

"What? I don't ... I mean, not until the paramedics came and dragged her up on a stretcher. He stayed in his car on the phone. Like I said, it was one of those car phones that you couldn't remove."

"Right. Right. You did say that. Thank you, Mr. Welling. That's all I have."

"Ms. Brent?" Judge Saul asked.

"Nothing further," I said. But I was seething. Matt had tried to plant a seed that Tucker Welling was lying about what he did or found that day. It was ludicrous. He'd been cleared in about two seconds at the time of the attack. He had an iron-clad alibi leading up to his movements when he found Denise already injured at the riverbed.

It was cheap. It was dirty. And I should have seen it coming.

Chapter 12

THE JURY HELD their breath as Denise Silvers wheeled herself to the front of the courtroom. She would not be able to move up into the witness box. Instead, the microphone was moved to a table near her.

Her face seemed hard as granite as she raised her hand, read her name loud and clear into the record, and swore to tell the truth.

"Good morning, Denise," I said. "Are you ready?"

She leveled her brown eyes straight at Neil Shumway. "I am," she answered.

"All right then. Denise, I want to take you back to your life as it was twenty years ago. The spring of 2000. Can you tell me what you were doing then?"

"I was going to school. I took classes part time at the University of Toledo. I hadn't quite settled on a major yet but I was leaning toward a biology degree. I thought maybe I'd go into nursing later. Or work with animals. I was twenty years old."

"How were you paying for school?" If I could help it, I wanted to interject as little as possible. Denise was the most powerful when she told her story, her way. I would keep her focused with open-ended questions where I could. But Denise had been waiting to tell this story, in this setting, every single day of those intervening twenty years.

"I worked," she said. "I had a part-time job working as a receptionist for Powell Insurance Company. I answered phones, made copies. Made appointments for the different agents we had working there."

"And where was that office located?" I asked.

"In Sunmeadow Court. At the corner of Jackson and Talbot. We were in Suite 207."

"Were you the only office in Suite 207?"

She shook her head. "No. It was a three-story building. I'm not even sure how many other offices were in there. Maybe seven or eight on each floor. Some of the offices were vacant. But on my floor, the second floor, it was Powell, Dr. Podney, he was an orthodontist. Then there was a dermatologist, Dr. Sweeney. Um ... there was another doctor, a family doctor. Joe Nicholson. There was us. And then there was an embroidering place. Gosh, I can't remember the name of it but they did mostly varsity jackets, you know?"

"Thank you."

"Denise, can you tell me what your day was like on April 14th, 2000?"

"It was a Friday," she said. "I worked three days a week. Monday, Wednesday, and Friday. On Tuesdays and Thursdays I took classes. I know that was the last full week I was going to work before taking off for exams. They were the following week but I never ..."

She folded her hands in her lap. I waited. So did the jury. Then she took a deep breath and leveled her eyes back at Shumway.

"I worked nine to five that day. Like every Friday."

"Do you remember who was in the office that day?" I asked.

"Mr. Powell senior," she said. "He was getting ready to retire and turn the business over to his daughters. One of them, Maisy, she was there too. When it got to be five o'clock, they were both still working in Mr. Powell's office. He was a really sweet guy. But ... at that time, he wasn't really running the business. His mind was starting to go. Maisy and Mary Ann were really running the show. Anyway, I checked with them to remind them what time it was. We usually left the building together. Maisy kind of waved me off. Told me to go on ahead without her. Her dad was having a bad day. Anyway, she told me good luck on my exams. And I remember telling her they weren't until the next week. Then I left."

"Where did you go?" I asked.

"There is a parking garage that connects all three suites at Sunmeadow. They're set up like a tower with the parking structure at the center of it. Like the hub. I left the office and headed to my car. I always parked on the second floor. 2b, actually. I liked it there because it was facing the right direction. I could back out and head down and out rather than circling up and out."

"Was anyone with you?" I asked.

"No. I don't remember if I saw anyone when I left that particular day. Sometimes people from some of the offices came out at the same time. I would hold the elevator if I saw someone ... but not that day. It was just me."

"Then what happened?" I asked.

"I had my purse. I had my keys out. I drove a blue Neon then. Anyway, when I got to the car, something seemed off. It looked, lopsided. I checked and my driver's side rear tire was flat."

"What did you do then?" I asked, thinking about Cass Leary's experience with Shumway. He'd slashed her tire and shown up when she pulled off to the side of the road. Two other suspected victims of Shumway's had similarly had their tires slashed. But because of the rules of evidence I was bound by, the jury would hear none of that.

"I walked around the car," Denise continued. "I didn't have a cell phone then, but I had triple A. I was going to go back into the office and make a call. While I was standing by the back of my car, someone came up behind me."

"Did you see who it was?"

"No," she said. "I never saw clearly who it was. I mean, I knew it was a man. I saw his reflection in my back window. He was tall. And he came up walking really fast. It all kind of happened so fast it took me a second to register it all."

"I was going to turn around. In my mind I thought he was probably going to ask me about my tire. I don't know, maybe even offer to help me put the spare on. But then, arms came around me like this."

108

Denise gestured, putting her arm across her chest.

"Across my chest," she said before I had to remind her to verbalize it. "Then there was a bag. Like a plastic grocery bag. He shoved it over my head and pulled it tight. Like the handles. I couldn't see through it. I couldn't breathe. I tried to kick out at first. He pulled me backward.

"I got lightheaded. I don't know. It finally occurred to me I had to figure out a way to rip the bag or I knew I was going to pass out."

"Did you?"

"He pulled me across the parking lot. Backward. I remember that. My feet dragging across the concrete. I'd been wearing heels and I lost a shoe. I got a hand up. I mean, thank God I got a hand up. I managed to tear a small hole near my mouth."

"He still had a hold of me across the chest. I was kicking out but not hitting anything. He had one free arm and he opened the back of his car. Then he just pivoted. Like his whole body. He threw me in the back of that car. I landed face down."

"Then what do you remember?"

"I was panicking. I mean part of me just ... you don't believe it's happening. It has to be a dream. It can't be real. I still had the bag over my head and I remember clawing at it. Trying to get it off.

"Somehow, I ended up turning around. On my back. He came at me then. I just saw this dark shadow through the bag. It was white, the bag. Almost opaque."

"Did you see anything unique about the car you were in?"

"It was dark inside. I don't know if it was black or dark blue.

But it wasn't wide like a full van. There was no backseat but there were ... it wasn't level. Like maybe it was a mini-van but the seats were all pushed down like you do."

"Objection," Matt said. "The witness is speculating."

"Sustained," Judge Saul said. "Ms. Silvers, I know this is difficult, but try to stick to facts you observed. Not guesses."

"All right," she said. When Denise looked back at me I gave her the slightest nod. She was doing great.

"He hit me then," she said. "With something hard and heavy. I don't know if it was a plank of wood, or a billy club. But it was like a big, hard stick. I got my arms up just in time. It ... I found out later that blow broke my right wrist. I tried to scream. To be honest, I don't know if I made a sound."

"Then what happened?"

She looked down. "He hit me again. In the shoulder. I tried to scoot further back, away from him. I could make out enough of him to know he was raising that club or whatever it was to hit me again."

"Did he?"

She nodded. Silent tears rolled down her face. "He did. I don't remember the blow though. I blacked out. Later ... when I woke up. When I made it to the hospital. I had a skull fracture."

I paused for a moment. Denise held the jury's rapt attention. Each of them looked at her, not Shumway. He kept his head down.

"What do you remember next, Denise?" I asked.

"When I came to ... I was ... I didn't have any clothes on. I couldn't see. There was duct tape over my eyes and over my mouth. My wrists and feet were tied with rope. The car was moving."

"What could you observe? By touch? Sound? Feel?"

"Well, I mean, like I said, I felt the car moving. And he was humming. It was familiar. 'Oh Susanna' or something like that. I didn't recognize his voice. Everything ... every inch of me. It was just pure pain. My shoulder. My head. And ... down there."

I clasped my hands on the lectern. "Denise, I know this is tough. But you need to explain what you mean."

"Down there," she said again. "I felt ... raw ... like he'd. My hands were tied in front of me at the wrists. I could still use my fingers somewhat. I felt the blood. It was running down my legs ... from in between my legs. I felt ... ripped open. Everywhere. My ... everywhere."

I'd asked her to describe what she felt about her injuries, in detail. She did. Shumway had brutalized her. Sodomized her. But the worst was yet to come.

"Denise, can you tell us what happened after that?"

"I don't know how long we drove. The corner of the tape over my eyes started peeling up so I could see little bits from my peripheral vision. Not straight on. I know it was dark out. I tried to yell out to him. I was begging him to stop. To let me go. I doubt he could hear anything but moaning through that tape. But ... finally, he did stop. But it was so much later. I didn't really have a good sense of time, but it felt like we'd been driving for hours. It went from dark to light."

"And then what?"

"I felt the light. The sunlight. And it was so cold. He pulled me forward by my ankles. In my head, I knew I should try to kick. I was just limp. He pulled me to the edge so my legs were dangling out of the car. Then ... he put his hands between them. And I knew ... or ... I was afraid he was getting ready to do that to me again. To rape me. So I did try to fight. My wrists were tied together but I got a hold of one of his arms. I tried to dig my nails in his skin and that made him angry. He hit me. With I think the back of his hand. Then ... I lost it. I started to kick. Tried to scream. He lay on top of me."

"Did he say anything?"

"No," she said. "Not even to tell me to stop. Not to threaten me. None of it. But I heard something scraping against the floor of the car. The corner of the tape over my eyes started to peel up even more and I saw that club. I rolled. Tried to get out of the vehicle. I had no idea where we even were. I fell to my knees, scraping them hard. It was the pavement."

"Then what happened, Denise?"

"He hit me. God. So hard. Across the lower back. Everything just ... stopped working after that. I know now that's when my spine was fractured. If he'd left me there. If he'd just left me there ... maybe I would have been okay. But he didn't. I blacked out again. And he threw me down or dragged me down that embankment and my back ..."

"Your Honor," Matt said. To his credit, he at least looked pained. "The witness just testified she was unconscious so how ..."

"Mr. Orville," Judge Saul said. "You'll have your opportunity to cross-examine this witness and explore it. For now, there's no need for this."

I cleared my throat. "Denise ... what happened next."

"I didn't come to again until I was on the bank of the river with a rope tied around my legs and the cement. The tape had come off by then. Blood and tears ... it just wouldn't stick anymore, I guess. It was Mr. Welling's voice I heard. He was ..."

Here, she finally broke down. "I thought I was in hell. I was in hell. But ... he held my hand. He told me ... he was ... His hand was so strong in my hand but so gentle too. And the way he talked. I just ... I wanted to die. I knew. Even through all of it ... I knew. Something was wrong. I was broken. It was bad. I couldn't feel my legs. And I could have died. I know it. They say you can lose the will to live. I did. God help me. I did. But Tucker Welling ... he saw me like that. He knew what happened. And he comforted me. He ... it was like he reminded me I was a human being again. If he hadn't been like that. If he'd acted scared or horrified. But he didn't. He was ... he was my friend."

Four members of the jury openly wept. I had heard Denise explain what Tucker Welling did for her that day maybe a hundred times since I met her. My throat closed up. I turned away from the jury for a moment.

"Denise," I said. "What has your life been like since that day?"

"My spine was crushed in two places," she said. "Below L3. I have no feeling beyond that. The last ... the last sensation I remember before I died below the waist ... was the damage, the tearing from the day that man raped me. And I feel it every day. Every night. When it's quiet. When it's dark. I sleep with the lights on. Because the minute I turn them off, I feel that pain down there.

"I was a virgin," she said. "Before that day. And there's been no one ... I've never had a boyfriend since then. Or a husband. Even if I could ... I could never be intimate. Both because of what was done to me physically and emotionally. I will never walk again. I cannot have children. My ... I can't go to the bathroom like normal people do. I was never able to return to school. Never graduated. He broke my body that day. But he didn't break me."

"How do you support yourself now, Denise?" I asked.

"My hands still work. Thank God for that. So, I learned how to knit. It gives me such joy to create something. It took a long time for me to come to terms with what I lost that day. But ... now ... I try to be there for other victims. Tucker Welling was my angel that day. So, I try to be an angel to other victims of sexual assault. A few years ago my sister and I formed a non-profit. The Silver Angels. We provide support to victims of sexual assault. We stay by their side at the hospital. We come with them to court hearings. We partner with battered women's shelters. We have legal advocates. I've tried to make something positive come out of all of this. But ... even with all of that ... I wish I could go back. I wish I would have waited to leave until Maisy and Mr. Powell were ready to go. I wish I would have called off sick that day. But then ... I think maybe someone else might have been his victim instead of me and that fills me with such guilt because sometimes I wish it was."

She sobbed. She took a tissue from the box on the desk beside her.

"Would you like a moment, Ms. Silvers?" the judge said. "We can take a brief recess."

"No," Denise said. "No. I want to continue."

"Denise," I said. "Before charges were filed, did you know who the defendant, Neil Shumway, was?"

She wiped her nose. "I didn't know Neil Shumway. When you told me that name, it didn't mean anything."

"But it has since?"

"I saw a picture ... his mugshot. You showed me, or the police did, I'm not sure. And still, it didn't quite look familiar. But then I saw a picture of him from when he was younger. And then I did recognize him. He had more hair. And he was smiling in it. When I saw that picture I knew who the man in it was."

"And who was that?" I asked.

"I knew him as Newt. I didn't know a last name."

"And how did you know the man you called Newt?" I asked.

"He was a drug ... a pharmaceutical rep. I can't recall which company. But like I said, there were a lot of doctors' offices around us in Sunmeadow Court. Newt would make the rounds. He was friendly. A talker. A salesman. And he'd often stop by my window at Powell and say hello. He'd give us pens, or stress balls, or whatever trinket he was passing out. He knew everyone by name. At least, I always heard him calling everyone by their first name. He was nice. He was handsome. And he ... he knew everyone who worked in that building."

"Thank you, Denise," I said. "I have nothing further."

I gathered my notes and turned away from the lectern.

"We'll adjourn for lunch," Judge Saul said. "After that, you can begin your cross-examination, Mr. Orville."

Chapter 13

BETSY SILVERS and a group from the Silver Angels closed ranks around Denise as soon as she left the courtroom. They were there to form a physical and emotional barrier between Denise and her attacker. Not that Neil Shumway had any chance of getting near her. The idea was to create a physical wall of supportive, female faces. For her part, Denise looked stronger than I'd ever seen her. She would have to be. Matt Orville was playing to win.

Kenya and I took a quick lunch at the coffee shop across the street. During trials, I had a standing order for bottled water and a grilled cheese sandwich. It wasn't glamorous, but it had become a ritual.

"She was good so far," Kenya said. She opted for coffee and a cruller. I could not for the life of me understand how Kenya Spaulding stayed so calm with the amount of caffeine and sugar I saw the woman consume on a daily basis.

"That was the easy part," I said. "The trick is going to be

keeping the jury engaged over the next two days when we put the science guys on."

"Oh come on," Kenya smiled. "I love the science guys. Everybody loves the science guys."

I took a bite of my sandwich. My stomach was a little unsettled. I was pleased with how Denise's direct exam went. She got in all the facts we needed from her. She established the timeline. Her description of the attack was gut-wrenching. The jury was riveted. And she'd painted a poignant picture of what her life was like today and every day since. Still, I had that feeling like being at the top of a roller coaster. At some point, we were in for a steep drop. I just didn't know when.

"You sure you don't me to handle Terry Martin?" she asked. Terry Martin was our DNA expert. He was brilliant. His lab was the number one in the country. But every time I'd ever had to call him as a witness, he tended to come off as arrogant. He had a droning voice that no amount of guidance from us could change. That said, his science was solid.

"I'm good," I said. "And I'm gonna need your eyes more than anything. Nobody reads juries as well as you do."

She nodded. "Well, so far, I'd say they believe Denise's every word. Matt's got his work cut out for him this afternoon. He'd be a fool to come at her too hard."

"Well, that's a double-edged sword too. If he plays the nice guy and gets in a point or two ..."

"He won't," Kenya said. "He's got nothing. The only thing he can underscore with her is that she can't identify her attacker. She never saw his face. Didn't get a good look at the vehicle.

He can only make that point and that's it. Relax. We're winning."

I liked her confidence but had the distinct urge to throw salt over my shoulder or something.

Kenya wiped her mouth with her napkin, folded it, and put it on her plate. "Come on," she said. "Let's go watch Denise wipe the floor with Matt Orville."

I stuck a twenty on the table and scooted out of the booth to join her.

The courtroom was standing room only when we returned. The Silver Angels took up the three rows toward the back. They wore silver wings on their shirts and sat with their arms locked. The bailiff opened the gate while Denise made her way back up to the microphone.

Judge Saul reminded her she was still under oath. Matt Orville shuffled papers on his table. Neil Shumway said something to him that made Matt lean down to hear him better. Matt nodded. He patted Shumway on the arm.

I didn't like the expression on Denise's face. Earlier in the day, I'd seen only steely-eyed resolve. Now she looked exhausted. I hoped the physical toll this was taking on her wouldn't impact her delivery. I tried to transmit a message of strength as Orville finally got his notes together and walked up to the lectern.

"Good afternoon, Ms. Silvers," he said. "I just want to start out by saying ... I can't imagine how difficult this is for you. And I know you probably look at me as the enemy. I'm not. I assure you. I'm just going to ask you some questions. That's all."

Denise set her jaw in a hard line. "I'm not a child, Mr. Orville."

There she was. Kenya made a fist and tapped it lightly on the table beside me.

"All right. Then I just want to clarify a few things you talked about in your direct testimony. I know it's been a long day already. If you need ... if you're uncomfortable for any reason or need a break, will you promise to let us know?"

"I promise I know how to speak up for myself, Mr. Orville, if that's what you're asking," she said.

"It is. Yes."

This too was strategy on Matt's part. Make the jury see him as an empathetic nice guy, sure. But also, if for any reason Denise misspoke and tried to claim she was getting tired or uncomfortable, Matt would undercut it by reminding the jury how he'd repeatedly checked in with her.

"All right," he said. "So let me ask a few things about the office where you worked. You said the parking lot is at the center. It's the hub of the building, yes?"

"Yes," she said.

"You claim you were completely alone when you left the building that evening?"

"I was the only one who left my office at the time. I didn't see anyone in the elevator or when I walked to my car. I didn't see another soul until the defendant grabbed me from behind and put a plastic bag over my head."

"But you didn't see your attacker's face, correct?"

"I did not, no," Denise said.

"And you didn't recognize his voice?"

"He didn't say anything to me at that time," she answered.

Orville looked through his notes. "At that time. Did this man say anything to you at all?"

"Like words? Conversation? No. He didn't."

"But you say you heard him singing. 'Oh Susanna'?"

"Yes,' she said. "He hummed it but he also sang the words."

Matt Orville took a pause to nod. He kept a puzzled expression on his face. "And it's your claim you didn't recognize this man's voice at any point during this attack?"

"No. I didn't," she answered.

"It didn't sound even vaguely familiar?"

"It did not," she said.

Matt stepped around the lectern. He leaned against it, crossing his arms in front of him. "You testified you believed Mr. Shumway was actually a man named Newt who worked in your office?"

"Not in my office. No. He was a drug rep. Several offices in the building were clients of his. He was a schmoozer, you know? He made it a point to get to know the staff at the front desks of the other offices."

"He made it a point," Matt repeated. "I see. How many times would you say you saw Newt while you worked at Powell Insurance?"

"I ... I don't know. Like I said, I worked Mondays, Wednesdays, and Fridays. I believe Mondays were when he came in."

"Every Monday?"

"I'm not sure."

"Did you look forward to it when he came?"

"Objection," I said. "This is irrelevant."

"Your Honor," Matt said. "I think the level of familiarity this witness had with the man she believes to be her attacker is extremely relevant."

"Overruled," Judge Saul said.

"He was ... Newt was fine," Denise said. "I mean, he was corny. Always calling girls sweetheart, that kind of thing. But there were a few drug reps that would frequent that building. They were all kind of the same. Super nice. Passing out free stuff. So yeah, we liked it when they came around and Newt was one of the few who bothered to pay attention to the Powell office. We weren't on his client list."

"I see. So you knew him. You were friendly with him. Were on a first-name basis."

She hesitated. "Yes."

"And you knew what his voice sounded like, didn't you?"

It was the first sign of alarm in Denise's eyes. Her breathing quickened and she looked at me. I tried to transmit calm. Matt was trying to raise questions where he could but this was nothing more than a smokescreen. Denise's terror-filled, likely concussed brain may not have recognized Neil Shumway's singing voice as he brutalized her behind a mask, but his DNA wouldn't lie.

"Ms. Silvers," Matt said. "Isn't it true that not only were you familiar with this Newt, you actually had a crush on him?"

Two red spots appeared in Denise's cheeks. "I'm sorry, what?" she asked.

"Didn't you in fact have a crush on Newt?"

"I don't ... I don't remember that. He was good-looking. Yes. I remember that. But he was just a schmoozy salesman who came into the office with candy every other week. I didn't know him outside of that."

"You rated him a ten though, didn't you?" Matt asked.

My back stiffened. Kenya was scribbling a note. She turned the paper toward me.

Where the hell is he getting this?

"Rate?" Denise asked.

"Rate," Matt said. "Let me ask you this. Who would you say your best friends either in the office or in the office building were at that time? Who did you socialize with the most?"

"I ... I mean, the Powells were who I saw the most."

"But you often went to lunch with Grace Sandford, Kiersten Marshall, Marcy Cross, and uh ... Ann Duffy, isn't that right?"

"Sometimes," Denise said. "Grace and Kiersten worked as dental hygienists next door. Ann was a receptionist on the first floor. Marcy was a nurse in Dr. Nicholson's office. Yes. Sometimes we went to lunch together. But they weren't my friends outside of work. We weren't close, if that's what you mean."

"But you were close enough to rate the men you encountered in that office, weren't you? And close enough to even make a bet over who could sleep with Newt Shumway first, isn't that right?"

My lungs felt like they'd just filled with acid. Kenya kept scribbling. I had to put a hand over hers to get her to be still. We couldn't look shocked by any of this.

"Objection," I said. "This is irrelevant, highly prejudicial."

"Your Honor," Matt said. "Do I even have to answer that? This question is extremely relevant to show the extent of this witness's familiarity with the defendant. And it goes to her credibility."

"I'll allow it," Judge Saul answered.

Denise was sweating now.

"Ms. Silvers," Matt said. "Do you need to take a break?"

"No," she said.

"Do you need me to repeat the question?"

"Yes," she said.

"Did you or did you not enter into a bet with Grace, Marcy, Kiersten, and Ann as to which of you could get Newt into bed first?"

"No," she said. "I do not remember that."

"But does that sound like something you *would* have done?"

"Objection!" I shouted.

"Sustained," Judge Saul said. She was glaring at Matt.

"I said I have no memory of that," Denise said.

"All right," Matt said. "Fair enough. Ms. Silvers, I don't relish having to ask you this question. But you have to understand that when you take the witness stand and make certain statements ... well ... truthfulness is always an issue."

"Objection," I said. "Counsel is giving speeches."

"Sustained," Judge Saul said.

"Ms. Silvers," Matt said. He squared his shoulders and looked straight at Denise. "Isn't it true that you in fact boasted at lunch the Friday before your attack that you had won the bet you made about bedding Newt Shumway before they did?"

"Objection!"

Judge Saul's face was purple. "She can answer, Ms. Brent."

"No!" Denise said. "I never made such a claim. It wasn't true. And if you're trying to imply your client's brutal rape and attempted murder of me would satisfy some sick fabricated bet on that score then you can just go straight to hell right along with him!"

The Silver Angels erupted behind me. Judge Saul banged her gavel. It took a full minute before the bailiffs had the courtroom calm and the Silver Angels cleared out. Kenya went right out with them, reading my mind. All of the women Matt brought up had been extensively interviewed by the police. I'd spoken to Ann Duffy myself before she passed away from breast cancer. At no point had any of them mentioned any such thing. I couldn't believe Matt would risk doing anything as stupid as throwing up lies in front of the jury.

I was fuming as we stepped up to the bench for a sidebar.

"I don't even know where to start," I said. "He's assuming facts not in evidence. He's ..."

"Look," Judge Saul said. "I don't like this any more than you do. I sure hope one of you is planning to call those girls in to explain themselves."

"Oh, you can take that to the bank, Your Honor," Matt said.

"Fine," she said. "For now, this witness has been asked and answered that line of questioning. Move on. Do you have anything else?"

Matt looked at his shoes. "Listen ... I might as well get this out now even though I do *not* have to give you a heads up on any defense strategy I plan to use. But ... I get the sensitive nature of this trial and what this witness has been through. But ... so we are clear, I wouldn't be doing this if she hadn't opened the door."

"What are you talking about?" Judge Saul and I spoke in unison.

"Denise Silvers is lying," he said. "She was very far from being a virgin the day she was attacked."

I felt sick. Judge Saul's face went a little green.

"This is improper," I said. "The Supreme Court has weighed in. A rape victim's past sexual history is *not* admissible."

Matt let out a breath. "It is when she's made an unequivocal statement that can be rebutted. I'm allowed to offer evidence to impeach her credibility. She made the statement that she was a virgin on direct exam."

"You piece of ..."

Judge Saul put a hand up, stopping me before I said the rest of it. "I hate everything about this. But Matt may have a point from an evidentiary standpoint. I want everyone's bases covered though. I want briefs by morning. For now, we're gonna let that girl go home."

"Absolutely not!" I said. "Denise is stronger than all three of us put together. If Matt's done with cross, I want to redirect before the jury goes home. We have that right."

Judge Saul nodded.

"Finish up, Mr. Orville."

I tore away from the bench and sat down hard. Kenya had yet to return. Near the witness stand, Denise had begun to cry. She held steady though.

"Ms. Silvers," Matt said. "I have just one last question. Is there any part of your testimony today—either what you answered for me or what you said when Ms. Brent was questioning you—is there anything you think you may have misspoken? Anything you'd like to clear up?"

My jaw dropped. He was tying a noose around her neck. And I had no legal basis to object. I knew what was coming, but if I asked Denise to either walk back or reconfirm she'd been a virgin, it would be more than opening the door. I'd blow the thing right off its hinges.

"No," Denise said into the microphone. "Every word I've told you here today is the truth. Every. Single. Word."

"Thank you," Matt said. "I have nothing further for this witness but would reserve the right to call on rebuttal."

"That's the State's right," I said. "Not the defense."

Matt's color went a little gray, but he stood his ground. With the bang of Judge Saul's gavel, we were adjourned for the day.

Chapter 14

"IT'S A LIE!"

Denise was almost hysterical. We brought her to the large conference room next to my office. Betsy sat beside her, rubbing her shoulder. She had kind, whispered words for her sister. She stared red murder at me.

"Where is he coming up with that stuff?" Denise asked. "There was no bet. There was no ... I don't remember a rating system."

"Not ever?" Kenya asked.

I shot a look to her, trying to silently convey a "not now" message.

Phil appeared in the hallway. He beckoned me with two fingers.

"Listen," I said. "We'll work our way through this. You knew Orville was going to try throwing curveballs. You held up, Denise. I'm proud of you. You didn't let him rattle you. Not on the witness stand."

"You're going to clean this up?" Betsy asked. Her face had gone ghostly white. I was beginning to worry whether she was calm enough to get Denise home safely.

"There's a lot of trial left, Betsy. If blaming the victim is the best strategy Matt Orville can come up with ... well ... I like our chances even more. Now, there's nothing more to be done for you two today. Go home. Get some rest. Let me do my job. Tomorrow's a big day."

Kenya was already out in the hallway talking to Phil. He looked even angrier than Betsy. I said a few more polite, reassuring things to the Silvers sisters, then headed out of the conference room. A group of Silver Angels waited for them out in the parking lot.

As soon as I was certain Denise and Betsy were headed out of the building, I went to join Kenya and Phil in Phil's office.

He was pacing in front of his desk. I walked in just as he swiped his hand downward and knocked a pencil holder to the ground.

"How?" he asked. "Where the hell is Orville getting this crap?"

I folded my arms in front of me. "My honest opinion? He's making it up."

"Matt Orville isn't that stupid," Phil said. "He gets caught doing that it'll blow up in his face."

Kenya was holding a purple file folder in her arms. It contained a copy of the main police file on the Denise Silvers assault. I gestured to her and she put it down on Phil's desk.

I stood over it and leafed through it until I found the witness statements. I practically knew them by heart. All the women Orville mentioned had spoken to the cops along with about a dozen other employees from the Sunmeadow Court building. There was no mention of Neil Shumway or Newt. There was no mention of Denise ever making a bet involving sexual exploits.

"Is she lying?" Kenya asked. "I mean ... no ... she's not lying. But do you think there's a chance she doesn't remember this being discussed on one of these lunches?"

I sank into a chair by Phil's desk. "No. I think she would have remembered."

"But ... at the time they were questioned," Kenya said. "Newt —Neil Shumway—wasn't a suspect. He was never even on the cop's radar. I mean ... I can kind of see why none of them would have mentioned this then. Denise was in critical condition after a brutal assault. What kind of asshole would you have to be to start besmirching her character to the police when they didn't even have a suspect. It would have made sense back then. And ... I'm just playing devil's advocate here."

"Who interviewed these women?" Phil asked.

I didn't have to refer back to the police report to know. "Mostly Ken Leeds," I answered.

"Sloppy," Phil said. "How thorough have they been going back over this file? They were supposed to have re-inter- viewed every material witness."

"Phil," I said. "Calm down. This is a distraction. I don't care if Denise had an 'I love Newt' t-shirt made and wore it to work for a month. She was brutally assaulted by this man. He raped her. He beat her nearly to death and was planning to make her body disappear. Even without the DNA, we still have a solid case against him. With the security footage, I can prove he was in that parking garage that day and left after the time Denise would have been attacked. His movements match our timeline. You're reacting exactly how Matt Orville wants you to. So don't. This is nothing."

It was and it wasn't. But I wasn't going to let Phil's anxiety set the tone for the rest of this trial.

"We have to get him, Mara," he said. "I had a long conversation with Emily Schultz today. They don't have enough to charge on the Jennifer Lyons murder. They had some problems with their labs. Degradation of the DNA samples or something."

"What?" I said. His words stopped me cold. Regardless of the outcome of my case, I expected Kalamazoo to issue an arrest warrant the minute I had a verdict. They'd been sitting on it to lessen the risk of tainting my jury pool.

"They're also having some trouble nailing down their timeline. An old boyfriend has resurfaced. A junkie who went up on possession with intent to sell charges. They've got a witness who claims he's made a prison confession. Emily thinks it's bogus. Their case is getting press attention and this witness came out of nowhere. It's not going to pan out but the cops up there need to do their due diligence to rule it out."

"When did this all go down?" I asked.

Phil shrugged. "The day before yesterday. It's not public knowledge. To be honest, I'm hoping to keep it away from Matt Orville for as long as possible. And I didn't want it messing with your head."

I let out a sigh. "Except now you're okay with that. Listen, I'm sorry if Kalamazoo's having trouble getting their house in order. But I'm not. We're going to get this guy. Don't fall apart on me now, Phil."

I knew there was more to this than just the so-called lunch club bet. Although I found it distasteful for Matt Orville to even bring politics into Denise's trial, he wasn't wrong about the damage a loss would do to Phil's reelection hopes next year.

"Let me get Ritter or Cruz on the phone. We should know for sure who interviewed them back in the day. One of those girls has flipped. It better be a surprise to them too."

Phil shook his head. "You should have followed up with those women too, the minute we had a name."

My head snapped back almost as if Phil had struck me. I'd seen Phil lose his temper before, but this was different. It made me wonder if something else was at play.

"Kenya," I said. "Get a hold of them now. I still say it's not as big an issue as you think it is, Phil. It doesn't negate what Shumway did. It doesn't even begin to touch the elements of the crime."

Kenya read my hint and excused herself from the room. I waited until I couldn't hear her footsteps anymore then turned to Phil.

"Okay," I said. "So what's with you?"

He let out a hard breath that deflated him. Then he sat down behind his desk.

"He's not fishing," Phil said. "I know Matt Orville too well.

He pulled the pin from a grenade with one of those witnesses today. It's going to go off at some point. You can mark my words on that."

"Again," I said. "It still doesn't matter. Neil Shumway raped and brutalized Denise Silvers. We have the physical evidence. We've got him on DNA and the timeline. And that jury believes Denise. I'm sure of it. At best, all Matt's got is a twenty-year-old innuendo from some woman she had lunch with. It's meaningless. And it's just as likely to backfire and make the jury hate him as anything else."

I let my words settle. Phil considered them and seemed to calm down. But I wasn't done. "You were here back then, Phil," I said. "Not me. You're worried about some kind of prosecutorial oversight with the sheriff's department back in 2000? Well, where were you on this case?"

Phil's eyes flashed. "There wasn't enough to indict anyone, Mara. There wasn't even a solid person of interest. If you're implying we didn't take this seriously back then ... you're wrong. Everyone wants to talk about Ken Leeds as a casualty. He wasn't the only one. I saw this case eat *my* predecessor. Dan Proctor took so much heat on this case. It took years off his life too. But we can't prosecute if we don't have a suspect."

"I know," I said. I'd heard all the stories about the legendary Dan Proctor, former Maumee County Prosecutor. He'd taken on corruption with one of the most powerful unions in town. Some credited him with keeping organized crime out of Waynetown when other port cities like ours fell. "I'm just saying that we are *all* doing the best we can with what we have. There's a reason cold cases are so hard to prosecute. We'll weather this. I know it."

"What if she's lying though?" Phil said. "You're right about it not mattering on the elements. But you told me Denise was thrown when you showed her that old picture of Shumway and she realized she *did* recognize him. You said you didn't like the looks she was passing with her sister. Like they were holding something back. What if this is it?"

"Then it still doesn't matter," I said. Though I was less sure, I wasn't about to admit that to Phil. Part of my job was managing his reactions to things. I needed to make sure he could take that confidence out in front of the media, even if it was just to utter an obligatory "no comment." If he looked scared, it could hurt us.

"It doesn't matter if they even had sex before April 14th," Phil said. "But it matters if Denise lied about it. Are you sure ... are you one hundred percent sure in your heart of hearts that didn't happen?"

The room fell silent except for the faint clicking of a wooden clock Phil kept on his mantle.

"I believe Denise," I said.

"If we lose," he said. "It's not just Denise and the Silver Angels I'll have to worry about. I'll be finished. You'll have a new boss next year. You watch, you'll get scapegoated right along with me. Howard will survive with his job intact because ... well ... he's Howard. And Kenya? She'll be the only thing that survives the apocalypse. And she'll do it however she has to. You can't think it was an accident she got loud about her wanting to try this case instead of you. I mean, she did want it. But it was theater too. She was covering her bases."

I knew he was right. I knew what she was doing at the time.

135

But I also knew that Kenya Spaulding wanted justice for Denise just as much as I did. The rest didn't matter now.

"It was one day," I said. "One insinuation about something that doesn't matter. Denise held up. The DNA is going to finish that bastard."

"When are you putting it in?" he asked.

"Tomorrow."

Phil nodded. He still seemed unsettled. I was giving him a pep talk when really it should have been the other way around. But our relationship was like that sometimes.

"What?" I finally said.

Phil steepled his fingers beneath his chin. "I just ... Mara, I don't want you to get hurt. And I'm kicking myself a little for not protecting you better."

"Protecting me? From what?"

"From Matt Orville. We both know he's the one who bought that information about Jason's infidelities. Don't think he's done using it. He's just biding his time."

"I'm not afraid of him," I said. "I've done nothing wrong."

"No," he said. 'But Jason sure has. And there's no way it won't get messier for you on the personal front while this case is going on."

"Phil, I'm done talking about this. As far as I'm concerned, my personal life is off-limits as a topic of conversation inside these walls. I know you care about me, but it's really none of your business."

Phil frowned. He at least looked pained as he uttered his next sentence. Though it didn't make it sting any less.

"That's the thing, Mara, it is exactly my business when it impacts the operation of this office. Denise's testimony should have been tighter. She should have been pushed more when it became clear Shumway meant something to her. There's some *there*, there. I feel that in my gut and the jury will too. Matt ... the stuff he does ... it's not random."

I rose from my seat. I was angry. And it was the last thing I needed as I prepared to call our most important witnesses.

"Nothing I do is random either, Phil. If Matt Orville is throwing up red herrings ... which he is ... it's because he knows how good I am. It's too bad you seem to have forgotten that."

Phil's jaw dropped and he had the decency to look horrified as I turned and left his office.

Chapter 15

TWENTY YEARS IS A LONG TIME. In civil court, and lesser crimes, it's the reason justice demands a statute of limitations. Memories fade. Witnesses die or become unavailable. And yet, there are some crimes we deem so heinous, no amount of time can pass in which we will not hold a perpetrator accountable. But it's the reason why most cold cases are so difficult to prosecute unless we have substantial, physical evidence that cannot be denied.

In Denise Silvers's case, I had many hurdles in front of me, but luck on my side in the form of nurse Whitney Scofield.

Whitney had been one of the first people to care for Denise once she reached St. Bart's hospital. And now, twenty years later, her memory of that day remained crystal clear.

Whitney still worked in the E.R. at St. Bart's. I was of the personal opinion the place would fall apart without her. Whitney was fifty years old with short, silver hair, keen gray eyes, and a trim, toned, tanned physique. She walked with a limp though, a bad disk she'd earned through decades of the brutal, physical work required of nurses. She was due for surgery but had been putting it off, unwilling to take the time off she needed to tend to it. Whitney knew St. Bart's would fall apart without her too.

"Ms. Scofield," I said. Whitney sat rod straight in the witness chair. I knew it was agony for her with her back but I also knew she would sit there as long as it took.

"Do you recall the extent of Ms. Silvers's injuries when she was brought into the E.R.?"

"Objection," Matt said, barely looking up from his notes. "Nurse Scofield is not a diagnostician."

"That's absolutely incorrect, Mr. Orville," Whitney said. "Patient assessment is part of my job."

"Overruled," Judge Saul said.

"Do you need me to repeat the question?"

"No," Whitney said. "Denise Silvers was suffering from a number of injuries. While Mr. Orville was right that it wasn't up to me to make a differential diagnosis or come up with a treatment plan, I can most certainly tell you what I observed."

"And what was that?"

"Denise had multiple contusions and lacerations on her face. One laceration was so deep you could see her skull. That was just behind her left ear. She was covered in bruises, abrasions, and small cuts all over her body. Her arms, torso. There was extensive bruising on her right breast. Her legs. She was smeared with so much blood it was at first difficult for us to determine where it was coming from. She had significant tearing to her rectum and perineum. Vaginal tearing was also extensive."

"Ms. Scofield," I said. "Was there any visual documentation of Ms. Silvers's injuries?"

"There was," she said. "Whenever a patient is brought in and we suspect she was the victim of sexual assault, we follow protocol. On that particular day that consisted of the attending physician, another nurse, and myself. I was lead sexual assault nurse examiner. I took photographs as Ms. Silvers's injuries were assessed. Our gravest concern at that time was a possible injury to her spine as she exhibited very poor responses to neurological testing. Unfortunately, those fears were well-founded as she did, in fact, suffer permanent injury to her spinal cord."

"I'd like to mark State's Exhibits twenty-three through thirty-seven for identification. Ms. Scofield, can you look at those photographs and tell me what they are?"

"Yes," she said. "These are the original Polaroid pictures I took that documented Denise Silvers's injuries as she was brought into St. Bart's E.R. on the morning of April 15th. Understand we use a digital camera now. But back then, this is what we had."

"And are they a fair and accurate representation of the injuries you personally observed on Ms. Silvers that morning?"

Whitney nodded. "They are."

"I'd like to move for the admission of State's twenty-three through thirty-seven."

My motion was granted. I was then able to project the

enlarged photos on the monitor for the jury to see. Whitney went through them with me one by one.

Several members of the jury covered their mouths in horror. Denise Silvers didn't look human. She lay broken on a hospital gurney, covered in blood. They saw the swelling around her right eye, the result of a blow to her head by what we believed was a billy club. That alone could have killed her. She was lucky it only broke her cheekbone.

They saw the worst of the photographs, the horrific injuries to Denise Silvers's most intimate body parts. I did not linger on those photographs too long. Seeing them for only a second impacted the jury enough. And they would take each of those Polaroid pictures back to the jury room.

"Were you able to collect a rape kit on Denise Silvers?" I asked.

"We did," she said. "Though we call it a SAFE kit. It stands for sexual assault forensic evidence kit."

"And what does that entail?"

"Well, understand, the kit itself contains the ... uh ... tools we use in the collection. Sterile swabs, collection containers, gloves. But if you're asking for what we actually collect, we swab for semen, blood, comb for pubic hair, the hair on the head. We pack the victim's clothes. In Ms. Silvers's case there was only her bra. The samples are then collected, labeled, secured and given to law enforcement. In Denise's case, the police were on hand almost immediately. I understand her ambulance had been followed in by two squad cars. By the time our examination in the E.R. was completed, Detective Ritter was already there."

I spent the next half hour going through Nurse Scofield's tedious collection process, safeguards against cross-contamination, and chain of custody. I left nothing to chance. She came across as calm, methodical, caring, and extremely competent. I knew she would play well to the jury. Whitney Scofield was exactly the kind of professional you would want at your side or a family member's side if God forbid something awful happened.

"Thank you, Ms. Scofield," I said.

"Patients can run together," Whitney said. Her voice took a far off quality. It made my heart skip. She wasn't responding to a direct question and I had no idea what she was about to say. That's never a good thing for a trial lawyer.

"It's been twenty years but I remember that day like it was yesterday. Every terrible detail. It's like that with some patients. And Denise Silvers was one of the ones that stuck with me."

"Thank you," I said, wanting to kiss Whitney Scofield. "I have nothing further."

With one sentence, Whitney had just undercut most of the things Matt might have done to chip away at her on cross-examination. If I'd been in Matt's shoes, I would have wanted her off the stand as quickly as possible.

"Ms. Scofield," he said. "When doing a rape kit like you described, you can't say for sure whether any of the samples you collected actually contained semen, can you?"

"Not usually, no," she said. "That's for the lab to analyze."

"Not usually," he repeated. "And even if you were aware or

suspected the presence of semen in your sample, you can't determine whether a rape took place."

"Of course not," Whitney said, her tone sharp and irritated. "But like I testified a minute ago, this girl had significant injuries ..."

"Your Honor," Matt interjected. "Can you please instruct the witness to only answer what she's been asked?"

Saul raises a brow. "Well, you just did."

"I understand," Whitney said.

"Thank you," Matt said. "I actually have nothing further at this time."

Whitney rose from the witness box and walked slowly out of the courtroom.

I then called David Seaver to the stand. He ran the State BCI laboratory and was responsible for performing the testing on Denise Silvers's rape kit.

Seaver was another stroke of luck for me in that he too, like Whitney, had remained in his position for twenty years. Though he ran the State's central criminal laboratory now, back in 2000 he was a lab technician without any supervisory role.

I took him through the dry parts of his testimony. This was the hard part of using DNA evidence. You have to establish the procedures in place at each lab. The jury must sit through highly technical and scientific explanations about collection techniques, variables, margins of error. But it's necessary before you can deliver the "punch" of DNA results.

As scientific experts went, David Seaver was good. He talked to the jury not at them, delivering his testimony in the simplest language he could, pausing in natural places to allow them to absorb what he was saying. He explained the process of performing a polymerase chain reaction most commonly used to analyze limited quantities of DNA. For the most part, the jury remained engaged. Finally, I was able to circle him around to the "goods."

"Dr. Seaver," I said. "Can you explain what samples you were asked to analyze from Denise Silvers's rape kit?"

"We had blood samples, hair samples, and semen samples."

"Can you describe your findings regarding the semen samples?"

"It was present," he said. "A substance positively identified as human ejaculate was present. We also had skin samples taken from beneath Denise Silvers's fingernails."

"What were the results of your analysis?" I asked.

"We analyzed several samples in connection with this case. We took what are called elimination samples from known subjects. People we knew to have been in physical contact with her after she'd been found. Tucker Welling, the responding medical personnel. We took a reference sample from the victim herself.

"We were able to isolate only two DNA profiles. One belonged to Denise Silvers herself. That was mainly from the blood samples presented. But we were able to isolate a different DNA profile in the seminal fluid and also the tissue found beneath her fingernails."

"What did it reveal?"

Seaver adjusted the microphone. "Twenty years ago, when the samples were submitted, though we had an intact DNA profile, it did not as I understand it match with any known profile within the BCI database or CODIS. That's a national database. The FBI's Combined DNA Index System. But a few months ago, we were given a sample of the defendant's blood to match that profile against."

"And what were your findings?"

"The semen sample taken from Denise Silvers's rape kit contained multiple loci or markers in common with the blood sample taken from Neil Shumway. It was inclusive."

"And what does that mean, in layman's terms?"

"It means there is a greater than 99.99% probability that the semen collected from Denise Silvers on April 15th, 2000 belonged to Neil Shumway."

I had a few follow-up questions, aimed mainly at underscoring the care in which Seaver conducted the testing. But they'd heard what I needed them to understand. It was Neil Shumway's body fluids on Denise's body. No one else.

"Thank, you," I said. "I have nothing further. Your witness."

Matt spoke in hushed whispers with Neil for a moment, then he rose.

"Dr. Seaver," he said. "You indicated that skin samples from beneath Denise Silvers's nails were also tested. Are you also claiming a DNA match to the defendant?"

"No," Seaver said. "We were not able to make a match from those skin samples."

"There was no DNA present? In skin? How is that possible?"

"There was DNA present. But the results were inconclusive. In this case, there were some environmental factors that appear to have accelerated the degradation of the skin samples. I understand that Ms. Silvers was found partially submerged in the Maumee River. There was bacteria growth in those samples that degraded it to the point we could not include or exclude the defendant as the source of those samples within a reasonable degree of medical certainty."

"You're saying the samples you tested from Denise Silvers's were contaminated?" Matt asked.

"Yes," Seaver answered. "I'm saying the DNA mixture regarding the skin test contained bacteria, likely from the river, that made it impossible for me to make a conclusive finding."

"Contaminated," Matt repeated. "I have nothing further."

"Ms. Brent?"

It was a red herring. We'd established the integrity of Seavers's lab. The skin DNA would have helped. But the slam dunk came from the blood and semen samples.

"Dr. Seaver," I said. "The defense seems to imply that your testing as a whole was contaminated. Is that fair?"

"It isn't," he said. "If anything, the issue with the skin sample only underscores the integrity of the testing process. The profile match on the blood and semen is as close as we ever get."

"When you say the results on the skin sample were inconclusive, can you contrast that with an exclusion result?"

"Of course," he said. "In layman's terms, it doesn't mean it wasn't Shumway's skin beneath Denise's nails. It could have been. We just couldn't produce a clear result due to the bacteria introduced to the samples from the river. I can't say it was Shumway's skin, but I can't say it wasn't."

"Thank you, Dr. Seaver," I said. "I have nothing further."

As Doug Seaver stepped off the witness stand, I felt the tide fully turning in our favor.

Kenya's reaction was subtle as I turned and walked back to the prosecution table. She hid a smile and mouthed "We got him!"

Chapter 16

DETECTIVE GUS RITTER didn't look good. In fact, he looked downright gray as he took the witness stand first thing Friday morning. He fidgeted with his tie and kept shifting in his seat.

I wrote a quick note to Kenya. "Find out if he's sick or something."

She nodded and turned back to the gallery. Gus Ritter was a lot of things. A blowhard. An old-school kind of cop who had very little use for lawyers on either side of the aisle. He'd never met a bridge he hadn't burned. But he was a good cop. And we rarely lost cases when Ritter served as lead investigator.

The trouble was, Gus Ritter hadn't been the lead investigator on this case. Twenty years ago he'd only been in the detective bureau for a few months. His partner, Ken Leeds, had headed up the Silvers investigation. Leeds's fatal heart attack fourteen years ago came two days before his retirement party. So, Gus Ritter was the next best thing and the only other person with firsthand knowledge of what went down back then.

ROBIN JAMES

We were stuck with each other.

"Detective Ritter," I said. We'd gotten through his establishing testimony and his employment background. I now had to confront the weaknesses of this case with him head-on.

"Who were your main suspects in this case back in 2000?"

He cleared his throat. "Well, we had physical evidence. The cement block. The ropes. The rape kit. At first we were very hopeful we'd be able to make a positive identification. But the DNA samples taken from Ms. Silvers didn't match any known profiles in the CODIS database at that time. And actually, not since."

"What does that mean, exactly?"

Ritter played with his tie again. "It just means that the guy whose DNA that was ... he hadn't found his way into the system. No arrests. No criminal convictions. No activity that would have subjected him to submitting a sample. Doesn't mean it was someone who hadn't gone on raping or breaking the law. It just means he hadn't yet been caught."

"Objection," Matt said. "Improper foundation. We request the witness's last statement be stricken as unresponsive."

Judge Saul's look told me it wasn't worth fighting for this one.

"So ordered," she said. "The jury should disregard the detective's statement speculating on any further criminal activity of the owner of the DNA sample. Continue, Ms. Brent."

"Where did your investigation lead you back then?" I asked.

"Well." Ritter sat a little straighter. "The nature of her injuries led us to believe her attacker probably knew her."

"Objection," Matt said, exasperated. "Calls for speculation."

"Your Honor, we've established Detective Ritter's credentials as a trained criminal investigator. His hypotheses during this investigation are based on that expertise."

"He can answer," Judge Saul said.

"This was a sustained, brutal attack," Ritter said. "This girl wasn't just raped. She was tortured. Beaten. Systematically. Over a period of time of roughly twelve hours. We worked from a theory that this attack might have been motivated by revenge. We started questioning people in her life ... men ... who would have had anger toward her. We identified one man she'd dated twice in the previous year but it wasn't a long-term relationship. In any event, he was quickly ruled out. He was out of town visiting relatives on the west coast. She had no other significant dating relationships. No jilted exes."

"Was there anyone else you focused on?" I asked.

"At that stage of the investigation, we were focused on ruling people out. A lot of times you arrive at the answer by process of elimination. We looked at Tucker Welling too," he said.

I turned back to face him. "And what did your investigation into Tucker Welling reveal?"

"He had an alibi," Ritter said. "From five o'clock on the 14th to about fifty minutes before that 911 call, Tucker Welling was at work. He worked the night shift at a machine shop on Fargo Drive. We were able to verify through witnesses, Mr. Welling's time card, and security cameras from the employee parking lot that showed him leaving at just past five o'clock that morning. His parents gave witness statements that are also in our report. He came straight home. Finally, the DNA we tested didn't match his."

"Thank you," I said. "So, then what happened? Did you question Denise Silvers's co-workers? Others who knew her at her place of employment?"

"Yes," he said. "It's all in Leeds's main report. I was with him on the majority of the canvassing interviews he did. Leeds had a very hands-on approach to investigations. He didn't farm out many of those interviews to field ops. And being a small town like we are, manpower is and was always an issue."

"Who was responsible for re-interviewing witnesses this year subsequent to the defendant becoming a person of interest?"

"Myself and my partner, Sam Cruz. Detective Leeds is unfortunately no longer with us."

"Did you interview Ann Duffy, the first-floor receptionist?"

"We couldn't, no. She passed away some years ago."

"Did you interview Grace Sandford, the dental hygienist?" I asked.

"Yes."

"Did her statement substantially change from the one she gave in 2000?" I asked.

"It did not."

"Did you interview Kiersten Marshall, the other dental hygienist?" I asked.

"Yes."

"Did her statement substantially change from the one she gave in 2000?"

"No. It did not."

"And did you interview Marcy Cross, the nurse working in Dr. Nicholson's office?"

"We reached out to her, yes."

"Did her statement substantially change from the one she gave to Detective Leeds in 2000?"

"She didn't respond to my request for an interview."

"And none of those re-interviews caused you to zero in on a particular person of interest beyond those you've already stated?"

"No, ma'am," he said. "No one knew anything. No one saw anything out of order. None of our leads at that time produced any viable investigative paths. Not at the time. Not now."

"So, going back to 2000, you made no other arrests in this case?"

"We didn't. The case went well and truly cold until earlier this year."

"What happened then?" I asked.

"A hit came through on the DNA sample taken from Ms. Silvers's rape kit."

"Can you explain how that came about?" I asked.

"About ten years ago, commercial ancestry research sites became available as a law enforcement tool. One in particular, Tree of Life, allows us to submit DNA samples without making them publicly available. We get a notification if there's a match. If someone submits their DNA to the front-facing, public DNA database at Tree of Life and their DNA profile matches one we've submitted we get a notification."

"Is that what happened in this case?"

"Yes," he said. "A close family match popped up to the DNA profile we had from Denise Silvers's rape kit. It turned out to be a parent-child match."

"Parent-child?" I asked.

Yes," he said. "Neil Shumway had a daughter who was apparently given up for adoption. She submitted her DNA hoping to get more information about her birth parents. That was the first break we had in the case in almost twenty years."

"What did you do with that information?"

"Once we had a positive match on the DNA, through the connection to the daughter, her lawyer shared with us her findings. They'd identified Shumway as her father. So, with that intelligence on the defendant, Detective Sam Cruz and I began to reconstruct his movements during the days surrounding Denise's attack. We showed his picture to the remaining witnesses ... those we could locate. We received a tip that Mr. Shumway was in fact working in the Sunmeadow Court building during the timeframe in question. We had secured security footage from the parking lot for the evening of April 14th, 2000. It was on a VHS tape we had still sitting in an evidence locker. Through that, we were able to confirm that a vehicle registered to Mr. Shumway used in conjunction with his employment with Blair Pharmaceuticals was recorded leaving the parking structure at approximately 5:28 p.m."

"Objection," Orville said. "This witness isn't qualified to testify to the authenticity of that videotape or what it shows."

"Sustained. Ms. Brent, let's do this the right way, shall we?" Judge Saul said.

I looked down at my notes. I had the parking lot security representative scheduled right after Detective Ritter. While Orville's objection was well-founded, he'd just helped me do my job. I could almost feel a few members of the jury's ears prick. They'd be only that much more interested in what my security guard had to say and to view that video.

"Detective," I said. "What did you do next?"

"Well, based on our review of the security footage, the DNA evidence, and a positive photo identification of the defendant from one of the witnesses who worked in the Sunmeadow Court building, Ann Duffy, I believed we had probable cause to arrest Mr. Shumway and I secured a warrant to do so."

"Thank you, Detective," I said. "I have nothing further."

Gus chewed on his thumbnail. I shot him a look. Matt came up to the lectern.

Kenya had a note for me by the time I sat back down. "Cruz says he's fighting a stomach bug."

Terrific, I thought. But Gus Ritter was a hardened soldier. I just needed him to keep it together for the rest of the afternoon. There was very little Orville could do with him on the facts of the case.

"Detective," Orville said. "To be clear, there are any number of scenarios where a suspect's DNA could wind up in a rape kit and not be due to rape, am I right?"

"Ms. Silvers was raped, Mr. Orville," Gus said.

Matt gave him a dirty look. "But there are many alternative ways it could have wound up there. Consensual sex, for example, correct?"

"Yes," Ritter said.

"When you say you re-interviewed the living witnesses in this case when the DNA profile came back, it's not true that you interviewed all of them, is it?"

"I beg your pardon?"

"Well, for example, you never bothered to speak to Marcy Cross again, did you? She was one of the witnesses Ms. Silvers claims to have regularly lunched with, correct?"

"That's two questions. Which would you like me to answer?" Ritter said.

"You haven't spoken to Marcy Cross in over twenty years, have you?"

"I have no idea," Ritter said.

"You didn't re-interview her in connection to this case, did you?"

"I didn't, no," Ritter said. "As I told Ms. Brent, the Cross woman didn't respond to our inquiries."

"So if she were to claim that Ms. Silvers and Mr. Shumway had a relationship, that would be news to you, right?"

"Objection," I said. "Assuming facts not in evidence."

"Sustained, Mr. Orville."

"You never bothered to re-interview every single witness from the original case file this year, did you?" Orville asked.

"No," Gus answered. "It wasn't necessary to establish probable cause."

"So, it's fair then, that once you had what you considered to be dispositive DNA in your hand, so to speak, that was all you needed."

"No," Ritter answered. "DNA was not the only fact we presented that gave us probable cause to arrest your client. He was in the building. He was seen leaving in a van right after Ms. Silvers was last seen uninjured. He had the means, motive, and opportunity to commit this crime ..."

"Your Honor," Matt said. "Can you instruct the witness to refrain from speeches?"

"Ask him a question," Judge Saul said. "Detective Ritter, when he does, answer it."

"You claim a vehicle registered to the defendant was seen leaving the parking garage of the Sunmeadow Court office building at 5:28 a.m. Isn't it true that the vehicle was registered not to the defendant but to Blaine Pharmaceutical?"

"They were the leaseholder, yes," he said. "But Mr. Shumway was the driver."

"Are you sure about that?" Orville shouted.

"Yes."

"Really? Were you able to personally identify Mr. Shumway as the driver that day?"

"It was an inference," Gus said.

"An inference," Orville repeated. "And how many other vehicles were seen exiting that parking garage from five o'clock on April 14th?"

"I don't have an exact count for you. But it was dozens and dozens. Most of the offices closed at five for the day so that was when the most traffic would have been leaving."

"And yet not a single witness you interviewed claims to have seen anything unusual that day?"

"No," Gus said.

"Nobody claims to have heard screaming or other sounds of a struggle?"

"No."

"Nobody claims to have even seen Mr. Shumway in that garage, did they?"

"No."

"Did you bother to ask any representative of Blaine Pharmaceuticals whether anyone else on occasion covered the Sunmeadow building?"

"Of course," Ritter said. "But it was a moot point since it was Shumway's DNA that was mixed in with Denise Shumway's blood, Mr. Orville."

"A moot point?" Orville said. I wanted to crawl under the desk. Ritter was rattled. This performance was so unlike him. Orville was trying to make it look like Gus had DNA and decided to make the rest of the case fit. Which was fine unless Orville could throw a Hail Mary and convince the jury not to trust the science. I always liked my odds better when I was in my seat instead of his. And yet, juries were juries. I found myself trying to mind-meld with Gus Ritter.

Hold it together. Just hold it together.

"I have nothing further," Orville said, surprising me.

"Ms Brent?" Judge Saul said.

"Detective Ritter," I said. I knew the answer to my next question. I wanted to give Gus a chance to clean up the mess Orville tried to make. "Did your investigation reveal any other Blaine Pharmaceutical reps who might have serviced the Sunmeadow building?"

"No," he said. "Mr. Shumway was the only name on the list we received from Blaine at the time of the assault."

"Thank you," I said. "I have nothing further."

Now, more than ever, I needed clean testimony from Sunmeadow's security guy. By the ashen look on Gus's face when he left the stand, he knew it too.

Chapter 17

"THE STATE CALLS Alexander Conway to the stand."

Alex Conway looked scared to death. In his early sixties, he wore his thick gray hair generously parted to the side. Thankfully, Kenya made sure he put on his suit coat. I'd seen him out in the hallway and he'd already sweat through his dress shirt.

Great.

This was supposed to be easy. Twenty minutes before, I'd lost my temper in the hallway when Kenya told me Judge Saul wasn't going to budge from her ridiculous pretrial ruling on the parking lot security footage. She was making me introduce the actual VHS tape rather than a digital copy. So now, I had the unenviable task of rolling in an ancient, clunky TV/VCR combo on wheels. I drew a few raised brows and snickers from the jury as I got ready to handle one of my so-called star witnesses.

"Mr. Conway," I said. "Can you tell me what you do for a living?"

"Um. I'm the security manager for Sentinel Security Systems."

"And how long have you held that position?"

"Well, I'm the general manager now. I've done that for four-teen years. Before that I was an on-site security manager. I had that job for six years, I think it was. Before that I was a security guard for Sentinel. Did that for almost a year before getting into management. Before that, I was a Lucas County sheriff's deputy. Ten years before I had to go on disability. I hurt my back."

"I'm sorry to hear that," I said.

"Don't be. Sentinel pays much better and there's a lot less administrative crap."

Conway's face went white. He looked at Judge Saul.

"Sorry, ma'am."

"Indeed," she said.

"Mr. Conway," I refocused him. "Let me take you back to April of 2000. Where specifically were you working?"

"That's when I was an on-site manager. I was assigned to the Sunmeadow Court office buildings."

"Do you recall what shift?" I asked.

"I was always second shift in those days. I'd come in at two o'clock and I'd work until midnight. Four days a week."

"Do you recall whether you worked April 14th, 2000?"

"I do."

"How can you be so sure you worked a date over twenty years ago?"

"Well, that was the weekend Ms. Denise Silvers got attacked. I remember because obviously the police had to investigate so I was questioned. Multiple times."

"Did you know Ms. Silvers?" I asked.

"She looked familiar," he said. "I mean, I knew she was one of the girls who worked in the building. You know. Just from seeing her coming and going. And sometimes I'd still walk rounds. Depending on the time of day ... I had two guards working under me in the building at that time. One manned the entrance to the parking structure. The other would walk the grounds, check on the different offices, be ready to respond if there was ever a security issue."

"And what were your duties?"

"I supervised them. Made sure all the safety checks were being made. I reviewed the security tapes at the end of every day."

"Security tapes. There were cameras?"

"There were," he said. "Not many in those days. It's different now. And even since Denise's attack. Now, that building has cameras on every floor. Down every hallway. But back then, in 2000, we just had cameras in the parking lot."

"How was that footage maintained?" I asked.

"We were on VHS tape at the time," he said. "Didn't go digital until a few years after that. It was pretty old-fashioned. VHS cameras. We'd take the tape out at the end of every shift.

I'd review them. Then we'd put the tapes back in the camera and start fresh the next day."

"So you were recording over the previous day's tapes each day?"

"That's right. I mean, unless there was something suspicious that warranted further investigation. Then we'd save that tape."

"What happened to the tape for April 14th, 2000?"

"Oh, we got a call from the Maumee County sheriffs the morning of April 15th. That was a weekend. So the tape from Friday night, the 14th, was still in the camera and hadn't yet been reviewed. I would have done that as a matter of course on Monday morning, the 17th. Anyways, when I got the call from our answering service that the sheriffs were interested in reviewing that tape, I ran right down there. We didn't have manned security from Saturday to Sunday because the building was closed."

"Were you able to retrieve the parking lot footage?" I asked.

"Yes, ma'am," he said. "You have to understand. There was only one way in and out of the lot at that time. I think it's the same now though I don't work on site there anymore. Well, I met the sheriffs at the site and removed the VHS tape under their supervision."

"Then what happened?" I asked.

"Well, we took it right over to the booth. The security booth where we could do playback."

"Did you review it?" I asked.

"We did. That tape had been running since Friday the 14th from about 12:30 in the afternoon. That's when I came in to refresh it from the 13th."

"What did you observe?" I asked.

"Well, I mean … nothing out of the ordinary. Unfortunately, the area where Ms. Silvers was last seen … like I said, we didn't have cameras there. Just at the entrance and exit. We could see the cars coming in and out on any given day. We had no recording of Ms. Silvers coming in because as I said, that would have been part of the morning tape that I'd restarted. But there was no footage of her leaving. Also, while the police were there, we searched the parking garage itself. We found Ms. Silvers's car still parked. It was a blue Neon. Couldn't find the keys to it. It was still locked. And she had a flat tire in the rear."

"Mr. Conway," I said. "I'm going to show you what's been marked as the State's Exhibit sixty-seven. Can you tell me what it is?"

"Yes, ma'am. This is the original VHS tape that we removed from the parking lot on the morning of April 15th. It's still got my signature on the front."

"Have you had a chance to review it again since that day in 2000?"

"Yes, ma'am," he said. "The police re-interviewed me a few months ago."

"Your Honor, we move for the admission of State's Exhibit sixty-seven."

"Mr. Orville?" Judge Saul asked.

Matt sat stone-faced. He flapped a hand. "No objection."

"So entered," Judge Saul said.

"Mr. Conway," I continued. "Can you please press play?"

He had a monitor in front of him. I held my breath as he picked up the remote and pressed play. Every single member of the jury leaned forward to get a better view.

The video was still in surprisingly good condition for as old as it was the last time I saw it. I knew we would see Neil Shumway's light-tan mini-van leaving the parking garage at the 5:28 p.m. mark. I had Scott, the intern, cue the tape up to the 5:26 mark so Conway would have time to reassure the court and the jury this was the tape he'd made and seen.

I waited. Alex Conway pressed the play button a second time. The screen crackled to life but only a silvery line of static rolled up the monitor.

I shot a look at Scott Farmer. His face went white. He shrugged.

Neil sat up a little further in his seat. For the entire week of trial, he had kept the same downtrodden, miserable look on his face. Now there was a glint in his eye. Matt put a hand on his arm. I read his lips as he told his client to calm down.

"Can you fast-forward a bit?" I instructed Conway.

Conway kept the video playing as he hit the fast-forward button. The silver line wobbled, but nothing else happened. I watched the counter at the bottom of the VCR. He'd gone far past the 5:28 mark.

Without my instruction, he rewound then fast-forwarded the tape, then hit play again. Nothing. White static.

I couldn't believe what I was seeing. We'd run through this three days ago. We'd checked the equipment this morning. This shouldn't be happening.

"It's not there," he said. "It's gone."

"Your Honor," I said. "May we take a five-minute recess? I think there might be something wrong with the player."

This was a disaster. The worst thing you want to happen in front of a jury. Exactly the reason I'd argued so hard *not* to use old equipment like this. I wanted to murder Scott, but I wanted to murder Vivian Saul even more.

Judge Saul looked properly horrified as well. "Five minutes," she said.

I popped the tape out of the VCR. The jury was sent out of the room.

"What's going on?" Conway whispered to me.

I turned to make sure Matt Orville and Shumway couldn't hear.

"I don't know."

Five minutes wasn't enough time to fix anything. The bailiff stepped forward.

"There's another TV/VCR combo in one of the conference rooms across the hall. The screen's only twelve inches but ..."

"Good enough," I said, heart racing. We'll make it work. "Kenya, grab the DVD copy and bring my laptop."

The bailiff, Kenya, Scott, and I sprinted across the hall. The

TV player was there just as the bailiff said and Scott plugged it into the wall.

I shoved the tape inside. The device sprang immediately to life and for a moment, my pulse felt normal again.

Until it didn't.

We were faced with the same silver line of static. The security footage was gone. Scott took the remote and rewound the thing all the way to the beginning. Still nothing.

"It's wiped," Kenya said. "The whole thing. There's nothing on it."

I opened my laptop and took the DVD Kenya had brought. I slipped the copy in and waited for my player to pop up. When it did, cold dread snaked up my spine.

Something was wrong. Very wrong. The DVD copy we'd been given by the sheriff's department showed the exact same lines of static. I'd never even looked at it before. I'd only watched the original tape.

"This isn't possible," I muttered. "I watched that tape two days ago."

"So did I," Kenya said. "I was standing right next to you."

"My God," I muttered.

"Do you have another copy somewhere?" the bailiff asked.

We didn't.

"This makes no sense," Kenya said. "How can the original and our copy be ruined?"

I took a staggering step back and shook my head.

"How do we fix this?" Scott asked.

"We can't," I said, my throat dry. I put my hands on the top of my head, feeling like it might just pop off.

The bailiff, Henry Lake, knew this was his cue to slide out of the room.

"We can't," I said again. "Not unless Alex has an independent recollection of the Shumway van and exactly when it left that parking structure."

"He doesn't," Kenya said. "He can only authenticate the tape."

"The tape that plays dead air?" Scott said. "What about Orville? He has the copy we gave him in discovery, hasn't he?"

I shook my head. "We didn't make one for him. He requested to view it with Detective Cruz and Ritter in their office."

"My God," Kenya said. "This is a train wreck."

I felt very strongly it was worse than that. It was deliberate sabotage. And two of the people who would have had access to commit it were standing in the same room with me. There was also Ritter and Cruz. Their office made the copy. None of this made any sense.

"Judge wants you back." Henry poked his head in the room. "Sidebar."

Dreading every step of the way, we walked back into the courtroom. With Matt Orville standing smugly beside the bench, I took a breath and explained what had just happened. "We're having technical difficulty with the videotape," I said. "It appears to have been altered."

"Well then you can't show it," Judge Saul said.

"Altered?" Orville said.

"Poor choice of words," I said. "It won't play. I need some time to look into it."

Judge Saul narrowed her eyes at me. "You came in here ready to play a videotape you haven't checked?"

"We've checked it," I said, though my explanation sounded thin even to me. I couldn't say what I was really thinking. If I let on my suspicions about a culprit in my own office or at the sheriff's, this whole case would fall apart.

"Fine," Judge Saul said. "Can your witness testify to what he saw on the tape?"

"He can," I said.

"Then let's finish this up."

Horrified, I went back to the lectern. I existed outside myself as Alex Conway retook the witness stand looking as confused as I felt.

"Mr. Conway," I said. "Can you tell me what you saw on that security footage?"

He looked at the now blank television screen. "I mean ... there were cars going in and out all day. I didn't ... I can't tell you if I recognized any of them. I can't even tell you how many there were or what time they came and went without reviewing the videotape."

"I understand," I said. "I ... I have nothing further."

I sat back down beside Kenya and watched as Matt Orville did exactly what I would have done.

"Mr. Conway, do you know what kind of car Mr. Shumway drove in 2000?"

"No, sir."

"And you didn't personally observe Mr. Shumway coming or going from the Sunmeadow garage on April 14th, did you?"

"No," he said.

"You have no knowledge about whether he was or wasn't anywhere near that building that day, do you?"

"No, sir. I'm afraid I don't. Not without the tape. I thought I was here to talk about the tape."

"As head of security for Sunmeadow, you'd be the guy who would ultimately take reports about suspicious activity within the building or the garage, right?"

"Yes, sir," he said.

"And in your years as on-site manager for Sunmeadow Court ... you never once had anyone complain about Neil Shumway, did you?"

"Um ... no."

"And to be clear, that tape Ms. Brent had you play, that *was* the only security footage from the Sunmeadow garage for April 14th, wasn't it?"

"Yeah," he answered. "That was my handwriting. That's what I handed over to the cops. But it didn't look like that when I did. It wasn't in that condition when I handed it over."

God. It was getting worse.

"Thank you," Matt Orville said, knowing full well to quit while he was ahead. "I have nothing further for this witness."

And with that, we were adjourned for the weekend.

Chapter 18

"THIS WASN'T US," Sam said.

I sat in my car, staring out at the river. I don't know what made me do it, but I drove straight from the courthouse to the Bennett Street overpass and stared down at Tucker Welling's God's Brew.

"Sam, that tape was fine two days before I tried to show it at trial. I was stupid not to look at the DVD copy. The copy that *your* office made for me."

"This. Wasn't. Us," he reiterated. I wanted to believe him. My mind ran through all the possibilities of people who had access to the tape and the DVD copy. In my office alone, it would have been around two dozen people, including support staff and custodial. Someone wiped the tape. That alone I could have even discounted as some kind of accident. But for the copy to also be wiped? Logic dictated someone had either switched it or it had come like that from Sam's office. I had no way of knowing and a dwindling circle of people I felt I could trust.

"Orville will ask for a mistrial," I said.

Sam Cruz made a noise into the phone that sounded down-right bear-like. Ritter was starting to rub off on him.

"On what basis?" he asked. "This just means it'll be harder to put Shumway at Sunmeadow Court at precisely 5:23."

I pressed my skull against the headrest. "He'll go to the A.G.'s office. He'll rattle his saber and ask for an investigation into the sheriff's department or my office. Alex Conway teed him up perfectly. Sam, he said point-blank, to the jury ... the tape was altered after it left his hands and went into yours. Not yours personally, you know what I mean."

"Son of a bitch," Sam whispered. "This is a mess, Mara. You gotta figure out a way to fix it. Chain of custody on our end was pristine."

"I need you to take a harder look at Alex Conway. I don't know. He seemed genuinely surprised by everything that went down. For that matter, so did Orville."

"He's a snake," Sam said. "Worse than that. Orville's the devil."

I didn't want to argue the point. Of all people who might have had access to that stupid security footage, Orville was at the bottom of the list. But I couldn't be sure he hadn't paid someone off. Maybe a janitor or another of the interns we had floating in and out.

"Just see if there are any red flags on Conway. But don't ... don't let on you're looking."

"Of course not," Sam said. "Gus feels awful about the other day. He knows he wasn't at his best. He was sick."

I bit my lip. "Sam, I don't care. And Gus doesn't either. My whole life is falling apart at the seams but I show up. I do my job. If Gus thought this trial would be a slam dunk, then shame on him. I need every single person at the top of their game. That includes you. There's too much at stake."

I didn't like the edge to my voice. I was projecting and was pretty sure Sam knew it too.

"Mara," he said. "You need to take a step back."

"I need everyone to do their jobs," I spat. "That's what I need."

I heard him take a deep breath. "I'll call you if I find anything out. Go have a glass of wine. Get some sleep."

Before I could respond, Sam hung up on me.

"Great," I muttered. We were on the same team, or supposed to be. The real problem with all of this, this screw-up had happened on my watch. Now if I could only figure out a way to fix it.

It was after seven when I finally pulled up my long, winding driveway. Lights flickered in the kitchen and living room windows. My mother's silver Mercedes was parked at an angle by the front door.

I took a breath for courage as I pulled into the garage and readied myself to walk inside.

Kat couldn't stay this weekend. She'd planned a trip with a guy she'd been seeing well before I got my trial date on Shumway. She offered to postpone but she did so much for me I couldn't ask her to upend her life anymore.

So, Natalie Roth Montleroy descended on my household to

be here for Will when I couldn't. She sat at the kitchen island drinking a glass of red wine. Every evening, like clockwork, my mother would pour herself that one glass and no more.

She was tall, thin, her jet-black hair still mostly natural and her skin white and smooth as porcelain. Like me, she went gray early, but only in one place, a thick hank of white hair on the right side of her part. In my mother's case, she immediately dyed it. She'd been at me for almost a decade to do the same.

"How did it go today?" she asked. I wasn't sure whether that was a rhetorical question or not. With the gag order in place, I prayed none of today's courtroom drama made it to her newsfeed.

"It went," I said. "Long day. Where's Will?"

"Bath," she said. "Then he wants me to watch some silver bullet program."

I smiled. "Magic bullet. They're re-airing some documentary on the forensics of the bullet that hit JFK and Governor Connelly. Consider it an honor. He won't watch that one with just anyone."

My mother's nostrils flared. "I don't know why you encourage that. It's ghoulish."

"He's interested," I said. "And you might find it fascinating yourself."

"It's a tragedy," she said. "Your obsession with murder is rubbing off on Will."

I laughed. "My obsession with murder? I'm a prosecutor, Mom. It's my job, not an obsession."

She finished the last of her wine. She had not a hair out of place. My mother wore a cream-colored silk blouse with linen pants. How she kept them from becoming horribly wrinkled by this time of day was her own secret magic.

"Well," she said. "It's a mess, Mara. You should have taken a leave of absence. Or you should have quit outright. Jason needs you right now."

My heart thundered behind my ribcage.

"Jason. Needs me," I repeated.

"Yes," she said. It came out almost like a hiss. "Mara, that man is wracked with guilt over what happened."

I shook my head, trying to clear it. "What happened. You say that like it was something that happened *to* him. Like an accident. I mean ... unless his dick fell in ..."

"Stop it," my mother said. "You don't have to be vulgar."

"It is vulgar. This whole thing. And it's not of my making. I'm doing the best I can to hold everything together for Will. Because he's all that matters. Even Jason will admit to that."

"What Jason's doing, he's doing for Will," she said. "Regardless of what you think of him as a husband, I know you believe in him as a public servant. Jason's the one. I told you that from the moment I met him and heard what he had to say. He's the real deal and he can make a difference for all of us. I know you know that."

The truth was, I did. Jason Brent had that certain unique factor that only very few politicians did. He inspired people, made them want to be better versions of themselves.

"It's his time, Mara," she said. "He's taken things as far as he can in the A.G.'s office. You both knew that was only ever going to be a stepping stone. What we've put in place has taken years. He has the full-throated support of the party. We are going to send that man to Congress. And in ten years ... maybe less ..."

She stopped. The rest of her sentence hung in the air between us. She'd never finish it out of a deep-seated superstition she had about jinxing it. But it was there. My mother's ambitions for Jason were almost greater than his were for himself. She aimed to put him in the White House, or very close to it.

"It's in his blood," she said. "Jason wasn't born into it like you were, but I believe in fate. I believe he was put in our path for a reason. This reason."

I went to the fridge and pulled out her bottle of wine. I had half a mind to just drink straight from the bottle. I didn't. I found a glass. I'd nearly finished it before I responded.

"Then maybe you should have married him yourself, Mom. I'm your daughter. Me."

"That's right," she said. "And everything I've done for Jason, I would have done for you. But you didn't want it."

"Nope," I said. "I didn't. But I supported my husband. I just wish he'd supported us."

My mother let out a sigh. I heard the water draining upstairs. Will would be down in just a few minutes.

"Mara," she said. "If you want a different life for yourself, then you can have it. Just ... not yet. You need to put on a brave face and stand by your husband until after this election."

I poured myself another glass of wine. I only dared have the two. Already, I felt my head start to pound. I wanted to sink beneath the bubbles of a bath myself. The weight of all of it. My mother's judgment. My husband's life choices. Alex Conway's borked security tape.

"Mara, you can do this. Lord knows my mother understood what was expected of her. And my grandmother before her."

Oh yes. I'd heard of the legendary martyrdom of Grandma Alice Lindsey Roth who'd borne the wrath and infidelities of my grandfather, Vinton Roth, Jr. as he made his way up the ranks of New Hampshire politics on the strength of his name. But it all came crashing down before he reached what was supposed to be the pinnacle of his career. He'd been caught up in an insider trading scandal that nearly landed him in federal prison. Then there was my great-grandfather, the original Vinton Roth, who'd been counted among F.D.R.'s brain trust and architects of the New Deal.

Both legendary men and legendary philandering bastards. And here was my mother trying to convince me this was all my birthright.

"Three minutes!" Will's voice cut through my swirling thoughts. He stood on the landing in his Iron Man pajamas, barefoot, his hair still dripping wet.

I took a fresh kitchen towel from the drawer and went to him.

"Come here, you," I smiled. "You'll drip all over the floor."

He let me pat the ends of his hair dry. He let me kiss his cheek.

"I missed you today," I said. "Did you have fun with Grandma?"

"Natalie cuts the crust off the tuna sandwiches. Aunt Kat says that's the most nutritious part, but it's just where the bread gets brown when they bake it."

My smile widened. "You like it Grandma's way better?"

He considered my question for a moment. "Yeah. This is the one where they do a 3-D rendering of Dealey Plaza. You know they said there was a street sign with a defect that could have come from a bullet. The angle was right. It might have obstructed Oswald's second shot. I think that's specious. Far too many variables over the last fifty-plus years."

My mother looked puzzled. "I agree," I said. "That would never hold up to the rigors of the rules of evidence."

"Or the scientific method. Still, it's interesting to think about. I'd like to have a look at it myself when we go."

"When you go?" my mother asked.

"Yes," I said. "I promised Will we'd take a trip to Dallas soon. He's been working on his wish list. All the 'must-see' attractions."

Will left my embrace and headed for the living room. He took his favorite spot in the middle of my L-shaped couch and tuned to the appropriate channel. We actually had every one of these documentaries either recorded on the DVR, on DVD, or part of our digital library. Will liked watching them when they aired or repeated best.

I nodded to my mother. For the first time since I'd walked in the door, she gave me a smile. She sat next to her grandson and my heart squeezed a little as I watched him put a hand on her knee. She understood it for the gift it was as well. Then she settled in for the next two hours of in-depth forensic crime scene investigation.

I put the wine away and came out to join them. As I watched the science experts knock down the magic bullet theories, I tried to keep my mind from drifting back to my day.

I'd need a fresh start and a clear head tomorrow if I had any hope of tackling the potential conspiracy theory forming around the Shumway case.

Chapter 19

A DREAM. Or a nightmare. Everything was normal and as it should be.

The late summer sun peeked through the lace curtains leaving dotted points of light along my arm.

I heard spoons clinking against bowls in the kitchen and Will's unbroken chatter as he outlined the plans he'd drawn for a mystery freighter possibly spotted a few miles off the Titanic's bow in the late hours of April 14th, 1912.

April 14th. It had only just occurred to me. The Titanic hit an iceberg on the same date Denise Silvers was attacked, just eighty-eight years apart.

My son's stream of words was gently interrupted by Jason's calm, steady voice from time to time. He was careful, deliberate, helping keep Will's passion focused and constructive. Together, they worked out a structural problem Will had identified.

I slid my hand across the bed. If I closed my eyes, I could

imagine the warmth still trapped on that side of the bed. I could still feel the solid comfort of Jason's arms as he wrapped them around me thinking me still asleep. Then he would carefully slide out from under the sheets and pad off to the shower, always letting me sleep in on Saturday mornings like this. He'd done it since I came home from the hospital with Will. I'd never even asked him to. And yet, Jason always seemed to know what I needed anyway.

I rolled to my side. Maybe it all *had* been a dream. Perhaps I could do exactly what my mother suggested and just pretend. Deny. Because it would be easier, wouldn't it? Better for all of us?

Then the pain flooded back in as I exhaled. That clawing tightness wrapped around my heart. I could imagine Jason's arms wrapped around someone else, offering her comfort. Touching her in all the ways that become habit between two people who've been together as long as we had.

No. I could never pretend. It would never be okay.

I washed up and got dressed quickly, then headed down the stairs.

Will and Jason were still in deep conversation, though they'd moved their meeting to the living room. I cleared the breakfast bar of their cereal bowls and slipped them into the dishwasher.

Will had spread a large sheet of construction paper on the floor near the fireplace. He knelt over it, scribbling furiously with a pencil. His father had given him an idea. I saw that spark in his eyes as he incorporated it into his design.

I leaned against the wall holding my coffee mug with two

hands. Jason finally turned. His eyes glinted. The corners of his mouth lifted into a smile and for that brief moment, the span of time it took for him to draw breath then exhale, I knew he lived in that space before it all came crashing down. As if only the thinnest of membranes separated our new reality from the life we used to share. It was still real. Still touchable. So easy to go back to.

And then it wasn't.

Because I was really the only one who had lived there. Jason had always known the truth.

"I didn't hear you come in," I said, keeping my voice low. Will was in the zone. I didn't want to disturb him. So I took a seat on the opposite end of the couch and watched my sweet boy's mind at work.

"Two hours ago," he said. "Will said Natalie was here yesterday?"

I nodded, setting my mug on the leather ottoman in front of me. I drew my knees up. I was still barefoot and my feet were cold.

"I'm glad she could pitch in," he said. "You know I'd be here if ..."

I put a hand up. "I know." That was the truth. And it was the only thing keeping me from feeling like I was well and truly drowning. No matter how much we'd laid waste to the thing between us, Jason would always be here for Will. I supposed someday that would be the thing that brought me to the other side. To forgiveness. For now, I just had no idea what that would look like.

"Look," he said. "I ... it's tricky for me to even bring up. But I understand Matt Orville's making some rumblings with my office. Are you doing okay?"

So he'd already heard about yesterday's courtroom catastrophe. It didn't surprise me one bit.

I shrugged. "I'm going to have to be."

"Is this ... survivable, do you think?"

I pulled an Afghan off the back of the couch and covered my legs with it. "Hopefully. It's just ..."

"You think it's someone just dropping the ball? Or do you really think someone's working against you behind the scenes?" he asked.

"You're right," I said. "This is tricky for us to even be talking about. If Orville gets his wish and your office has to look into the sheriff's department or ... who knows ..."

"You've still got the same prima facie elements to prove, Mara," he said. "Two plus two equals four, but so does one plus three."

I smiled. This was vintage Jason. He had the same calming effect on me as he did with Will. If I started to spin on emotions, he would draw me back with logic. My rock. My touchstone.

"What else can you do to place Shumway in that building the afternoon of the 14th?" Jason asked.

This was a dangerous conversation we were having. There was a gag order in place. Jason himself was supposed to be walled off from this case within the A.G.'s office. And yet, he still knew exactly what happened in trial yesterday. It wasn't a big mystery how. All politics are small-town politics. It was the same with the legal system. Everybody knew everybody and Jason had a vested interest in what was going on with me.

"Denise doesn't remember if she saw him that day," I said. "And at this point, even if she did, putting her back on the stand comes with risks that would outweigh any benefit."

"You've gotten nowhere with Blaine Pharm?" he asked.

"We're talking about a single day, twenty years ago. Shumway didn't punch a time clock. He had territories, calls he made. He was salaried, drove a company car. So his expense reports didn't include day-to-day mileage by location. They just paid for the gas, maintenance, vehicle insurance. Most of the records we have are sparse."

"No logs at any of the doctors' offices he visited in the building?"

"Nope. The cops weren't focused on him back then. If they had been, maybe there would have been something to verify. But not now. A lot of the practices in that building in 2000 aren't even there anymore. They've all been bought out, taken over by Alliance Health and centralized."

"But the DNA is solid," he said. "You've proven Shumway was a regular visitor of the building. His presence in it or even in the parking garage if anyone saw him wouldn't have drawn suspicion. It'll be enough, Mara. You're a brilliant closer. It'll be enough."

I exhaled. The emotion hit me so suddenly, I had to blink back tears. Jason reached for me instinctively. I felt his warm hand on my knee and I froze.

I wanted more. Dammit. In spite of it all, I wanted more. I

craved it. It never occurred to me how long it had been since I'd enjoyed even the simplest affectionate touch.

My mother wasn't demonstrative like that. My father had been. But he'd been gone for almost ten years now. I'd been six months pregnant with Will when we lost him when he'd died of a heart attack behind the wheel.

For Will himself, physical affection was hard-won. Even when it came, it was just a subtle touch or brush against my shoulder or the way his body relaxed as he allowed me to hug him instead of going rigid. Those moments were gold. This one was supposed to be too.

Jason took his hand away. He looked down, emotion making his own eyes glisten.

"Don't," I whispered, knowing full well what he was about to say. *Don't say you're sorry. It's just the bare minimum and it's never enough.*

"Do you have support?" he asked. "From Phil, Kenya Spaulding."

I wanted ... needed ... to talk through the rest of it. Something happened to that tape. And something happened to the DVD copies. I was sure of it. It could have been on Ritter and Cruz's watch. I'd never reviewed the DVDs. I'd only taken the copies they made and viewed the original tape.

Ritter. His performance on the stand had been so unlike him. I didn't care if he had the flu. That man could have been gut shot and I knew he would still do his job. And yet ...

"What's going on in that head of yours?" Jason asked.

"Trust me. You don't want to know."

I meant it as a light joke. It made Jason go still.

"Well, like I said. You'll kill them in the closing, no matter what. What about the lawyer you were working with in Delphi? The one who represented Shumway's secret daughter?"

"Cass Leary," I answered. She'd been such an integral part in helping the cops nail down Shumway's identity.

"I can't call her as a witness," I said.

"But you said he tried to attack her too," Jason offered.

"It doesn't matter. You know I can't bring in evidence of other crimes the man might have committed. Too bad I don't know someone in the A.G.'s office who could work on changing that pesky rule of evidence before my trial ends. It's small consolation, but he's facing assault charges in Delphi over what he tried with Cass. But that's small potatoes, Jason. If I can't nail him and that's all we've got, we'll be lucky if he does six months for it. It's not enough. It's not nearly enough."

Jason smiled. "You'll get him, Mara. I know you. You'll find a way."

"Got it!" Will shouted. He leaped up from his drawing and spread his hands wide. "Check it out, Dad!"

Giving me a grim nod, Jason left the couch and went over to our son. Sure enough, he now stood over a fairly impressive blueprint for his mystery freighter and all the pieces fit.

Just Jason being here had helped quiet Will's brain long enough for him to find his solution. At that moment, I might have given anything if he could have done the same for me.

Chapter 20

AT SIX A.M. that Monday morning, Sam Cruz waited for me in his unmarked Lincoln two blocks over from the courthouse and my office. I slipped into the passenger seat. He stared straight ahead.

"Tell me something good," I said.

"There was no break in the chain of custody on that videotape or the copies. None. Nobody got near it that shouldn't have. Not from our end."

"So you think it was from mine," I said.

Cruz looked over at me.

"What about that clerk you've had helping out?"

"Farmer?" I said. "He's a law student. He's never been left alone with any of the evidence. His basic job is to play gopher with the witnesses and hand me stuff in the courtroom."

I noticed a twitch in Sam's jaw. "That was a rhetorical question, wasn't it? I surmised. You've already looked into him. Crap. You've already had him followed. Sam. What is it you're not telling me?"

He chewed his bottom lip. "Nothing. And yeah. I've poked around a little. The kid's clean. He went home after court Friday. Spent the weekend at a girlfriend's house."

I put a hand up. "Maybe you don't tell me any more about your methods." I had a sneaking suspicion Sam had probably needed a warrant for at least half of whatever he did in regards to Scott Farmer over the weekend.

"What's your read on Kenya?" he asked.

His question shocked me. "Are you kidding? You think she'd actually sabotage this case? Why?"

He shook his head. "No. Not really. I just know how driven she was trying to get first chair on it."

"She wouldn't torpedo the case out of spite, Sam."

He nodded. "Yeah. The motive makes no sense. You win this case, it makes her look good. You lose it, it's a blight on the whole office. That's got to be eating at Halsey."

"He's up for reelection next year, after all," I said, not even hiding the bitterness in my tone.

"It never should have mattered," Sam said. "This is Wayne-town. Nobody ever unseats an incumbent. Especially not one with a family name like his. Or yours. But now ..."

"You sound like my mother," I said.

He kept on chewing his bottom lip as if he were trying to work up to say something. I stopped just short of asking him to spit it out. Then it hit me.

"Great," I said. "Let me guess. The running theory in the sheriff's department is that I screwed this all up somehow. Is that it? Took my eye off the ball?"

"Mara, look. I'm not ... I ... I know you. I know how good you are. And no, I don't personally believe this screw-up with that parking garage tape is on you. Not that."

"Wait a minute," I said. "What happened to all the support I had from the task force? Sam, I know it was you and Gus who had my back most of all. They've met behind my back now, haven't they? That's it, isn't it?"

His whole body tensed and I knew I'd hit on the answer dead center. I no longer had the confidence of the men and women on the Shumway task force.

"So what's the consensus?" I asked. "At least tell me that."

"It's just bad timing, Mara. And now with Orville rattling the cage of the Attorney General's office ... Word is he's getting help from Jason's opponent's team. Evan Simpson's opposition research group."

"I see," I said. "So they've already decided who to scapegoat if I lose this trial. Me. Because of Jason. He's the one who cheated ... who brought this house down on my head. And I'm going to be the one who pays for it. Halsey will have cover. The task force, and even the A.G.'s office will have cover. The little wifey let the stress get to her. This is bull, Sam. That's not what's going on."

I punched my fist against the car door. To his credit, Sam at least looked miserable.

"Everyone's going to get what they want," I said. "Jason will beat Simpson. I know that in my soul. Hell, I'm even going to vote for him. And what, Halsey has to fire me after this?"

Sam shrugged. "That's not up to me. It's not up to the task force. I backed you for a reason and that reason hasn't changed. I just ... I wanted you to be prepared."

"Well that's just great," I said. "How about this? You can all just plot how to further screw up my life. I'll just do my job and get Shumway. You know who loses the most out of all of this? It's Denise. I don't really give a damn what happens to me."

"You should!" he barked. "And don't give me that crap because I know you do. I'm telling you to watch your back. Christ. Do you know how far I'm sticking my neck out just telling you any of this? Mara ... I know what you're up against. I meant what I said about how good you are. So go be great. The hell with the task force and Jason and even Halsey. You've got enough. Put that monster away."

I clenched my fists so hard I carved little half-moons into my palm. I stopped just short of drawing blood.

"I guess you want me to thank you." The truth was, I did know how risky this conversation probably was for Sam. I wanted to be grateful, but I just couldn't bring myself to say it. Not yet.

For now, I had to pull myself together and do exactly what he said. I had no more witnesses to call. I had to march into that courtroom with a case that was still bleeding, and I had to rest my case.

I took a breath for courage and left Detective Cruz's car.

I STOOD BESIDE KENYA. Behind me, I felt Denise Silvers's eyes boring into me. I'd managed to spend most of last night talking her through what to expect for this next phase of the trial. It would be harder. I had no idea how much longer it would take. Then, once again, everything would be entirely out of our hands.

"Ms. Brent," Judge Saul said. "Are you ready to proceed?"

She knew what was coming. I knew what was coming. Matt Orville rose to his feet as well. He reminded me of a sprinter coming up to the starting line. Neil Shumway remained stoic, glassy-eyed. Today, he wore a beige suit with a rose-colored tie. He'd lost weight since the trial started. From the moment I first set eyes on him, he looked much younger than his sixty-four years. Now, he'd finally aged in front of the jury's eyes.

"The prosecution rests, Your Honor," I said.

"All right," she said. "Mr. Orville, I take it you have a few things you'd like to say?"

"Absolutely," Matt said. He made his way to the lectern.

"Before you tee up," she said. "Let me remind you I've already ruled on your motion for a mistrial. It's denied. I don't want to hear it again. Are we clear?"

"Crystal, Your Honor," he said. "I believe I've preserved the matter for appeal."

It was an unnecessary comment. One aimed to basically

thumb his nose at the judge. I couldn't fathom why he'd do it if he were about to ask her for another type of relief two seconds later, which he did.

"Your Honor, the defense moves for a directed verdict under Rule 50. The prosecution has failed to meet its burden of proof on its prima facie case. Never mind the evidence tampering that one of their own witnesses testified to ..."

"Mr. Orville," Judge Saul snapped. "That's exactly the kind of grandstanding I'm not going to tolerate. I know you know what I mean. Try again."

Undaunted, Orville did. "The prosecution has failed to prove as a matter of law that the defendant was even in the vicinity of Waynetown at the time of Ms. Silvers's alleged attack. Whether you're willing to entertain the issue or not, their single establishing witness cannot place him there. On the contrary, he testified to the opposite. As a matter of law, we believe we are entitled to a directed verdict of not guilty."

"Ms. Brent, would the State like to respond?"

"Absolutely," I said. "Mr. Orville cannot turn a factual matter into a legal matter just by proclaiming it so. In essence, that's what he's doing here. We've provided ample evidence that Mr. Shumway served the Sunmeadow Court building. More than enough to allow the jury to infer his presence on the evening in question. Even if we hadn't, we've provided definitive proof through DNA evidence that Mr. Shumway, and only Mr. Shumway assaulted Ms. Silvers. The interpretation of this evidence is a question of fact within the jury's purview. Quite frankly, I can't think of another example with more genuine issues of fact than this one."

Judge Saul wrote something on the pad of paper before her.

"May I be offered the chance to rebut Ms. Brent's argument?" Orville asked.

Something about Judge Saul's look made Matt Orville change tactics on the dime. "We're ready to hear the Court's ruling," he said instead.

"Fine," she said. "I find the State's arguments to be well placed. Whether Mr. Shumway was present at the time of the attack is a question of fact. The DNA alone raises the issue. You'll have plenty of time to rebut that evidence in your presentation, Mr. Orville. But this is not a matter of law for which the Court must decide. This case will proceed. If you're ready, I'll have the jury brought in. Are you?"

"Absolutely, Your Honor," Matt said.

"Fine," she said. "Then you may call your first witness for the defense."

For a moment, Neil Shumway's posture changed. He sat far forward in his seat and it looked like he was about to stand up.

I couldn't believe it. Matt Orville was way too good a trial lawyer to let his client get on that witness stand. My heart skipped. I'd waited for this. Denise had waited for this. A chance to look this man straight in the eye and make him literally answer for his crimes.

But it didn't happen. Shumway settled back down. I waited breathlessly as the jury was led back into the room. As Matt turned back and gathered a notebook from his table, I took a pen, poised to sketch out any changes I needed to make in my cross-exam as he went.

"The defense calls Marcy Cross to the stand."

I heard a sharp intake of breath behind me. It came from Denise herself. I couldn't help it. I turned and gave her a look. As Marcy Cross made her way up the back of the courtroom and stepped into the witness box, Denise's reaction made me think the bottom was about to fall out from under me.

Again.

Chapter 21

MARCY CROSS LOOKED straight at Neil Shumway as she was sworn in. I tried to gauge his reaction. He kept his hands folded, resting on the table. Orville whispered something to him as he leaned across the table but Shumway gave no sign of a response. Then Orville turned and adjusted the microphone at the lectern.

"Ms. Cross," he said. "Can you state your full name for the record?"

"Margaret Catherine Cross," she said. She had a husky quality to her voice that would have come from years of smoking. It made deep lines around her mouth as well. I'd last seen Marcy in a photograph attached to her statement in Ken Leeds's police report.

"Ms. Cross," Matt continued. "Can you tell me how you know the defendant, Neil Shumway?"

She leaned more forward than she needed to, until her lips were almost pressing against the microphone.

"When I was in my twenties, I worked for Dr. Nicholson. Um ... Dr. Joe Nicholson. He was a family doctor with offices in the Sunmeadow Court building. I was a nurse. I mean, I still am. I do home care. Anyway, Neil was one of the drug reps who would frequent our offices, um, Nicholson's back in the late nineties and early 2000s."

"So you met him at the office?"

"That's right," she said.

"Can you tell me when, approximately?"

"Um, it was probably '98."

"What was your relationship with Neil Shumway?"

She cast a furtive glance toward Denise. "He was ... we began dating in the later part of 1999."

"You were romantically involved?"

"Yes," she said. "But ... we weren't open about it."

"Why was that?"

She coughed into her hand. "Well, at the time, he was married. His wife lived further north into Michigan. I'm not proud of that. But it was different with Neil. He told me he had an open marriage. His wife was ... well ... I understood it to be more of a business relationship between them. I don't know. And they didn't have any kids."

"How long did this romantic relationship with the defendant continue?" he asked.

My spine stiffened. I had Marcy's multiple statements to the police in front of me. At no time had she ever mentioned this connection to Shumway. And she'd refused contact with the cops when Ritter tried to re-interview her.

Marcy picked at her thumbnail. "About a year," she answered. "Through most of 2000."

"Can you tell me what brought an end to the relationship?"

"Well, I did. I was ... well, it was starting to become more serious between us. But I understood that Neil was probably never going to divorce his wife. And that just didn't sit well with me. I was coming up on my twenty-fifth birthday and I wanted more. I wanted a husband. I wanted kids. And Neil traveled so much. Even if he did get a divorce, I just didn't think that was the kind of life I wanted for myself. It was tough though. And he took it very hard."

"I see," Matt said. "I'd like to take you back to the spring of 2000. Were you also acquainted with Denise Silvers?"

"Oh yeah. She was a friend of mine. She was the receptionist for the insurance company down the hall from us. I had to pass by their office to get to mine. I'd stop and talk to her every day. We'd take turns getting coffee for each other from a shop that was at the corner from Sunmeadow. And we'd very often take our lunches together. There was a group of us. Me, Denise, Ann Duffy, Grace Sandford. Um ... Kiersten Marshall. She ... Denise ... was a friend. A good friend."

"I see," Matt said. "Are you and Denise still friends?"

Marcy put her head down. "No. I'm sorry to say that we aren't. It's all so trivial now. And with everything that happened. I feel bad about it."

"What happened, Marcy?" Matt asked.

"We had a falling out."

"When was that?"

Behind me, Denise was furiously scribbling something on a pad of paper. Kenya leaned back and took it from her. She lay it on the desk between us. It read, "Don't believe a word out of her mouth!"

I didn't like this. Not one bit.

"Denise and I stopped hanging out not very long before she had her accident. I mean ... at the time that all happened, we weren't even speaking. That's why I feel so bad for what happened to her."

Accident?

"Can you tell me why you had a falling out?" Matt asked.

"I knew she had a thing for Neil," Marcy answered.

"How did you know that?"

"Well, it was something she told me."

"Objection," I said. I couldn't actually believe Matt was trying this. "This entire line of questioning calls for hearsay."

"Sustained, Mr. Orville. Ms. Cross? You will not be permitted to testify about anything you claim Ms. Silvers said to you. Do you understand that?"

Marcy nodded. "Okay. I mean, I'll try."

"Ms. Cross," Matt continued. "Is there anything you can tell me that you actually observed regarding Denise Silvers and Neil Shumway?"

"Oh yes," she said. "Neil was super friendly. Charming. He had a smile for everyone. I mean, I know it was his job. He was a salesman, after all. A good one. I'd frequently see him leaning into Denise's window. He'd bring her candy; I mean, not specifically for her. For her office. But Denise ... I observed her talking to him. Her face would light up when he came by. They were flirting. Definitely it was a flirtatious exchange. And that didn't bother me so much. I understood it was part of Neil's job. You know, to have a good rapport with everyone in that building. But Denise ... I think she didn't understand the distinction."

"Objection," I said. "To the extent this witness is speculating about what the victim was or wasn't thinking, it's improper."

"I agree," Judge Saul said.

"Ms. Cross," Matt said, all smiles and gentle words. "Let's just try and stick to what you objectively observed if you can."

"Of course," she said. "I ... listen. This is really hard for me. It was a terrible time in my life. I did things I wasn't proud of. Being with Neil ... it wasn't something I'm proud of now. I justified things because I wasn't in a good place. I mean, self-esteem wise. Regardless of what his situation was, he was married."

"Ms. Cross," Matt said. "Let me ask you this. Was there a specific reason or incident that caused you to end your relationship with Mr. Shumway?"

"Yes," she said.

Marcy Cross was sweating. Her cheeks flushed and her breathing got a little ragged.

"Objection," I said. "Your Honor, whether this witness did or didn't have a relationship with the defendant is wholly irrelevant."

"Mr. Orville," she said. "I tend to agree."

"Your Honor, if the witness would be allowed to answer the question, I believe the relevance of their break-up has a direct bearing on this case."

"All right," she said. "Overruled for now. But let's get to the point, shall we?"

"Ms. Cross," Matt said. "Why did you end your relationship with Neil Shumway?"

"Because I saw him with Denise. I saw them together. In the north stairwell of the Sunmeadow Court building. I was ... God. I was trying to be more healthy. You know, take the stairs instead of the elevator. I was leaving to go to lunch and I opened the stairwell door, went down one flight, and I caught them together. They were ... he was ... they were having sex."

There came a collective gasp from the courtroom. Behind me, I heard a sob from Denise. Then, very quietly, she whispered, "She's lying."

I kept still. Cool. I couldn't let Matt, Shumway, or most definitely the jury see any reaction at all from me.

"Ms. Cross," Matt said. "How do you know they were having intercourse?"

"She was sitting on the stairs. He was in front of her with his pants down. I mean ... he's got a birthmark on his um ... oh God. Left cheek. She had her skirt up. I mean, there really isn't a way to mistake that ... activity for anything else. And she certainly seemed to be enjoying it. It wasn't rape. I mean, she kept saying yes over and over again."

I gritted my teeth. A hearsay objection at this point seemed fairly useless.

"Can you tell me when this was? The date?"

Marcy shrugged. "No. I'm sorry. I don't remember the exact date. But it wasn't long before Denise's um ... what happened to her. At most it was a few days before that. Very close in time. I wasn't speaking to her after that. I couldn't even look at her. I never confronted her about it. I was working up to it, but then ... well ... all that awful stuff happened and I mean, what would have been the point? I did break it off with Neil the next day though. Over the phone. He didn't ... it didn't seem to upset him. He was pretty matter of fact about the whole thing and I took that to mean he'd moved on. With Denise."

"Thank you, Ms. Cross, I have nothing further."

Blood roared in my ears as I made my way up to the lectern.

"Ms. Cross." My tone was sharp. My words coming out in staccato. "You were questioned by the police in April of 2000, two days after Denise's attack, weren't you?"

"Um, yes," she said. "I was."

"I have your statement in front of me. Do you recollect what you told them in 2000?"

"I told them I worked the day of her incident. On the 14th. I told them I saw Denise that day and that I didn't see anything unusual."

"So you failed to mention your claim of a sexual relationship between Denise Silvers and Neil Shumway, isn't that right?"

"That's right," she said.

"And in fact, you were asked point-blank whether Denise had a boyfriend. Remember, I have your statement right here."

"No," she said. "I didn't mention what I'd seen in the stairwell."

"And then, six months ago, you were again contacted by the Maumee County sheriffs in connection with this case, weren't you?"

"Yes," she answered. She was crying now.

"And at that time, you were fully aware that Neil Shumway was a suspect in this case, weren't you?"

"Yes."

"And isn't it true you refused to cooperate with them?"

"I didn't ... I didn't not cooperate."

"I see," I said. "You claim to have explosive information about Denise's relationship with the defendant but you didn't see fit to come forward with it? Not in 2000, and not this year?"

"I didn't lie," she said. "They never asked me about Neil back then."

"They asked you if you knew about any dating or romantic relationships Denise had!" I shouted.

She started to sob uncontrollably. I had the overwhelming urge to leap across that witness box and shake her.

She nodded. "I'm sorry. Yes. But I'm telling you the truth now. These things happened. Just like I said."

"And you lied to the police at a minimum by omission. You were aware that the defendant was being charged with brutally raping, torturing, and attempting to kill Denise Silvers. And yet you say nothing about this concocted version of events that you only now see fit to regale us with."

"Objection," Matt shouted. "Counsel is badgering the witness. There's no question in there."

"Ms. Brent," Judge Saul said, though I could see her own skin had gone entirely colorless.

"I didn't lie," Marcy Cross sobbed. "I just didn't want to be involved. I didn't want it to come out that I was sleeping with a married man. My family is very religious. You don't understand. I never meant to hurt anyone. But Denise, you can't keep lying. It's horrible what happened to you, but you know the truth. We both know the truth."

Judge Saul banged her gavel. But the damage was already done.

Through the commotion, I said I had no further questions for this witness. In the wake of her testimony, Judge Saul called for a recess.

The Silver Angels gathered around Denise and wheeled her out the back of the courtroom.

Chapter 22

"Denise, you have to breathe!"

Betsy Silvers knelt next to her sister. I stood in the doorway of our conference room. Every staff member in the office, from Phil, the paralegals, to the cleaning crew, crowded the office. A group of Denise's Silver Angels tried to bar my way in.

"We're all on the same side, ladies," I said. "I'm going to need you to give us a little room and a place to talk."

Kenya proved to be a godsend in the situation. She offered to take everyone but Betsy and Denise into another room so she could explain our next step. Now I just had to figure out what that even was.

After some dirty looks and a few more tense moments, the room was all but cleared. Denise cried silently, but at least she'd stopped hyperventilating.

Weary, I took a seat opposite Betsy and waited another moment to allow Denise to say something first.

"She's lying," she finally managed. "Marcy Cross is lying."

"Why would she do that?" Betsy said. The sharpness of her question startled me. I realized I'd mistaken her emotion for sisterly concern. Instead, Betsy Silvers quaked with anger.

"All of it," Denise said. "I was never in that stairwell with Newt. I never even talked to him beyond the times he'd come to my window with candy or whatever. I told the truth about all of that."

There was something in the way her sentence ended I didn't like. We kept a pitcher of water on the conference room table. I poured myself a glass and another for Denise.

"Is there anything you haven't told the truth about?" I think she thought I'd follow that up with "now's the time to come clean." It wasn't though. It was twenty years too late if she was lying about anything at all.

Denise met my eyes. I'd stared across a table from her maybe a hundred times over the last eight years. I'd heard her tell her story so many times, I practically knew the words by heart. Not once in all that time had I even detected a hint of deception. The details never changed. Ever.

"I wasn't having an affair with Newt Shumway," she said. "Or anyone else."

"But?" I said. The word hung in the air.

"I *was* at lunch ... once ... where the rest of them were talking about him the way Marcy described it."

I sipped my water. "The rating system," I said.

"It was something like that," she said. "A stupid game. Like something you'd play at a slumber party. Screw, marry, kill. Do you know the one?"

"I didn't go to a lot of slumber parties, Denise," I said. And Natalie Montleroy Roth didn't lead any Girl Scout troops or bake cookies either.

"It's juvenile," she said. "They were going around the table and naming three men. Of them, which one would you screw, marry, or kill."

"Ah," I said. "And you played this game?"

"I don't even remember. Marcy was there. Mara, I don't even remember the names they were throwing out. You have to understand who I was back then. Those girls were raunchy. They'd all lived on their own, gone away to college. I was the goody-two-shoes. They used to do things like that around me all the time to get a reaction. They liked embarrassing me. But everything I said on that witness stand. Everything I've been telling you and the cops and everyone who'd listen, it's been the truth."

"But why would Marcy Cross lie like that?" Betsy asked.

I had theories. It did me no good to voice any of them in front of these women. There were far too many unknowns. I still had no idea who might have tampered with the parking lot security footage. Now I had a witness who may well have perjured herself on the stand to protect Neil Shumway.

I needed to think. I needed to scream.

"Can you prove she's lying?" Betsy asked.

"With any luck, the jury will see through what happened today. It makes no sense why Marcy Cross would have with-held that story until today. You heard me cross-examine her. She was questioned by the police multiple times. Twenty years ago she was asked directly whether she knew of any romantic relationships you were in. She said nothing. I could even buy it ... maybe ... if she didn't at the time know Neil was involved. But the moment he was arrested, she still didn't come forward to tell that particular story."

I was angry at Sam Cruz and Gus Ritter. Ritter shouldn't have taken no for an answer when Marcy Cross ignored his calls. It should have been a red flag.

"Will it be enough?" Denise asked. She slowly raised her eyes and stared at me. "Mara ... is he going to get away with what he did to me?"

I leaned across the table and took her hands in mine. I'd never once in all our years made her the one promise she wanted to hear. I couldn't do it now either.

"This trial isn't over yet, Denise," I said. "Marcy Cross was by no means a perfect witness. In fact, if I know anything about Detectives Ritter and Cruz, it's likely they were waiting for her when she left the courthouse. What she's done ... she could be charged with obstruction of justice or giving a false statement to the police."

"But that's only if they can prove she was lying," Betsy said. She stood in the corner of the room now, her hands folded.

"I need you both to go home now," I said. "Get some rest. And then I need you to show up tomorrow. There's a gag order in place, but I can't promise you Marcy Cross's little bombshell won't hit the internet. If you hide now ... it won't look good. So, you show up in force tomorrow morning. You and as many Silver Angels as you can get. Then we keep going. All of this ... everything Marcy said ... it still doesn't touch what happened to you."

"But now he can explain away the DNA," Betsy said. "That was the whole point of that, wasn't it? He's going to argue that my sister had some nooner with Shumway on the day she was attacked. And that's why his DNA was on her even though it was somebody else who tried to kill her."

"What?" Denise said, starting to hyperventilate again. "But ... we know that's not true. We know what Shumway is. All those other girls ... they ..."

"Enough," I said. "I've told you from the very beginning, we do this one day at a time. Today was a rough one. Tomorrow is tomorrow. Now go home. Then show up and we get ready to fight again."

For the first time since I met her, I saw genuine doubt in Denise Silvers's eyes as her sister wheeled her out of the room.

***

"Get me absolutely everything we have on Marcy Cross," I barked. It was nine o'clock at night. Kenya stayed, so did Scott Farmer. Some of the things Sam Cruz had said to me played in the back of my mind. Was it possible that one of them had either actively or negligently messed up this case? Regardless, they weren't responsible for the train wreck that was Marcy Cross's testimony and I needed more hands and minds on this problem.

"We know all of this," Kenya said. We had multiple copies of Marcy's statement to the cops laid out on the conference room table.

"I know," I said. I stood over the table, hands on hips.

"She was nothing," I said. "She barely registered on anyone's

213

radar. The cops were pretty much checking off a box in interviewing her. Both in 2000 and this year."

"So why now?" Kenya said. It was more rhetorical. "If she's feeling jilted by Shumway, or wants revenge for him not leaving his wife ... why on earth would she go in there trying to defend him?"

"Do you think any of this matters?" Scott asked. "I mean ... Cross doesn't come off as the most credible of witnesses, but if even one member of that jury thinks twice about what she said ..."

"It's enough for reasonable doubt," Kenya answered for him.

I grabbed a stapled stack of papers from the edge of the conference room table. It was part of the Detective Leeds's original file. It contained a directory of every person working in the Sunmeadow Court building in the spring of 2000.

"This one's alphabetical," I said. "Do we have one that's organized by office?"

"What do you mean?" Scott asked.

"I mean I want the names of every single person who worked directly with Marcy Cross in that timeframe."

Scott rose from his seat. He leaned over the table and started rummaging through more stacks of paper.

"She was in Dr. Nicholson's office, right?"

"Right," Kenya and I answered in unison.

Scott licked his finger then produced a single sheet of paper and handed it to me. It was a mercifully short list.

There were two receptionists, Louise Lensky and Carrie Jarvis. Dr. Joe had a single nurse practitioner by the name of Peggy Hollister. Then there were two nurses who worked alternating days, Marcy Cross and Lisa Casteel.

"Do we have current contact information on these people?" I asked. Dr. Joe himself died a few years back.

Scott fired up his laptop and started plugging in names. He got lucky on the first couple. They were still listed as being local to Waynetown. I gave Kenya the two receptionists. That left the nurses and nurse practitioner.

"Call them," I said to Kenya. "Do whatever you have to to get them on the phone tonight. Be careful what you tell them about the substance of Marcy Cross's testimony. But ... feel them out."

"The cops should have done this twenty years ago," Kenya muttered.

"They did," I said. There were statements in the file from almost every employee working at Sunmeadow. Only about three dozen had actually been working in the building on the day in question.

"This was before Shumway was a suspect, remember?" I said. "They were flying blind. And once we had positive DNA and that security tape, there was more than enough probable cause to arrest Shumway and for us to indict."

Kenya nodded as she took her list of names and headed down to her office.

"Here are the other two nurses, Hollister and Casteel," Scott said.

He wrote down an address and phone number for each of them. I took them from him. "Keep at it," I told him. "Trust your instincts and report back to me when you have info on everyone else."

"Got it," he said.

I went into my office. My first call to Peggy Hollister went unanswered. I left a message and hoped for the best. Then I tried Lisa Casteel. According to Scott's note, she, like Marcy, was doing home care now. But she'd moved away and was now living outside of Columbus. If I had to, I'd figure out a way to get her through the agency she worked for.

I got lucky that night. The number Scott found was Lisa's cell phone. She answered.

"Ms. Casteel?" I said. "My name is Mara Brent. I'm a prosecuting attorney in Maumee County. I know this is going to sound strangely out of the blue, but I was hoping you could talk to me about a former co-worker of yours from Dr. Nicholson's office. Marcy Cross?"

I heard an audible sigh on the other end of the line. "Lord," she said. "Is Marcy dead?"

"What? No. Oh goodness. No. I don't mean to upset you. Look, this is a fairly long story and I'll try to be brief. I'm in the middle of an ongoing criminal trial. I'd really prefer to have this conversation in person, but I'm afraid time is of the essence."

"Do I have to talk to you?" she asked. "I mean, don't you need a subpoena or something?"

It was such an odd thing for her to say. The hair stood up on the back of my neck. "Ms. Casteel. You're not in any trouble or anything. And anything you tell me ... your decision to talk to me is up to you. I'm calling about some things that might have happened in your office between Marcy Cross and Neil Shumway. Do you know that name?"

"He's dead," Lisa said. There was real distress in her tone. "The poor old guy is dead. Isn't there some kind of statute of limitations on this stuff?"

"Dead?" I said. "No. Neil Shumway is still very much alive."

"Dr. Joe is dead," she said. "I mean, what good will it do dragging him through the mud now?"

Dr. Joe? What mud?

My heart stopped cold. Columbus, Ohio was a two-and-a-half-hour drive. I took a breath and a leap of faith. Then I begged Lisa Casteel to get in her car and meet me halfway.

Chapter 23

I REALIZED WELL after the fact, this was probably one of the craziest ideas I'd ever had. By the time I reached Kenton, a little town halfway from Waynetown to Columbus, it was one o'clock in the morning. I'd told no one where I was going, not even Kenya or Scott. Will was staying with Jason for the remainder of the week until the trial was over. But there I was, parked outside an all-night diner off Route 68.

I recognized Lisa Casteel right away from her Facebook profile photo. She told me she drove a red Ford Fusion and I saw it parked two spots over from the single handicapped space. I parked beside her. Lisa was watching from the window and acknowledged me with a nod.

"Well," I said to myself. "In for a penny and all that ..."

I found some comfort in the fact there were two other occupied booths in the diner. One was oddly a family of four with two small children, perhaps on their way to some family vacation or event. The other was an older couple. Husband and wife, maybe. I got a polite smile from the man as I walked in and approached the first booth by the door where Lisa sat.

She was pretty, with short blonde hair and a wide jaw. She wore tortoise shell glasses with a rhinestone chain. She was fifty years old and twenty years ago, she would have been very well known to most people in Waynetown through Dr. Joe Nicholson's office. And now, she knew something that made her scared to meet with me except for far out of town in the middle of the night.

Lord. Yes. This might have been one of the craziest things I'd ever agreed to.

"Thanks for meeting with me," I said. "I know this is all … strange."

"I just don't understand why now," she said. "After all this time. I don't know why it still matters to me. I mean, the man is dead. It's just … this all caused me a lot of grief and I worked really hard to put it behind me. No one would listen when I could have done something about it. It's too late now but … I don't know. When you called … I guess I've always known someone finally would."

I found a smile. I had a distinct impression Lisa Casteel and I had two very different objectives for this meeting. I knew from experience I'd get better information if I just let her work her way around to hers rather than injecting my own.

"Who did you try to tell your story to besides me?" I asked.

Lisa ran a thumb over the handle of her now empty coffee mug. "That office … Dr. Nicholson was a saint in Waynetown. It seemed like everyone went to see him. And he was really great to work for. At the time, my daughter was just a baby when I first got hired. She had some health problems in those years. There were a lot of specialists we had to see and appointments. Evie's fine now, my daughter. But I know if I were working for anyone else, I would have lost my job over all the missed days. Dr. Joe never questioned it."

"He was a good man," I said. "At least that's what I've heard. I didn't grow up in Waynetown so I didn't really know him. But you say Dr. Joe and everyone still knows who you mean."

Lisa nodded. "He was like Santa Claus to some people."

"Lisa," I said. "It's … it's actually a bit dicey for me to be talking about this. I'm in the middle of a trial and the judge has issued a gag order. That limits what I can say outside of the courtroom. But … primarily it's to do with anyone talking to the press. You understand my role though, don't you? I'm working to secure a rape conviction against Neil Shumway. You are familiar with what happened to Denise Silvers?"

She nodded. When she raised her cup to take another sip of coffee but finding it still empty, she set it back down. Her hands were shaking. It caused my heart to skip a beat.

"Lisa," I said. "Marcy Cross has made some claims about Shumway and Denise. Claims that I think aren't true. You worked with Marcy in that office for years. Did you also know Denise?"

"Of course," she said. "We were all friendly on that floor."

"Did you ever see Shumway and Denise together? Or Shumway and Marcy, for that matter?"

She set her mug down. "God. You're missing the point. Everyone always misses the point."

221

"So help me find it. Marcy Cross testified that she caught Denise and Neil Shumway together the week Denise was attacked. I think she made it up. I think maybe you know why."

Lisa rolled her eyes. "She was so gullible," she said. "Marcy actually told me I was jealous. To my face. She said I'd be lucky to have someone like Newt even look my way."

"She was in love with him," I said. "Newt."

"She was in love with what he gave her," Lisa snapped.

"And what was that?"

"Are you taping me?" Lisa asked, panic rising in her voice. "I should have asked you that straight off."

"No," I said quickly. I put my purse on the table and emptied the contents. I unlocked my phone and slid it across to her.

"No," I said again. "For right now, this is an off-the-record conversation. It's between you and me. I have one interest and one interest only. Marcy Cross did some damage in court the other day. She claimed that Neil Shumway and Denise Silvers were having sex in the stairwell a few days before Denise's attack. Denise insists that's a lie. Do you have any opinion on Marcy's story one way or the other?"

"I don't think Denise was having sex with Neil Shumway, no."

"But Marcy was," I said. "She's at least made no secret of that."

Lisa got a pained expression on her face. She pinched the bridge of her nose with her thumb and forefinger.

"So Marcy was jealous of any attention Neil paid to other women," I said. "Did you ever see her talking to Denise about that?"

"No," Lisa said. "I don't think Newt, Neil, whatever his name is cared at all about Denise in that way. It was only after people started asking questions. Then everyone assumed it was me. I wasn't the only one though."

Once again, I felt like Lisa Casteel and I were having two different conversations.

"Lisa," I said. "I need to be very clear here. And I need you to be. You're saying you absolutely knew Marcy and Neil ..."

"There was no romance," she interrupted. "But did I know they were banging each other? Yes. And Marcy was dumb enough to think he was going to leave his wife for her. She had no concept of the fact he was only with her to keep her quiet."

"Quiet about what?" I asked.

Lisa looked over her shoulder.

"Lisa, you understand Neil Shumway is standing trial for raping and nearly killing Denise Silvers. She was beaten almost to death by him and has remained in a wheelchair ever since. It was him. I have no doubt. We have a positive DNA match from Denise's rape kit. Marcy has stayed silent all these years. Now she's painting a picture that Denise and Shumway had a consensual sexual relationship that Denise adamantly denies. I need you to understand how serious this is. With what Marcy said in court ... it's very possible she may sway the jury. Shumway could get away with what he did."

I stopped just short of saying the rest of it. I'd already skirted an ethical line telling her this much. I had to hold back what we suspected about the serial nature of Neil Shumway's crimes. I needed it to come from Lisa.

"I went down this road before," Lisa said, on the verge of tears. A new cold horror formed deep in my gut. Was I sitting across from yet another one of Neil Shumway's victims?

"Lisa," I said. "Did that man hurt you too? If he did ... and you've kept quiet for this long ... I can help you. I need you to trust that there are people—powerful people—trying to make sure Shumway pays for what he did."

A tear slid down her cheek. If he'd victimized her too, it might not be enough to help with Denise's trial. His other criminal acts wouldn't be admissible.

I reached for her, taking her hand. She let me.

"Lisa," I said. "You don't have to go through this alone. There are people ... experts. With everything that's happened to Denise, even she has turned it into something positive. She's formed an advocacy group for sexual assault victims."

Lisa slid her hand out of mine. "My God," she said. "Neil Shumway didn't rape me. To be quite honest, I have no idea if he raped Denise. You say Marcy claims they were having sex. They might have been. I don't know one way or the other. But ... Denise wasn't attacked by some rapist. She was attacked by someone who wanted to keep her quiet. I thought you knew that."

I felt like I was standing on quicksand.

"Quiet about what?" I asked.

Lisa dropped her shoulders. "Ms. Brent, you seem like a smart lady. This was a mistake. I thought ..."

"You said Marcy was more in love with what Shumway could give her. What was he giving her, Lisa?" I asked. Bits and pieces started falling into place about what Lisa Casteel had already said.

"He was supplying her," I said. "Was Marcy selling drugs for Shumway?"

Lisa's rapid blinking gave me my answer. I'd finally hit on it.

"What was it?" I asked.

"Benzos, Ritalin, even Oxy by that time. At first ... I mean, I believed what everyone else said about him. That man was beloved in Waynetown. I knew if I said a peep, well ... I'm ashamed to admit it. I am. But it wouldn't have been Denise in that ditch, it would have been me."

My head spun. *That man was beloved*. She wasn't talking about Neil Shumway at all. She was talking about Dr. Joe Nicholson.

"It was all off book," I said. "Or mostly. Shumway would get Dr. Joe the samples he needed? Is that it?"

Something broke inside of Lisa Casteel. Her armor cracked. She had a story to tell and she'd been holding it inside for almost twenty years.

"I don't know how long it went on. And it wasn't every patient. But ... little by little ... he knew how to fudge the records so nothing would draw suspicion. But I knew they were making a fortune toward the end. I asked too many questions. Then one night I got followed home. Run off the road. Then my phone rang and the voice on the other end told me I'd end up at the bottom of the river if I didn't watch my mouth."

I sat back hard. "And then you found out that's exactly what happened to Denise Silvers."

She nodded, sobbing. "I don't know how she found out about Dr. Joe's operation or Shumway's part in it. But ... I was so scared when I found out what happened."

"Lisa," I asked. "Did you ever talk to the cops about any of this? I mean ... you were questioned after she was attacked. Everyone in the office was."

Lisa had of course been listed as a possible witness as an employee of the building. It's how I even knew who she was. But we'd found nothing in the old case file beyond that basic information.

"They interviewed me, yes," she said. Her posture changed. She looked uncomfortable. "A week or so after Denise's attack. You have to understand. At the time, I didn't think what happened to her was connected to what was going on with Dr. Joe. It was only after I got threatened too. At first, I didn't know anything."

"But later," I said. "After you were threatened. Did you go to the police then?"

"I wrote a letter," she said. "I left my name off of it. I sent it to the address they had on all the posters. Crimestoppers or whatever. I never heard back. I was scared for a really long time after that. I ... I quit my job at Dr. Joe's about two months after what happened to Denise. I couldn't get hired anywhere else in Waynetown though. Working for Dr. Joe was supposed to be a dream job, so everyone kept asking me why I left. I didn't want to deal with it. So ... eventually I moved down to Columbus. My brother lives here. I make better money doing home care."

226

"What did you say in your letter?" I asked.

She shrugged. "I was really scared. I *needed* to keep my job. Evie's medical bills would have buried me if I lost my insurance. I told the police they needed to look at Dr. Joe's records. I told them I believed they were running illegal drugs out of that practice. I told them to ask Denise what she knew."

"You never mentioned Shumway by name?" I asked.

"I knew him as Newt back then," she said. "I don't remember if I knew his last name. And I had no idea he was the one who attacked Denise. When I saw his picture in the paper a few weeks ago, it came as a shock."

"Why didn't you come forward then?" I asked.

She blinked rapidly. "I...I don't know. I lost a lot twenty years ago. Just from asking questions. Dr. Joe's dead now. And back then...nothing happened. I sent that letter and nothing happened. Dr. Joe knew a lot of people. They all loved him. Nobody believed me then. Why would they now?"

"I understand," I said, though cold fury ran through me. "Lisa, did you keep a record of the patients of Dr. Joe and Shumway's customers?"

"Not a list, no," she said. She looked even more uneasy and I knew she had something even bigger to tell.

"But if you saw them, you'd recognize them?" I asked.

"I know how they were fudging the charts. A lot of back pain complaints. And there was a pattern to how frequently they'd come in. I was getting ready to start making copies. Then ... I got scared. It all came to a head.

"If you had access to those charts again," I said, "would you know what you were looking at?"

She nodded. "Why hasn't she said anything?" Lisa asked. "Denise, I mean. When I heard Shumway got arrested ... I just assumed now finally everyone would know. I never understood why she didn't tell them about Dr. Joe and Shumway back then?"

"Do you believe it was Shumway who threatened you?" I asked. "Did you recognize his voice. His face?"

She shook her head. "No."

I took a breath. "Lisa, you've helped more than I can even express. Neil Shumway is the man who attacked Denise Silvers. Only ... I don't think keeping her quiet was his motivation. At least, I'll have to talk to her again ... but I'm about one hundred percent certain Denise had no clue about the prescription drug ring Shumway was running through Dr. Joe's office."

She snorted a bitter laugh. "What ... so he's just like some serial killer?"

She said it as a joke. My silence rolled through her and her color went gray. I reached for her again.

"It's going to be okay," I said. "I'm going to help make it so this asshole never sees the light of day again except through razor wire."

I'd made that promise before. To Denise. Once again, I felt the weight of it settle over my shoulders for Lisa Casteel.

Chapter 24

I WAS on forty-eight hours of no sleep. At six a.m., we were three hours from Judge Saul taking the bench for what would probably be Matt Orville's final day of witnesses.

"You want me to what?" Sam asked. I was still wearing the clothes I'd had on in court yesterday. I wouldn't have time to go back home, but always kept a fresh change of court attire in my office. That said, I knew I looked rough and Sam Cruz looked worried.

"Somebody never wanted Neil Shumway looked at back in 2000," I said. I'd given Sam the highlights of what Lisa Casteel had told me.

Sam shook his head. "This Casteel woman thinks this whole thing was about keeping Denise Silvers quiet?"

"Except she's wrong about that," I said. "Denise never had a clue about what was allegedly going on inside Dr. Joe's office. She was just in the wrong place at the wrong time and had the bad luck of being Neil Shumway's type."

Once again, we sat in Sam's unmarked cruiser in a back alley three blocks from my office and his. Though the engine was off, he gripped the steering wheel hard.

"Was Ritter one of Dr. Joe's patients?" I asked. I should have used more finesse. But I was at the end of my rope and I was tired.

"I have no idea," Sam said. "But if you're suggesting Gus Ritter would have tanked the case against Shumway ... let him get away with rape and attempted murder ... just to save his own skin? No. Absolutely not."

"What about Leeds?" I asked.

"Mara, we're sitting here spinning our wheels. You're throwing out baseless accusations."

"Lisa Casteel tried to blow the whistle on Joe Nicholson and Shumway. She said she sent a letter in using the Crimestoppers address. That would have landed on Leeds or Gus's desk. I've never seen it. Have you? She was wrong about the motivation for Denise's attack. But Lisa Casteel was afraid. She was threatened, Sam."

"None of it is going to help Denise," he said. "You said yourself, you believe Shumway's attack on her had nothing to do with his drug racket. Wrong place. Wrong time. Right girl."

"It matters," I said. "It matters because Matt Orville trotted Marcy Cross out and let her tell a bunch of lies about Denise screwing Neil Shumway. Marcy was protecting Shumway and herself in 2000. She's still doing it now. And now we know why. She's still in love with him and she was in on what Nicholson was doing. Her credibility is at issue. I can get to all of this on rebuttal."

Sam looked at me, his brown eyes flashing. "That's if you can get Lisa Casteel to testify."

"Already writing up the subpoena. She's ready, Sam. I know it. This thing cost her her career. Her life in Waynetown, basically. She's not afraid anymore. Not like she was. Joe Nicholson is dead and Neil Shumway's in jail. Now she's just angry."

"Still," Sam said. "It's gonna be her word against Marcy's."

"That's why I need you. Get me Nicholson's patient list and records from 2000. However you can. And Sam, you understand I need you to do this quietly."

"Mara, more than half the town saw Dr. Joe in those days. This goes beyond needle in a haystack territory."

"Maybe," I said. "But Lisa knows what she's looking at. She said there was a pattern of complaints Nicholson would have them write down in their charts. She knows where the bodies were buried in those records, so to speak."

"You realize how big of a hornet's nest you're kicking with this?" he said.

"Yes," I said. "And I have every reason to think what Shumway was doing in Waynetown, he was doing other places too. What if part of the reason he's gotten away with his attacks on these women is that he had dirt on the right people? More than just here."

"Christ," Sam said.

"I need you," I said. "Sam, no matter who this touches, the truth has to come out. You know what kind of monster we're dealing with."

His knuckles turned white as he gripped the wheel. I touched his shoulder.

"Sam," I said. "Look at me."

He did.

A muscle twitched in his jaw.

"Yeah," he finally said.

"This has to be just you and me for now," I said. "We can't bring this to the task force yet. Not until we have a clearer picture of who might be involved. Someone is actively working against me. Against you. That security footage was tampered with. I know you know that. Matt Orville is going to come after your department hard on this. Mine too. This is the way to fight back. And it's not too late to save this trial."

I realized it was me who had taken the biggest leap of faith of all. If it turned out Gus Ritter or someone else Sam idolized had been one of Dr. Joe's special patients there was a chance he'd try to protect them now.

But all I had left was faith. I just prayed I hadn't misplaced it. Sam put his car in gear and drove us out of the shadows.

Chapter 25

ORVILLE SAVED his DNA expert for last. He was Dr. Gerald Siefert. He'd been one of the pioneers in the use of DNA evidence in criminal trials, making a name for himself in the late nineties after he switched sides and started testifying in cases for the Delayed Justice Project.

Orville did a decent job getting Siefert through his qualifications without boring the jury. The trouble was, with these kinds of witnesses, the jury already knows what the witness will likely conclude based on who called them to the stand. At this late stage of the trial, their patience would quickly wear thin.

"Dr. Siefert," Orville wound up. "In your expert medical opinion, can you estimate or give a range as to how old the DNA evidence collected from Ms. Silvers's person might have been?"

Siefert straightened his jacket. "It's impossible to say exactly," he said.

"I think we all understand that," Matt said. "But can you give a timeframe? A window, if you will."

Siefert was a born actor. He squinted, tilted his head, pondering the question as if it were a surprise to him he was even asked it.

"Well, we can safely assume the samples taken were at several hours old based on the victim's claims about her activities, medical response times, etcetera. So, they were not fresh ..."

"Objection," I said. "The witness by his own admission is assuming facts in his answer."

"Dr. Siefert," Orville said.

"Mr. Orville," Judge Saul interrupted. "Are you not in the habit of waiting for a ruling on a pending objection?"

"My apologies, Your Honor," Matt said. It was a rare slip-up on his part.

"Doctor," the judge continued. "Let's be clear that any speculation you make is based on your medical expertise, shall we?"

"Of course," he said. "If I may rephrase the beginning of my answer, I think I can satisfy the prosecution's objection."

"By all means," Orville said.

"In general," Siefert said, "the semen sample collected could have been as much as seventy-two hours old. Perhaps even longer. That's why it's standard procedure to compile a list of sexual partners a victim has had in that timeframe. So elimination samples can be gathered."

"So there is a range ... a window, if you will?" Orville asked.

"Yes," Siefert answered.

"And to be clear, it's entirely possible that this sample could have come from consensual relations several hours or even days ... as you stated ... prior to the physical assault on the victim. Is that correct?"

"Absolutely," he said. "Again, that's why taking a complete history of a victim's sexual behavior in the days leading up to an alleged attack must be done."

"Thank you," Matt smiled. "I have nothing further."

I stepped to the lectern. "Dr. Siefert, to be clear. You've just testified that you can't say for certain whether that sample was a few hours old or older?"

"Correct," he said. "I testified to a window of time, not a precise time. That's for you to establish."

"And you're aware that Ms. Silvers's injuries included visible signs of forced penetration."

He looked uncomfortable, at least. "I am."

"And you've read the reports submitted along with the various fluid samples. So you know they were collected at the sites of her injuries."

"I do," he said.

"And you're not disputing that the samples collected from Ms. Silvers, other than her own DNA, belonged to a single individual?"

"Um ... no."

"And that individual was the defendant, Neil Shumway," I said.

235

"Yes," he answered.

"Dr. Siefert," I said. "How much were you paid to be here today?"

"Objection as to the form of the question," Matt said. "To the extent counsel implies ..."

"Overruled, Mr. Orville," Judge Saul said.

"Shall I repeat?" I said.

Dr. Siefert stayed cool and calm. We both knew this was standard cross-examination for any defense expert.

"I've been compensated for my time, Ms. Brent," he said. "An hourly fee to review the records in this case, write an opinion, and for the time spent testifying today. I do not have an exact dollar amount I can report today. My office will bill for my time."

"What's your hourly fee?" I asked.

"I believe it's three hundred and fifty dollars per hour."

"And how many hours would you estimate you've got into this case?" I asked.

"Again, you're asking me to estimate so don't hold me to an exact figure. I would say probably twenty hours total including my time spent answering all of your questions."

"Thank you," I said. "And isn't it true, you are not qualified to render an opinion on whether or not Ms. Silvers was raped."

"That's correct," he said.

"Thank you," I said. "I have nothing further."

"Dr. Siefert," Matt popped up quickly. "Do you ever turn down criminal defense consulting work?"

"Yes," he said. "To be honest, I turn down more cases than I take, these days. I don't do this for the money, counselor."

"Thank you," Matt said.

"Ms. Brent?" The judge offered me re-cross. It was petty of me, but I had just one question. A beat I couldn't let go unplayed.

"Dr. Siefert, you sure as heck don't get up there for free, do you?"

He scowled at me. So did the judge.

"Objection!" Matt hollered.

"Withdrawn," I said. I'd made my point.

"The witness may step down. Mr. Orville?"

Matt rose again. He took his time walking to the lectern. He waited until Gerald Siefert had made his way out of the gallery then leaned into the microphone.

"Your Honor," Orville said. "At this time, the defense rests."

Chapter 26

JUDGE VIVIAN SAUL's toothache ended up being a gift from the heavens for me. Rather than having me begin my rebuttal case right then and there, she adjourned for the afternoon. It meant I had roughly sixteen hours to pull a Hail Mary that might yet secure Shumway's conviction.

Because, as it stood right then, I knew he was about to walk free.

Kenya hadn't come to court that morning. I'd trusted her with another task and as I walked outside, her text popped up. She delivered.

My pulse skipped as I crossed the street and headed back to the office. She had things set up in the smaller of our conference rooms. Phil paced outside as I approached. His face turned two shades of purple.

"This is a waste of time," he managed to somehow shout and whisper all at once.

"Did you hear what he had to say already?" I asked. Behind

Phil's shoulder, I could see Kenya talking to a thin, handsome man with dark hair and even darker circles under his eyes. He sat alone. Shockingly, he hadn't thought to bring a company lawyer.

"Oh, he's a talker all right," Phil said. "Do you want to clue me in how you're planning on getting one word of his story in front of the jury?"

I took a breath and went with honesty. "I have no idea."

I didn't wait for more from Phil. I walked into the conference room. Phil followed close behind.

"Mr. Prentice?" I said, extending a hand. "I'm Mara Brent."

His eyes darted to Kenya, but he took my hand and shook it, half rising out of his chair.

"Tell her what you told me," Kenya said, the excitement in her voice evident.

"I was Neil Shumway's regional manager from 1993 through 2005," he said.

"I'm happy you agreed to come talk to me today," I said. "I know this was very short notice and probably out of the blue."

"No," he said. "I've been contacted ... well ... no ... not me personally. I know the company reps have been contacted by some detectives in other cities."

I had to be careful. The task force investigation into Shumway's other suspected rapes and murders weren't public knowledge. Any questions Blaine Pharm got had to do with Neil's travel schedule over a fifteen-year period. But it wouldn't be hard for someone with half a brain to put it all together. Earl Prentice had to know what charges Neil was facing here in Waynetown. Kenya had no choice but to tell him.

For now, I had another angle to work.

"Did you stop being his regional manager in 2005 because he left or you did?" I asked.

"I told your colleague all this," Prentice said, annoyed. "I work in Blaine's corporate office now. Neil resigned in 2005."

"I understand," I said. "And I also understand how difficult a position that puts you in. I'm not asking you to throw anyone under the bus."

"Personnel records aren't public knowledge," he said. "There are privacy laws."

"I'm not trying to hurt Blaine," I said. "Or you or anyone you're still friends with. I'm sure Ms. Spaulding has explained to you the delicacy of the situation we're in. This is about Neil. I need you to tell me everything you can about his separation from the company."

I turned back to Phil. He held a folded piece of paper in his hands. I smiled. I had no idea what kind of dance he had to do to get a judge to sign off on this, but he came through. I wanted to hug Phil Halsey just then.

He gave it to me and I handed it to Prentice. I watched his face go through a series of changes.

"That's a subpoena, Mr. Prentice," I said. "You're right. There are privacy laws. But that's how we circumvent them."

"Did you lure me here for this?" he asked, folding the subpoena and putting it on the table in front of him.

"I think you did your due diligence," I said. "I think you were put in a tough situation. And I think you probably saved Blaine Pharm from a mess. Today, I'm not here for any of that though. Today, I want to know about Shumway."

Prentice took a breath. I hoped I'd be able to get his story without having to mention Lisa Casteel. Of course, he wouldn't know her personally, but the fewer people knew her name, the better I could control any leaks.

"We'd gotten some ... complaints," Earl Prentice said. "Neil's numbers were off a few quarters in a row. We have controls, you see. Safeguards in place. It's as you said. All those mechanisms worked the way they were supposed to."

"But you didn't fire him," Phil interjected. "You didn't bother to report your suspicions to the D.E.A. or any authority. You all just swept it under the rug and what ... had him resign instead of firing him?"

I looked back, wanting to murder Phil. The last thing I needed was to scare Earl Prentice more than he already was.

"Look," I said. "All that is out of our jurisdiction. The only thing I care about is whether I have a witness lying to cover up Neil Shumway's shady dealings with doctors' offices. I know Ms. Spaulding has explained to you the relationship Shumway had with a nurse in one of the offices he served. Are you aware of any other improprieties like that?"

"Yes," Prentice blurted. "Okay? Yes. There was an issue with the numbers. The recording of the drug samples he had access to. And we received a harassment complaint from another nurse in a pain clinic we served in Cleveland. There was a similar issue at a doctor's office in Ann Arbor, I think it was."

242

"What kind of complaints?" I asked, heart racing.

"Look," Prentice said. "I don't know what was going on. I'm a family man. I can't dictate the personal lives of the people who work for us. But I knew Neil had a wife. But it also came to my attention that he was ... catting around with women while on the job. It started to look like a girl-in-every-port kind of situation. Then, when the accounting stopped making sense where he was concerned, we thought it best to give him a choice."

"Resign or be fired," I said.

"Yes," Prentice answered.

"These harassment complaints," I said. "Were any of them violent in nature?"

"No!" Prentice shouted. In the back of my mind, I knew he was lying. We'd find out soon enough through the subpoena. I would demand the names of the complainants.

"As I said when I walked in," I said. "I really do appreciate your coming in to talk to us. You understand that we'll have more questions. And you'll likely be contacted by even more members of law enforcement."

"I knew I shouldn't have agreed to come down here. I want a lawyer." Great, I thought. Now he thinks of it.

"You should speak with one," I said.

Personally, I didn't give a single care about what happened to Earl Prentice after this. I tried not to think about what might have happened if Blaine had done the right thing and turned over what they suspected about Shumway to the D.E.A.

What if he'd been charged and convicted back in 2005? How many innocent women might have been spared his horror?

I couldn't let any of that derail me. I had to stick to the matter at hand. For the first time in a long time, hope sparked in my gut. Lisa Casteel was telling the truth. I had enough to put her on the stand and shred Marcy Cross's testimony.

I just prayed it would be enough to close the cell doors on Neil Shumway forever.

Chapter 27

THE HOUSE ALARM PINGED. I woke from a dead sleep into the pitch blackness of the middle of the night. It took me a few seconds to figure out whether I'd overslept or just where I was.

Then the doorbell rang. I grabbed my phone off the charger and pulled up my doorbell app. It was Sam Cruz, hair disheveled, with a thick package under his arm.

I grabbed my robe off the bedpost and flew downstairs. Breathless, I opened the door.

Sam towered over me. It was something I didn't notice much anymore but that night—or rather, that early morning—he just seemed to loom so much larger than normal.

"Sorry," he said. "I knew this couldn't wait." He gestured to the package he carried.

I opened the door wider. "Come on in," I said.

"You might want to put on a pot of coffee."

"Welcome to the new twenties, Sam. Who uses pots of coffee?"

I pulled pods out of the drawer and quickly brewed two cups. I brought them to the kitchen island where Sam had already set up camp and started spreading the contents of the package he brought. It contained mounds of documents.

My heart raced as I took the stool opposite him. From just a cursory glance, I could see they were portions of medical records.

"Good lord," I said, sipping my too-hot coffee. "How many? How did you ..."

He put a hand up. "Better if you don't know the how."

"Right," I nodded.

"Back pain," he said. "That's the chief complaint from all of these. I have more files in my car. But these are the ones Dr. Joe was repeatedly seeing through late 1999 all the way to the summer of 2000. Marcy Cross was doing intake on all of them. There are hundreds total. You think Nurse Casteel can make sense of all of this?"

"I do," I said. I picked up one random file. The patient's name was Delores Fraser. She was a new patient to Dr. Joe in 1998. Just like Sam said, her chief complaint was chronic back pain.

"There's something else," Sam said. He had a dour expression on his face. He reached into the back pocket of his jeans and pulled out a well-worn leather book. He tossed it on the island and it skittered across to me.

"What is this?" I said, picking it up. The pages were wrinkled and stiff as though the thing had gone through the washing machine and left to air dry.

"It belonged to Ken Leeds," he said. "It's his day planner from 2000."

I threw a glance at Sam and opened the book to April. It was covered in scrawling cursive, short-hand for meetings, appointments, personal notes.

"Where did you get this?" I asked.

"Joyce Leeds," he said. "Ken's widow. I went to see her yesterday. We talked about the case."

"Why are you giving me this?" I asked. "Why now?"

"I don't know. And that's the God's honest truth. What happened to that videotape ... this list."

Sam sifted through the pile of records and pulled out a single piece of paper. He gave it to me. It was a visit summary from January, 2000. It was different from the others in that it detailed flu symptoms, not any kind of pain management. But the patient's name struck a chord.

"Ken Leeds was a patient of Dr. Joe's," I said. I checked the date. In Leeds's day planner, he had written down an appointment reminder for the same day.

"There are two other dates in there," Sam said, his voice devoid of all emotion. "March 28th. Then in June. He's written down appointments with Dr. Joe but there's no corresponding visit summary in Nicholson's records."

"Sam ..." I started.

"It doesn't have to mean anything," he said. "Ken also interviewed Dr. Joe in connection with this case. His whole staff. That's noted in his day planner. It's noted in the case file. We either have full witness statements or at least an impression in Ken or Gus's write-up."

"Sam," I said again. "If Ken Leeds was one of Dr. Nicholson's special patients ... if Shumway was supplying illegal narcotics to the lead investigator in Denise's assault case ..."

"None of this proves that," he said.

"And you wouldn't have brought it to me if you weren't thinking the same thing. What did Joyce Leeds tell you?"

He shrugged. "Nothing out of the ordinary. She doesn't have any reason to think Ken had been taking drugs he shouldn't have. Ken never even drank."

"Are you sure?" I said, looking Sam straight in the eyes. "How well did you really know Ken Leeds?"

He met my gaze. "I knew him well enough. And Gus knew him like a brother."

I sat back. "How much does Gus know about all of this?"

Sam blinked. He took a breath. "Zero."

It took me a moment to process all of that. Sam and Gus worked as partners on this case. If Ken Leeds and Gus Ritter had been close as brothers, I knew Sam's relationship with Gus now was just as tight. And yet, Sam didn't trust him with what we now knew about Dr. Joe and Neil Shumway.

"Sam," I said.

"Enough. Whatever happened with that tape. Whatever happened with Lisa Casteel ..."

"What happened is she wasn't taken seriously twenty years ago. She said she tried to tell her story to Ken or Gus ... maybe both. And yet it never even made the report."

Again, Sam's face changed. The realization hit me. I may very well be holding the answer in my hand. I opened Ken Leeds's book to April 2000. Slowly, methodically, I flipped through the pages. He'd written down names in the margins of each day in the few weeks after Denise's attack. There were no observations, just the names and times. I would have to cross-reference them with the police report, but I was reasonably sure they would correspond to interviews he conducted on the Silvers case. On April 30th, there was a single name listed at 4:45 p.m.

Lisa Casteel.

I put the book down. *She was in Ken's book but never made it into his official report.* It could mean nothing or it could mean everything. Lisa had already told me she'd been interviewed by the police. But, at the time, she hadn't thought Dr. Joe's illegal activities were connected to the attack. That came later. Only, Ken Leeds's report was thorough. Even if it was just a line or paragraph, he made a note of the substance of every interview he conducted. Except Lisa's.

"Sam," I said again. He knew exactly what I read.

"It isn't what you think," he said. "Mara, I know it in my gut."

"He talked to her," I said. "Ken Leeds talked to Lisa. And yet her statement isn't in the case file. The letter she sent into Crimestoppers is missing. Why?"

"Who knows," he said. "You said yourself she was rambling about her suspicions about Dr. Joe. She didn't have anything relevant to say about Denise's attack. Ken could have made a judgment call. Her info was tangential. Not related to the crime he was investigating. The Crimestoppers letter was anonymous. Ken wouldn't have even known Lisa sent it."

My shoulders dropped. "This doesn't pass the smell test, Sam."

"I don't know," he said. "And we don't even know Ken was getting anything he shouldn't have been from Dr. Joe. Run it by Lisa. I don't care."

"How do you know Gus hasn't been trying to keep this from coming out the whole time? He could have ..."

"No!" Sam shouted, rising. "Dammit. No. This wasn't Gus. It doesn't make sense, Mara. What good would it have done for him to risk his career, his freedom by tampering with that security tape now? That's insane. Gus isn't ... there are a million ways to make a guy disappear," he said. "If Gus wanted to keep Shumway quiet ..."

"Don't say another word," I said.

"Yeah," he said. "I won't. What are you going to do now? Do you have to take this to that weasel, Orville?"

I ran a hand through my hair. "No."

"No?" he asked.

"No," I said again. "None of this exculpates Shumway. It makes things worse for him. I have no ethical duty to disclose this information. If anything, it's evidence of someone on the inside trying to protect Shumway, not frame him. I'll use it the way I have to."

"How's that?" Sam asked.

"By putting Lisa Casteel on the stand and blowing Marcy Cross's testimony right out of the water. No matter who else gets hurt by it."

Chapter 28

FOUR HOURS LATER, my final witness and last hope took the stand. Lisa was steady and confident and wearing a crisp, light-blue suit. Gone was the angry, timid woman I'd met a few nights ago. Now that the day had come, she'd gone into warrior mode.

Good. I would need it.

"Nurse Casteel," I said after taking her through all the biographical questions the jury needed to hear. "Are you acquainted with Marcy Cross?"

"I am," she said. "Marcy was the other nurse who worked in Dr. Joe Nicholson's office in the Sunmeadow Court building with me."

"Can you tell me how long you worked together?"

"I think it was five or six years. I left the office in the summer of 2000. Marcy had been there longer than me. I can't say for sure how long, but she was employed by Dr. Joe for the entire length of time that I worked there."

"Were you also acquainted with the defendant, Neil Shumway?" I asked.

I snuck a look behind me. Neil sat unnaturally straight, almost as though his body was receiving an electric charge. Even Matt Orville noticed. It occurred to me Orville had absolutely no idea about what was to come.

"I knew Neil," Lisa said. "I knew him as Newt though. He was one of the drug reps that serviced Dr. Joe's office. He came in once a week. Always on Fridays."

My heart skipped. "Fridays," I said. I'd never asked Lisa this before. She'd just given me gold. April 14th, 2000 was a Friday. From the corner of my eye, I saw Kenya scribbling a furious note. Oh yes, I'd just mentally written a new line for my closing argument.

"Were you aware of a relationship between the defendant and Nurse Cross?" I asked.

"Yes," Lisa said. "Marcy and Newt were romantically involved. Marcy was in love with him."

"Objection," Matt said. "This witness isn't qualified to speculate on Marcy Cross's emotional state regarding the defendant."

"Your Honor," I said. "Nurse Cross testified to as much herself."

"Overruled," Judge Saul said. "But let's stick to objectively observed facts. Not hearsay. Not speculation."

"Noted," I said. "Do you have personal knowledge about how serious the relationship was between Marcy Cross and Neil Shumway?"

"Yes," she said. "I saw Newt and Marcy together many times. They were all over each other when they thought no one was looking. I'd come around a corner and find them kissing in the office when he stopped by. There were times when Marcy would leave to meet Newt or she'd leave with him on her lunch hour. But I was worried."

"Why is that?"

"Well," she said. "Newt was married. I never really believed he would leave his wife for Marcy. And ... later I learned Newt was seeing other women in other offices on his rotation."

"How did you learn that?"

Lisa cleared her throat. "One day, one of his other girlfriends came to Dr. Joe's office looking for him. Marcy wasn't working that day. The girlfriend, I think her name was Louise. She waited in our waiting room for him. He showed up about twenty minutes later. He looked surprised and upset that she was there. He kind of strong-armed her and took her out in the hallway but I could see because the door didn't shut all the way. Newt was really angry. He shook her."

"Then what happened?" I asked.

"He gave her something," Lisa said. "Medication. I don't know what kind. Then she left."

"Did you tell Marcy about any of this?" I asked.

"I tried to," Lisa said. "But you couldn't say anything to Marcy about Newt. She'd get livid. She was very protective of their relationship. And I started noticing other things. Marcy was ... she was showing some signs of being unwell."

"How so?" I asked.

"She started losing weight. Like a lot of it. Marcy was thin to begin with. And her skin got kind of mottled in appearance. I noticed some sores on her skin. She had tremors."

"Did you ever confront Marcy about her health?" I asked.

"I tried that too," Lisa said. "She blew me off. Then she started getting kind of desperate in the days leading up to Newt's visits. At one point, I overheard Newt talking to her in one of the back rooms. He said ... he told her he was going to have to cut her off. He said, you started sampling the product. I told you not to do that. If I can't trust you then I can't use you. If I can't use you, then there's no reason for me to be around you."

"Product," I said. "Do you know what he meant by that?"

Lisa looked down. "Oxy. Newt was supplying Marcy with OxyContin."

"How do you know that for sure?" I asked.

"Because I saw him give them to her. And once ... when Marcy was in the bathroom, I searched her purse. I found packs of samples. They were all marked with Blaine Pharmaceutical labels. They were coming from Newt."

"Objection!" Matt finally said. "Your Honor, this is all speculation and irrelevant."

"It's not speculation," I said. "Nurse Casteel has already testified to her medical expertise. And she has testified about what she observed, not anything she was told."

"Overruled," Judge Saul said.

"Nurse Casteel," I said. "What other concerns did you have about Mr. Shumway in the office?"

Lisa took a great breath. "Newt Shumway and Dr. Joe Nicholson were running a side business selling narcotics to patients."

"Objection!" Matt said. "This testimony is completely irrelevant, unsubstantiated ..."

"Sidebar," Judge Saul said.

We met in front of the judge in hushed whispers. She covered her microphone with her hand.

"Where are you going with this, Ms. Brent?" Judge Saul said.

"Your Honor," I said. "Marcy Cross sat in that chair and claimed Denise Silvers was sleeping with the defendant. That is a lie and this witness can prove it. Marcy's credibility is at issue. Her mental state at the time she claims to have observed the victim with the defendant is at issue. Her bias ... her willingness to do anything she could to protect her lover and her own crimes is at issue."

Judge Saul raised a brow. "I'm inclined to agree, Mr. Orville."

Matt turned purple. But I'd won the argument. It was now time to deliver the coup de grace.

"Nurse Casteel," I said. "Were you aware of any relationship between Denise Silvers and Neil Shumway?"

"No," Lisa said. "I never saw them together. I never heard Denise talk about him. I never heard him talk about her."

"Did you ever have lunch with Denise Silvers?"

"I did," Lisa said.

"Was there ever a discussion of Shumway or the man you knew as Newt during any of those lunch dates?"

"Not that I recall, no."

"Did you ever confront either Dr. Joe or Mr. Shumway about your suspicions about their illegal activity?"

"I confronted Dr. Joe. He denied everything. But this was after Denise's attack. A few weeks later, I received a threatening phone call. The caller said if I wasn't careful, the same thing would happen to me as to Denise."

"Objection!" Matt shouted. "Your Honor, the witness's last statement should be stricken. It's hearsay. She has no idea who even made that statement."

"Sustained."

"Nurse Casteel, did anything else happen after you brought your concerns about the defendant to Dr. Nicholson?"

She looked down. "I was fired," she said. "That was June 2000. I could have fought it. Or maybe I could have. But with everything that happened with Denise, I was afraid. I just ... I wanted to put it all behind me. I felt terrible for years. I tried to get someone to listen to me, but nobody would. Everyone idolized Joe Nicholson. Everyone loved Neil Shumway. I had no allies. So I left and started over somewhere else."

"Thank you," I said. "I have nothing further."

Matt's face was white as bone as he took to the lectern after me. He drew in a hard breath. He paced for a moment.

"Ms. Casteel," he said. "Isn't it true you were actually fired by Dr. Joe for incompetence?"

"No," she said. "That's not true."

"How convenient you're just now coming in here and making these outrageous allegations?"

"Is that a question? No. I'm not doing this for convenience. And it's not just now. I tried to talk to the cops back in 2000. No one cared. And like I told you, I was scared. I thought Denise's attack ... that caller threatened to do the exact same thing to me."

Matt was literally spinning. He took a turn as if he meant to walk back to his table. He circled back to the lectern. Then, inexplicably, he leaned far into the microphone and uttered the words that ended the case.

"I have no use for this witness," then he sat down.

I swallowed hard as the judge looked just as shocked as I felt. "Counselor?"

I rose slowly. "Your Honor," I said, my eyes on the jury. "We have no further rebuttal witnesses. The prosecution rests."

Chapter 29

THERE WAS NOTHING LEFT. There were just the twelve
members of that jury and me. I approached the lectern and
folded my hands in front of me.

At this stage, juries are so hard to read. They know a seismic
shift is coming. The power reverts to them. They are anxious,
probably excited even. I believe most of them have probably
made up their minds at this point. I hope they will still listen
if their minds are against me. And I never know what detail,
what tiny event or fact, or mannerism of a witness may have
stuck with them and blossomed into a fully formed opinion or
bias.

"Ladies and gentlemen," I started as I always do. "I do not
wish to be in your shoes. Your job is harder than mine. We
have asked you to take time away from your lives, your families, your jobs. We have asked you to take a hard look at something ugly. Something out of our worst nightmares. And we've
asked you to decide the fate of two people. The defendant,
Neil Shumway, and the victim, Denise Silvers.

"The judge will instruct you on the law and the rules you must follow as you weigh the evidence you heard. But before all of that, I want to thank you. No matter what you decide, I know your lives won't be the same after you walk out of this courtroom. None of ours will be.

"There has been a lot of drama in this trial. I won't deny that. The defendant's lawyer is going to stand up here in a few minutes and try to get you to focus on that drama instead of the facts. He's going to make a great issue out of videotapes that didn't work as we planned. Tests on skin samples that he thinks should have told a different story.

"Don't fall for it. See through it. Smoke and mirrors are all the defense have left when the cold, hard facts are staring you in the face.

"Only the defendant was in the parking lot that fateful evening with Ms. Silvers. Friday night. Lisa Casteel told you as much. Shumway's rotation in Sunmeadow Court was always on Friday. He was there. Period.

"It was Neil Shumway's DNA alone present in Denise Silvers's rape kit. You heard irrefutable, scientific proof of that. You saw the photographs. This was not some consensual liaison. This was a brutal, violent, almost fatal attack. Neil Shumway did that. DNA doesn't lie. Only guilty people do.

"There are other liars in this case. Marcy Cross is a liar. Now you know why she lied. Her first story to the police was the correct one. She said nothing about some contrived relationship between Shumway and Denise because it never happened. She made it up. She did it to save the man she might still love. She did it to cover up her truth. Shumway was her supplier. He used her and threw her away. And yet she came into this courtroom and told you all the most heinous lie of all to try and save this monster and herself. That alone should convince you even more of his guilt."

For each point I made, I pulled up the evidence on the screen behind me. I methodically walked the jury through all of it, allowing the cadence of my voice to crescendo.

At each turn, I fell back on the DNA. Denise's injuries. The timeline.

They listened. I couldn't read their minds, but I had their attention. In the end, it was all I could ask for.

Denise sat just behind Kenya. Her sister held her hand. For every second of my closing argument, Denise kept her gaze fixed and steady on Neil Shumway. I hadn't told her what to do. I wouldn't have dared. And yet, of the things I would remember most about that trial, the way she stared her monster down seared its way straight through my soul.

I prayed it would be enough. I wasn't sure if I could live with myself if it weren't.

I left the jury with a single image. Of all the crime scene photos, it was probably the least shocking in terms of its graphic nature. I almost wondered if it had been merely an afterthought. The hospital rape team member had simply taken it and nearly discarded it. But it was a long shot of Denise Silvers lying broken on that gurney in the E.R. She'd been unconscious for most of her time there but for one, single moment, she'd opened the only eye she could and stared straight at the camera. Blood caked her skin. The swelling distorted the outlines of her face. But that one, clear eye held questions.

Do you see me?

Will you help me?

I turned back to the jury and voiced those questions for her.

"Thank you," I said. "From the bottom of my heart. Thank you."

I took my seat beside Kenya. She reached beneath the table and squeezed my knee.

"Good job," she whispered. "You've done all you can."

I hoped it was enough.

Matt Orville took his time getting to the lectern. I felt like I could write his closing for him. I hoped I'd undercut a lot of it by broadcasting to the jury what I knew he would say.

He didn't disappoint.

"Ladies and gentlemen," he said. "There's no denying the horror Denise Silvers went through. She is a survivor. Maybe the strongest person any of us will ever meet. This may seem like a strange thing for someone like me to say. But I feel honored to have gotten to know her a little through her testimony."

Denise made a noise behind me.

"I can't imagine the fear Denise must have felt. The hopeless-ness. It's natural for us to want to make whoever did that to her pay. There has to be meaning in it. If it could happen to her, it could happen to anyone. And therefore none of us are safe. So, we cling to something. If we catch Denise's monster, then we can all sleep better at night. It would be so easy to make ourselves feel better by putting Mr. Shumway behind bars. The prosecution has given us someone to project our fears onto.

"The problem is, the facts just don't line up. The problem is, Mr. Shumway is an innocent victim in all of this too. He's the victim of a rush to judgment."

A twenty-year rush? Kendra wrote on the pad beside me. I rolled my eyes.

"DNA," Matt said. "Almighty DNA. It's the only thing the prosecution has. They want you to ignore logic. Facts. The law. Their own burden of proof.

"And no matter how much you want to do something to help Denise Silvers, it's not enough. They have failed to meet their burden.

"You know the truth. And the judge will tell you that Mr. Shumway has a right to benefit from the burden of proof. Reasonable doubt. If there are two inferences that can be made from a piece of evidence, one leading to guilt, one leading to innocence, you must choose the one that leads to innocence. It's the law.

"You were presented with two versions. Only one of them was backed up by facts. Marcy Cross is no liar. She's an imperfect witness. I'll grant you that. But she's no liar. She told you what she saw. Neil Shumway is no saint. He may even be a scoundrel. He probably played two very nice women along. Maybe he told Marcy one thing then turned around and told the same to Denise."

"Objection," I said. "Your Honor, I've kept quiet long enough. It is entirely improper for defense counsel to speculate on what the defendant would or would not say."

I stopped short of suggesting the defendant should have got up there and told his own story. To do so would give Orville more footing in an appeal. A criminal defendant can't be compelled to testify and any mention of their choice not to testify was improper. But this was bull. Likewise, Matt couldn't stand there and speak for him.

"Mr. Orville," Judge Saul said. "Stick to the admitted evidence, please."

"If Neil Shumway's DNA was found in Denise's rape kit, it's because the two of them were having an affair. You heard the experts. The presence of certain body fluids doesn't prove rape. It just proves the presence of body fluids. The law requires you to find Mr. Shumway not guilty. He gets the benefit of the inference, ladies and gentlemen.

"And what about that DNA? Dr. Siefert and the prosecution's expert both told you they can't say for sure how long those samples were present on Ms. Silvers's body. Could have been days. And they might have gotten there through consensual intercourse. Marcy Cross told you that's exactly what she saw.

"I find it interesting that Ms. Silvers never got up here and denied those allegations. Did she? Why do you suppose that is?"

"Objection," I said. "She absolutely *did* deny it in her direct testimony. Your Honor ..."

"The jury will disregard Mr. Orville's last statement. Ms. Brent. If you want to say anything on rebuttal, you may. For now I suggest you hold it."

Orville was flustered. Good.

"Ladies and gentlemen," he said. "The State hasn't met its
burden. You know it. You saw it. Now, it's up to you to say it. I
don't envy you. I want justice for Denise Silvers too. I have a
wife. I have a daughter. If something like what happened to
her happened to them ... well ... I can't even let my mind go
there. But Neil Shumway is an innocent man. There was no
reason for the police to suspect him in 2000. He and the
victim had a consensual relationship. If the DNA found on
her belonged to him, it only proves what Marcy Cross said.
You must acquit Mr. Shumway. I hope with all my heart that
someday, Ms. Silvers's real monster is brought to justice. But
that day is not today. Thank you."

I rose. "I just have one thing I'd like you to ponder about what
defense counsel just told you," I said. "If Neil Shumway was
having a consensual relationship with Denise, why didn't he
come forward after her attack? Why didn't he tell the police
that? He had to have known about the attack. He knew her.
Everyone in the Sunmeadow building and all through town
was talking about it. At the time, there was a ten-thousand-
dollar reward for information leading to her attacker. And yet,
Shumway said nothing. He acted ... well ... like a guilty man
who didn't want to get caught. Because that's exactly what
he is."

I left it there. I noticed two jurors looked surprised by what I
said. I hoped that meant good things. But for now, I'd done all
I could do. In the next few hours, we might argue about which
versions of jury instructions the court would read. It was a
tedious process and one of my least favorites. Then those
twelve men and women would retreat to a small conference
room just a few feet from here and decide Neil Shumway's
fate.

ROBIN JAMES

It was Denise's fate too. It might be the fate of each and every one of Shumway's other victims. And it was my fate. If it came back not guilty, no one but me would be blamed for this. Orville would try to take me down. He'd try to take down the Waynetown justice system regardless of the outcome if the money was right.

As I took my seat at the prosecution's table, I knew in my heart he might succeed. Part of me hoped he would. Something was wrong. Very wrong. I would take the blame for this loss but it wasn't my fault. And not one bit of that would bring comfort to Denise or the thirty other women Shumway had tortured and raped. And in a lonely grave outside of Kalamazoo, his murder victim, Jennifer Lyons, would never rest easy.

Chapter 30

THE MORNING after the jury got the case, Jason brought Will home. I waited for them on the back porch sipping lemonade, soaking in what felt like the final moments of summer. It was the first time I'd even noticed, really. I'd spent it inside my office or a courtroom.

"Mom!" Will said. His cheeks were flushed as he tumbled through the back screen door. He wore his favorite t-shirt. Blue with the Georgetown University bulldog on it. He had no particular attachment to Georgetown. But we'd picked it up last summer when the three of us went to D.C. so he could visit Arlington Cemetery. He liked the feel of it. Soft cotton with a reinforced hem around the sleeves. I wish I'd thought to buy three or four more in bigger sizes for when he outgrew this one. But I never knew just what Will might love best.

"You okay?" Jason said. He read my expression, I think, and decided I wasn't in the mood to be hostile. I wasn't. I was just bone tired and glad to see my son.

Will stood beside me and let me run my hands through his

hair. It was too long, the cowlick at the crown of his head an unmanageable, feathery peak.

"How was the art museum?" I asked.

While I delivered my closing argument in the Shumway case, Jason had taken Will to the Toledo Art Museum to see a Titanic artifact exhibit. I'd gotten the rundown on the phone last night as Will grappled with whether he thought the archeologists amounted to grave robbers. He came down on the side of education. The more we knew about the tragedy, the less likely we would be to repeat it.

"I missed you," I said.

"Me too," he said back. "Did you win?"

"I don't know yet. The jury has been deliberating for just about twenty-four hours. They're taking their time. That's a good thing." I hoped.

"I put your lunch on the table," I said.

He turned and started to walk back toward the kitchen.

"Oh shoot," I said. "Will, just don't touch anything on the island."

I got up and followed him. Jason fell in step behind me. All of the Nicholson patient files were still spread out in not-so neat stacks all over my kitchen counters. Will bypassed them and went to the dining room table where I'd left his lunch plate.

"What's all this?" Jason asked. He picked up a random file and started leafing through it.

I took a seat at the bar. "It's a lot," I said. "And you probably shouldn't know about it. I don't know. Maybe you should. I don't know where the lines are anymore sometimes."

"You look tired," Jason said. He reached for me. For the first time in almost six months, I didn't recoil. I was too tired for that too.

"I'm surprised you haven't already heard rumblings about this," I said. "It seems that Dr. Joe Nicholson was running an illegal prescription drug scheme through his office. Neil Shumway was his supplier. Shumway was forced to resign over it. It's going to blow up."

"Damn," he said, sitting down hard on the bar stool opposite me. He put one file down and looked through more.

"It's a mess, Jason," I said.

I watched Jason's eyes dart over the files as his mind worked. I didn't have to explain it. Jason Brent's brain worked on a different track than most people's. Our son was more like his father than I think even Jason realized.

"Christ. Mara. This is going to get to us." He looked at file after file. "These are people we know. You're saying these are the patients he was supplying?"

"Some of them, yes. I think so."

"You're going to need an outside investigation. This can't go through Maumee County. Dammit. We'll need a new task force. Who has this right now?"

I hesitated. For some reason, I didn't want to bring Sam Cruz into it with Jason just yet. Jason had carefully and wisely not asked me how I came to be in possession of these documents.

"It's early days, Jason," I said. "And this impacts the existing task force on Shumway. If he was engaged in this here in Waynetown, of course he was doing it in other jurisdictions."

"How do you think this is going to impact deliberations?" he asked.

"I'm not sure. Maybe not at all. It came in ... at least the tip of this particular iceberg ... to discredit Marcy Cross. She was the one claiming Denise was having an affair with Shumway. We believe she was in on the criminal enterprise here. If she's smart, she's already been talking to a lawyer. I'm not even sure of the statute of limitations on all of this. Shumway hasn't worked for Blaine Pharm in fifteen years. It's a lot to sort through."

"Ken Leeds?" Jason asked. He'd zoned in on Leeds's medical file. "God. He was a patient of Dr. Joe's. Mara ... I was a patient of Dr. Joe's. So was Kat. My mother was ..."

He stopped short. His mother. Jason rarely talked about her. She died of a heroin overdose when he was fourteen years old. That was twenty-six years ago. Well within the timeframe that Neil Shumway worked for Blaine Pharm and serviced Nicholson's office.

"You don't think ..." Jason backed away from the table; his face went white.

"Jason," I said. I scooted around the island and went to him. He kept his fists curled at his sides, going rigid as I approached him.

"Jason," I said again.

I'd been here with him so many times before. It was a side of him no one else ever saw. Not even Kat. He was vulnerable. His mind going back to those awful years when he and Kat were just kids and their mother couldn't take care of them. He was a man. Strong. Capable. Probably a genius. But that rejected little boy was still deep inside of him too.

"Maybe," I said. "Maybe Dr. Joe did give your mom drugs she couldn't handle. But so far she doesn't fit what I think is emerging as the profile of who he and Shumway sold to. She didn't have any money, Jason."

He slammed his fist against the counter, breaking the skin. The blow echoed, but Will didn't look up. He had his drawing pad beside him and was busy sketching something out.

"So what if she wasn't," he said. "There would have been others. Who knows how many people were hurt. They're going to hate you for even asking these questions, Mara. Maumee County won't want to get their hands dirty. There are probably plenty of the old-timers in the department who went to Dr. Joe ..."

His face fell. "Mara."

"I don't know," I answered the question he hadn't given voice to. "But yeah. I think there's a distinct possibility that all the little anomalies about this case could trace right back to Dr. Joe's clientele. Somebody didn't want me to find out too much about Shumway. Or Shumway had the clout to lean on some-one. I just can't prove any of it yet."

"And you can't trust the people whose job it is to help you," Jason said.

He went back to the island. His ears still burned red from the rage he'd let out. He grabbed a stack of the files.

"You need to leave this," I said. "Just like you said, it's going to have to be an independent investigation. Too many conflicts of interest for this to be handled locally."

He threw the file on the table. Another stack overbalanced, sending papers floating to the floor.

"She told you not to touch anything, Dad," Will said, finished with his lunch. He brought his plate in and put it in the dishwasher. Shaking his head, my son looked back at me with his father's eyes.

The two of them were convinced a monkey could load that dishwasher better than I could. Perhaps they were right. Will set about rearranging the bowls into neat rows. Jason's anger passed; he smiled and went to help our son. For once, I was glad of their shared annoyance with me. It felt normal.

I went back to the fallen papers and started to pick them up. Somehow, I was going to have to make sense of all of this. I didn't yet want to bring any of it into the office. I wondered if I could trust one of the interns to come out there and start scanning and categorizing everything.

"Are you staying today?" Will asked Jason. His innocent question sent a spear of panic through me. I froze, clutching the last three pages I'd picked up off the floor.

"That's up to Mom," Jason said. It was an off-the-cuff comment and his dropped jaw told me he realized how unfair it was too.

"Why is it up to Mom?" Will said.

"It's not," I said quickly. Not now. I just couldn't deal with this right now. Jason could sleep in the guest room if he liked. But someday soon, we were going to have to figure out once and for all where we went from here.

A muscle jumped in Jason's jaw. As Will turned away to slide the last of the bowls in place, Jason mouthed a "thank you."

Hot tears sprang to my eyes and I turned away so he wouldn't see. I busied myself with the paperwork mess in front of me. I started to slip the papers in my hand into a waiting pile.

Then I froze. They were upside down. I hadn't seen the name clearly when I first grabbed them. I did now. My lungs burned as though they'd just filled with acid. My hand shook.

"Mara?" Jason asked. "You okay? Hey, Will, why don't you run down to the mailbox? I forgot to grab it when we drove up."

That would take him at least fifteen minutes as our mailbox was at the end of the winding drive. Generally speaking, Will would get distracted along the way inspecting grasshoppers and various other flora and fauna on the edge of the woods.

As soon as Will left through the front door, Jason came to me.

"Mara?" he asked again.

Before he could see, I slid the three pages from the patient file into the stack, effectively burying them for now. But the name on them seared into my brain and made my pulse roar in my ears.

It was 4:02 in the afternoon. Friday, September 4th. As Jason came toward me, concern still carving deep lines in his face, my phone rang on the counter beside me.

I noted the date and time on the lock screen as I picked it up. I brought it to my ear, my eyes still on Jason's. The words reached me as if I were underwater. It was Kenya. Since Will was coming home, I'd left before noon today. Kenya stayed.

"Mara," she said. "The clerk just called. The jury's in. Just meet us at the courthouse by five. We're already making arrangements to get Denise there. Mara, we have a verdict."

She spoke loudly enough Jason heard it all too.

"I'll call Kat," he said. "Tell her I'll drive you in."

"I'll be ready," I said to Kenya, willing it to be true.

Chapter 31

DENISE AND BETSY sat at the back of the courtroom. At least fifty members of the Silver Angels lined the walls, surrounding her.

Matt Orville was late. The sheriffs would bring Shumway in through a side door. As he had been throughout the trial, they would remove his leg irons before anyone in this courtroom saw him. That way, he could march in clean-cut in his crisp suit. Just a regular guy.

My ass.

Kenya sat beside me. Phil showed up for the verdict reading too. Kenya offered to let him sit at the table with me, but Phil wouldn't hear of it. It was a classy thing to do on the one hand. On the other, he might already be trying to distance himself if the verdict went the wrong way.

Shumway came in. Matt Orville didn't look right. He was sweating. In all the hours of heated testimony and verbal jousting, I'd not seen him do that.

Shumway was different. For the past two weeks, I'd seen him look meek, passive, overwhelmed by what was happening around him. Not today though. Today he strode in with his chin up, his hair freshly barbered. His eyes clear. For the first time, he looked straight at me and smiled.

"Good afternoon," he said. I froze. It looked like the bastard was actually about to shake my hand.

"Come on," Matt said, stopping him. They took their seats at the defense table as the bailiff came in.

"All rise!"

I took a breath. Beside me, I saw Kenya's hand trembling as she held a pen poised to take notes. Lord. It was as if all the oxygen had escaped the room.

Another deputy led the members of the jury in. They all looked straight ahead. Shumway preened. Something occurred to me just then. In about two minutes, he would cease to be the center of attention in the room. Whether he was convicted or acquitted, he'd have to be led away by the deputies for processing one way or the other. This was his big moment. His big show. If that jury form read not guilty, I expected Shumway had a whole speech prepared for the press waiting outside.

Orville would have to try and tackle him not to give it. Though this was our best shot at nailing him, his legal troubles would be far from over.

"Ladies and gentlemen of the jury," Judge Saul said as she rifled through some papers in front of her. "Have you reached your verdict?"

The foreman was juror number two, a retired dentist who'd

only moved to Waynetown two years ago. She was sixty-five, never married, and lived in one of the more affluent communities on the west side of the river.

"We have," she said.

Judge Saul went through all the legal preambles necessary. The clerk handed the jury form to her. She read it, her face betraying nothing. She cast a quick glance at Shumway then gave the form back to the clerk. With a nod from Judge Saul, her clerk leaned forward to read the verdict into the record.

"We the jury in the above-entitled cause, on the count of felonious assault pursuant to ORC Section 2903.11 find the defendant, Neil Shumway, guilty ..."

The air rushed back into the room. I heard a guttural cry from Denise Silvers behind me. Matt Orville went rigid. Neil Shumway sank into his chair. Only a jerky motion from Orville reminded him to stand back up.

The clerk read the rest of the charges. Kidnapping. Guilty. Rape. Guilty.

On all counts. A clean sweep. Beside me, Kenya's shoulders dropped. She put her head down and started to cry. Each word from the clerk went through me like the crack of a gunshot. I couldn't breathe.

Guilty.

My God. We'd done it.

For the next few minutes, I existed outside myself. The jury was polled. Their verdict was unanimous. Judge Saul thanked them and gave them their final instructions. One last time, they were led out of the courtroom to the waiting press. It would be their choice whether to talk to them.

I turned. Juror number two, our foreman, stopped only to say a word to Denise. With tears streaming down her face, Denise reached up and hugged her.

"Mara," Kenya said, her voice choked. She pulled me into an embrace and for the first time in months, I felt myself exhale.

DENISE WAS STILL emotional by the time I made my way back to her.

"Thank you," she whispered. "My God. Thank you."

"I love you," I told her. I did. But for now, that was all I had time to say. Later, when things died down, I'd go visit her, I promised.

Phil was at my side. "Let's go," he said. "Now's your time to shine."

I smiled at him. "You do it," I said.

His mouth dropped. A look passed between him and Kenya. "You're up for election in a year, Phil. I'm not running for anything, remember?"

Wordless, he nodded. Kenya stood with me as Phil made his way out of the courtroom and up to the bank of waiting microphones. While we had remained in the courtroom, Matt had already started his grandstanding.

"He'll appeal," Kenya said.

"Of course," I answered.

We stood off to the side. Several members of the Shumway task force had started to gather in the hall as Phil made his speech about justice being served. He gave me credit. I stood in the background and tried to force a smile.

I was happy. But I was still numb. Twenty years. Eight since I met Denise. So many victims. The weight of it crushed me.

"You okay?"

Gus Ritter appeared seemingly out of nowhere. I found myself looking for Sam. He wasn't here. My heart raced, knowing exactly where he was. On a task I'd set it in motion. Once he finished, there would be no turning back.

"We did it." I turned my attention to Gus. Sam's absence went unnoticed in the euphoria of the moment. Gus had tears in his eyes. He grabbed me into a bear hug and sobbed into my shoulder.

Chapter 32

THE OFFICE WAS ALL but empty with most of the lights out. I had missed calls from Jason, Kat, Denise Silvers, Cass Leary, and at least a dozen others. I let each and every one go to voicemail.

I waited until all the celebrating had died down. I embraced my coworkers. Said the right things. I thanked each and every member of my team. And then they all went home.

A single file folder sat on top of my desk. I tapped my fingers over it. The faint strains of an orchestra reached my ears. Then Maria Callas's voice rose clear and sharp. A live performance of Bellini's Norma. It was one of my favorites as well.

I picked up the file and walked across the hall.

"I figured you were still here," Phil said, smiling. He stood facing the window, one hand in his pocket, the other holding a rocks glass with an amber liquid in it.

Scotch whiskey. He kept it in his lucky drawer at the bottom of his desk. He went to it now; pulling out another glass he poured a shot for me.

"Thanks," I said. We clinked glasses as the flute solo from the opening of Casta Diva began to play again. He'd put it on repeat.

"I'm proud of you," Phil said as I took a seat at his desk. His eyes glistened with tears and I believed him. My own throat thickened. I thought of my father. He would have loved this. He would have wanted to wrap his own hands around Neil Shumway's neck.

"I just got off the phone with the Seneca County Prosecutor from Tiffin. They're confident their cold case from 2006 matches Shumway's profile. Her name was Amelia Garner," he said.

I nodded. "I know the case. They never found her body."

"They're gonna proceed with the grand jury. That's what the call was about. It's a death penalty case, Mara."

I shook my head. "So much loss," I said. "So many women."

Phil leaned forward. "And he'll never touch another one again, Mara. Thanks to you."

I looked out the window. Downtown Waynetown was eerily quiet now. The Friday before Labor Day and everyone had lit out of town for the lakes.

"I want you to take some time," Phil said. "I mean, I need you to be available to the Shumway task force. But you've earned some air. You and Jason both."

My eyes darted back to him. "Phil ..."

"I mean it. Believe me, I know how badly he screwed up. I'll never forgive him either for putting you through this. Especially now. But Mara, just ... well ... I hope things get easier for you."

"How much air are we talking about?" I asked.

"Jason's election is eight weeks away," he said. "Come back after that. Take a leave of absence, Mara. Trust me. It'll do you a world of good and your job will still be waiting for you when you get back."

"I appreciate that," I said. "I really do."

A moment passed. "What is it?" Phil asked.

"He'll appeal," I said. "Shumway. And you and I both know he'll probably win. We were on thin ice from the moment I tried to enter that security tape."

Phil waved me off. "Immaterial. You had him on the DNA and that's all that matters."

"That tape though," I said. "Orville will make good on his threat to open an A.G. investigation into the Maumee County Sheriff's Department. And us."

"Let him," Phil said. "It's all posturing. Shumway's a monster and nobody is going to care what the A.G. finds. Somebody'll get a slap on the wrist and on we go. Don't worry about it."

I nodded and finished off my whiskey. When Phil pulled the bottle out, I waved him off. I didn't drink often and one shot was all I dared try.

I had that thin file folder on my lap. I put it on Phil's desk. He barely registered that it was there.

"Shumway will go down," I said. "But I no longer think it'll be for Denise. Orville *should* have been granted a mistrial. Evidence was tampered with. That tape was tampered with sometime after Alex Conway handed it over. Everyone thinks it was Ritter or Cruz's fault. I thought that too. But it wasn't."

"Mara ..."

"The whole thing ... wiped," I said.

He let out an exasperated sigh. "Don't torture yourself anymore. You've done your job."

"Thirty-seven patients," I said. "It's not as many as I feared. And Lisa Casteel might be wrong, but right now it's looking like Dr. Joe and Shumway were supplying thirty-seven patients in and around Waynetown, with Oxy mostly. Got in right at the ground floor of the opioid epidemic. Right here in our little town, Phil."

He said nothing. He just slowly sipped his whiskey. He was going to make me do it.

"You were one of them," I said, pulling out the pages from my file. There were three of them. Visit summaries and other chart notes on Phil himself. They detailed eight visits to Dr. Joe between early 1998 through 2001.

"Stop it."

"For how long?" I asked. "Christ, Phil. Are you still using now?"

"You're tired," he said. "This case has taken more out of you than you realize."

"Who approached you?" I said. "Was it Orville? Shumway? God. Was it Shumway?"

There would be records. As we spoke, I knew Sam Cruz was busy getting a search warrant together to search Phil's phone and computers.

"Phil," I said. A tear escaped my eye. "You know what that man did to her. You were there right after it happened. You had my office back then, right? It was staring me in the face for weeks, only I couldn't see it. I didn't want to believe it. I should have put it together when the tape went haywire. I looked it up. Did you know a simple magnet could do that? And I knew it had to be someone who had access to the copies Ritter and Cruz made for us. I hate myself for thinking for even a half a second it could have been Kenya. I wondered if she wanted me to fall on my face."

"This is ridiculous," he said. He shoved the file back at me.

"If I'd never met Lisa Casteel, it might have ended there," I said. "And Neil probably would have been acquitted outright. Unopposed, Marcy Cross raised reasonable doubt. Now we at least stand a ghost of a chance of prevailing on appeal. But then Lisa came into the picture. Ken Leeds got an anonymous letter from her twenty years ago. It went through Crimestoppers. Before that, I know he met with her. It's in his day planner. But any statement she gave isn't in the case file. Her Crimestoppers letter disappeared. None of it ever made it on to us."

"Ken met with you in *my* office how many times, Phil? The thing is, I don't even need your answer. It's all right there in Leeds's day planner. He wrote your name down. It seemed routine. He met with a lot of people."

His lip quivered. "You don't know what you think you know."

"I know enough, Phil. I think you slipped her letter right out of that case file twenty years ago. Probably while you were sitting at my very desk. It was innocuous anyway to anyone but you. She was probably ranting and raving about office irregularities. She didn't have anything useful or corroborated to say about the Silvers's assault so Ken probably never even noticed it was missing. If he followed up with Denise, she wouldn't have known anything about Lisa's accusations. I asked her. She doesn't even remember Ken asking so if it happened at all it was quick. Whatever was going on with Dr. Joe, it wasn't connected to Denise so Ken dismissed it. He was getting so many leads and wild gooses to chase down, it got lost. Overlooked. And that's what you were hoping for."

Phil's face went white. He gripped his shot glass so hard I thought it would crack. The window behind Phil's head flooded with light as two unmarked cruisers pulled into the parking lot.

Phil never even turned to look.

"Was it worth it?" I asked. "You would let Denise suffer. You would risk letting Shumway walk, for what? So you could keep your job? So no one would find out you're a human being with a disease? But then you were a criminal. God. Phil. You make me sick. Jennifer Lyons. Now Amelia Garner. Those women are dead because of you. We could have stopped him so much earlier."

He opened his bottom drawer. The bottle of whiskey was almost empty and I felt sure he had another ready.

I was wrong.

It happened almost in slow motion. Phil showed me his hand.

He had a small black pistol in it and he pointed it straight at me.

"Phil," I said, my throat running dry.

Maria Callas's soaring soprano reached a crescendo. I rose to my feet, stumbling backward.

"You don't know what you think you know," he said, cocking the pistol. "And now you never will."

"Will!" I cried out. I saw my son's face swim before me. No. I closed my eyes and prayed for him. Stumbling, I backed up. There was nothing to hide behind. Nowhere to run. I felt Jason's strong arms around me as if he were a ghost. My whole life. All of my failures. It would all be gone in a split second.

The front door of the office opened. Heavy footsteps fell. My heart thundered and my knees went weak. I opened my eyes and stared down the barrel of that gun. I took a breath and held it, waiting for the shot.

An odd smile spread across Phil's face. He turned his hand and put the pistol in his mouth.

I screamed. Behind me, I heard a deep shout. I heard my name.

Then Phil squeezed the trigger and blew out the back of his head.

Chapter 33

PHIL HALSEY WAS BURIED on Sunday afternoon under a cloudless sky. The circumstances surrounding his death hadn't yet reached the internet, but that was only a matter of time. Jason stood beside me looking stoic, handsome, powerful. I leaned on him. That day. And two days before, it had been Gus Ritter who called him to come get me from the office.

I didn't fall apart. Not then. I gave my statement to Sam and Gus, remembering every detail. Every sound. Every word. It was only later, as Jason put me in the passenger seat of his black Lexus. He leaned over me to snap my seatbelt and that's when he noticed the spots of blood staining my sleeve.

Phil's blood.

That's when I cried. Jason's arms came around me and for the first time in over six months, I didn't pull away. I needed him then and he was there.

But this was today. We stood side by side as Phil Halsey was

eulogized by Mayor Kratz, retiring Congressman McCardle, whose seat Jason hoped to win, and Judge Vivian Saul.

Then it was all over.

"Come on," Jason said. "Let's get you home."

"I'm fine," I answered. In the distance, I saw trouble brewing. For some ungodly reason, Matt Orville had shown up today. Sam Cruz stood off to the side, his face reddening as the two of them exchanged words. Then Sam turned and looked straight at me. They both did.

"It's okay, Jason," I said. "I know you want to have a moment with McCardle."

"Mara," he said. "I think I can put politics aside for one day."

I smiled. I don't know what made me do it, but I reached up and touched his cheek. "No, you can't. And neither can McCardle. Phil's in the ground today because he couldn't either."

"I'll see you back at the house," I said. Lane McCardle was already making his way toward us after shaking hands with a few other city officials.

Jason let out a sigh. He leaned in and kissed me on the cheek. Then he headed for McCardle.

I turned. Sam had made his way to me. Adjusting my purse strap on my shoulder, I met his gaze.

"Hey, Sam," I said.

"You doing okay?"

"I am," I said. And it was the truth. "But I think I'm going to go to ground for a few days. I trust you can present my statement to the task force."

"Yeah," he said. "We just got the forensics back on Phil's home computer. He's got some searches on there about erasing VHS tapes with magnets from a few weeks ago. We're reviewing property room logs and tapes. But there's no doubt about what he was trying to do. The bastard wiped the tape on the eve of trial and swapped your DVD copies. It'll still be a few weeks before toxicology comes back, but we found pain medication in his house that he wasn't prescribed. Quite a lot of it. And some ... paraphernalia. You were right about all of it, Mara. Phil was using. We're trying to prove if he cut some kind of deal with Shumway personally. But, it's looking like it. We found a burner phone in Phil's house. He only called one number from it. Repeatedly. Seven calls. We've traced them to Shumway's cell. Mara...it looks like Phil tried to tip Shumway off even before we got the arrest warrant."

My throat ran dry. I hadn't wanted to believe it. "Even after he knew," I whispered. "Maybe he really didn't suspect Shumway twenty years ago. Maybe he believed the Lisa Casteel letter wasn't related to Denise's case. But when the DNA came back and Phil *knew* what that man had done to Denise and the others."

"Yeah," Sam said. "The running theory is Phil was just hoping to buy himself time and kick this particular can to another jurisdiction and save his own reputation in the process. He was a very sick man, Mara. I'd like to think this all just snowballed on him. Maybe he was dumb enough to believe Marcy Cross's lies too."

"But Ken Leeds," I said. I knew when the truth came out, the deceased detective's reputation would take a hit.

"Yeah," Sam said. "He...I don't know. I wasn't there back then. Gus thinks he just got overwhelmed. They got hundreds, probably thousands of anonymous tips coming in about that case in those first few months. Understaffed, overworked. And Lisa told you her letter focused on Dr. Joe and what was going on in his office. Maybe Ken thought it was too tangential. We'll never know whether Ken and Phil even discussed that letter. For all we know, Phil just happened on it in Ken's case file. I don't know. Ken *knew* Dr. Joe. He wouldn't have wanted to believe anything bad about him. Phil slipped that letter out of the file and I think it was just out of sight out of mind for Ken. It's unforgivable, but maybe understandable."

I blew out a breath. It was all just too much to wrap my head around.

"What's the deal with Orville?" I said, jerking my chin to the left. Matt had stopped to talk to a few people, but he was heading this way with a determined look on his face.

"Son of a bitch," Sam said. He turned, putting his body between Matt Orville and me. I put a hand on Sam's arm. Down the hill, closer to the cars, Jason saw it all. He narrowed his eyes but I made a downward gesture with my hand. I had enough Alpha males to deal with at the moment.

"I just need a few minutes," Matt said.

"Mara, I can get a couple of the uniformed officers to throw him out of here."

"It's a public cemetery, Sam," I said. "And there's no need for a scene."

Matt's eyes darted between us. "I just came to deliver a message."

"And I told you to stay the hell away from her," Sam said.

"How's your client?" I asked, not able to keep the acid out of my voice.

Matt let out a sigh. "He's not my client anymore. Shumway and I have parted ways. It's just one last thing he wanted to convey. I know what happened here. Both of your offices have things to answer for. You know Saul should have granted my mistrial. You know Shumway's conviction won't stand if he chooses to appeal. He'll at least be granted a new trial if not an outright reversal."

I said nothing. Those were almost the exact words I said to Phil right before he ate his gun.

"Why do you care?" Sam asked. "I thought you just said you and Shumway parted ways."

Matt chewed his lips. "I need you both to know this is against my advice. But like I said, I agreed to relay a message. Neil wants to talk."

A chill went through me.

"To you," Matt said, staring straight at me. "He only wants to talk to you, Mara."

For the second time in three days, I had the sensation of standing on quicksand. I don't remember reaching for him, but the next thing I knew, I held Sam Cruz's arm in a vice grip.

He said some choice words of his own to Matt. I ignored it all. I locked eyes with Matt and took a step forward.

"Tell Shumway he's got my attention," I said. "Set it up."

Chapter 34

In ten days, Neil Shumway would likely be transferred for processing into the Ohio State prison system. For now, he remained in solitary confinement at the Maumee County Jail, still just three blocks from my office.

As I walked through the metal detectors, the place was even more silent than the Woodfield Cemetery where we had just laid Phil Halsey to rest.

Sam waited for me, pacing an almost perfect circle.

"I still don't like this," he said.

"Sam," I said. "Shumway's made it pretty clear he'll only talk to me."

"He's just jerking your chain. He's figured out he's about to fade into oblivion. He loved every second of that trial and I'd bet Orville had to pretty much sit on him to keep him from taking the stand. I wish you would let me do this."

"I can handle it," I said. "And I appreciate your concern. I'm a big girl. And I'm not afraid of Neil Shumway."

The moment I said it, I realized it might be naive. We both knew exactly what this man had done. And here I was, about to sit across the table from him.

"I'll be right outside," he said. "He's chained to the table. He so much as looks at you funny, you just say the word and we're in there."

"Got it," I said.

"It's probably all a game to him anyway," Sam said as he led me further down the hall to one of the interview rooms where Shumway waited.

"You're probably right," I said. I half expected Shumway to get us all keyed up to simply tell me to go to hell.

We stood outside the steel door. Two deputies stood guard beside it. As Sam opened it, there were two more deputies inside standing next to Shumway.

He looked so much different than he had just a few days ago in trial. Gone was his tailored suit, his neatly combed hair. He wore a baggy orange jumpsuit, his blond hair with touches of gray stuck out in peaks at the sides. But he flashed those pale-blue eyes and I saw a hint of the handsome smile he'd used on Marcy Cross and perhaps countless victims before he got to Denise. It occurred to me Marcy likely had no idea how lucky she was to be alive. At the moment, she was facing perjury and obstruction charges.

One of the deputies approached me. On instinct, I raised my arms, waiting for the inevitable pat-down. Sam stepped in with a scowl on his face and the deputy stepped aside.

I turned to him. My voice barely above a whisper. "I've got this now."

He gave me a grim nod and followed the deputies out. I stood for a moment as the heavy metal door clanged shut behind me. The rest of the world fell away and I stared into the eyes of a monster.

I waited for a moment. Then I set my briefcase on the table and pulled out a single sheet of paper and a pen.

"Sign it," I said. "You understand that your Miranda rights are still in effect? By talking to me, you're doing so against the advice of counsel. And you're waiving those rights?"

"I understand," Neil said. His voice was clear and deep. His hand was steady as he picked up the pen and signed the Miranda waiver.

Only then did I take a seat opposite him. I couldn't help but stare at his hands. He had long fingers. Little blond hairs dusted his wrists and all the way up his arms.

I imagined him closing those fingers around Denise's neck. Curling his fists and striking her. Cruel hands. An evil heart.

"What's this about, Neil?" I said. I tucked the waiver into my briefcase and set it on the floor.

"Sorry about your boss," he said. "Suppose that's good for you. Career advancement."

I didn't respond.

"You'll need it," he continued. "You'll have extra time now that your hubby's found other amusements."

I didn't take his bait. Of course he'd know about Jason. I wondered how long he'd been waiting to try to stick me with the point of that particular knife.

"Orville says I have a stellar case on appeal. Sloppy of you, really. Sorry about the mess it'll make for you. I mean, when it's your husband's office that has to look into yours. They say Phil Halsey blew his head off in front of you. I think maybe you helped him. Take the focus off you, right?"

"This was a treat, Neil," I said. I rose and picked up my brief-case. I turned to leave.

"Wait," he said. "Sit back down."

I turned. Something ignited inside of me. I slapped my hands against the table and leaned in. "I'm not one of your victims, Neil. You don't have control this time. You're caught. It doesn't matter what you try to do on appeal. You'll never see the outside of a cell again. And you know what else is coming. Amelia Garner ... from Tiffin? She was a mistake, wasn't she?"

I sat back down. Just a tiny flicker in Neil's eyes told me I'd hit on something. "Your victims," I said. "I mean, there was a pattern in having no pattern. Except there was. But Amelia. That kind of struck me. You killed Jennifer Lyons. Michigan doesn't have the death penalty. You attacked Denise in Ohio but you left her alive, just barely. I've been wondering. Would you have called 911 yourself if Tucker Welling hadn't shown up? But Amelia. She died on you. So now, you'll face the needle when they convict you for that. They've got you on DNA there too. It was all over her car. They found enough blood to prove a murder without a body. Did you know that?"

He curled his fists. "You're not as smart as you think you are."

"Oh, I'm exactly that smart," I said. "That's why I'm sitting here and you're in a cage, Neil. You finally faced up to a woman you can't victimize. That's what's got you the most teed off about this, isn't it? They chose a woman to convict you."

He actually snarled. Neil jumped forward, but his chains held him in place. It took everything in me not to flinch. But I didn't.

"What is it that you want?" I asked. "You figured out you couldn't come after me in the courtroom, but here? You throw my personal life at me. You threaten me?"

"I won't face the needle," he said. For the first time since Neil Shumway came into my life, I sensed a trace of fear from him.

"But you will," I said. I knew the indictment in the Garner case would come down by the end of the week. I suspected Orville already told him that before he slithered off.

"You didn't mean to kill her, did you?" I asked. "Amelia would be alive if she'd just submitted to you like the others. If they didn't submit, you knocked them out like you did to Denise. They were closing in. Blaine Pharm was about to take away your best weapon. It was going to get harder to have a reason to be in so many other towns. You had people like Phil in your pocket but that was all about to end. They were on to you and your drug-selling schemes. If you didn't stop ... if you made trouble for Blaine and didn't just go quietly, you'd have faced charges on that. Amelia Garner might be your last. You knew that. You wanted to make it count. But she wasn't supposed to die."

"Shut your mouth," he said. There he was. He wasn't Newt. Not some charmer. The perfect salesman. Here was the devil.

"They say it's a peaceful death, lethal injection. It's not

though. Sometimes they get it wrong,' I said. "I know of one right here in Ohio. Took the poor man twenty-five minutes to die. And he felt every second of it. Struggling. Gurgling. Gasping for air the entire time. Nasty business. Let's hope they use better drugs on you, Neil."

"I'll kill you," he whispered.

"No,' I said. "You won't. You'll never get to kill again."

His eyes flicked to mine. "I'll give her to you," he said. "But you have to take the needle off the table."

My heart pounded in my chest. A deal. He was looking for a deal?

"I have no authority in Seneca County," I said.

"Yes," he said. "You do. You can make it work."

I could. Probably.

"Where is she, Neil?" I said. "What did you do with Amelia Garner?"

"Get it in writing," he said. "I will not face the death penalty in Ohio. Not in Indiana. Not in Florida."

The air itself seemed to choke me. Neil was right. I wasn't as smart as I thought I was. He'd killed more women than we knew.

"I can't promise you that," I said. "Like I told you. I don't have authority in those other jurisdictions. Now, if there were more victims here in Maumee County."

"Stop your filthy lies!" he shouted. "And here I am saving you!"

"Saving me?" I said.

"Mara Brent. Just the hapless little wifey who couldn't keep her man happy. And the whole world knows it. How embarrassing for you. But this ... you can make a name for yourself if you're the one who brings in my confession. Maybe it could be your name on the ballot next time."

"I'm not interested," I said.

Neil smiled. The salesman was back.

"You can make it happen. I'm counting on you, Mara. You'll get the other boys to fall in line on your task force. But you better hurry. All I have to do is stop talking."

I thought about Denise. As much as I hated every ounce of it, I knew what our exposure was on appeal. And I knew the nightmare Amelia Garner's family and Jennifer Lyon's family faced.

I could end it. Neil's confession on even one of those cases would put him behind bars for life. If I took away the needle.

I pulled a blank piece of notebook paper out of my briefcase and placed it in front of him.

"You show me yours, Neil," I said. "Then we'll see."

He fixed a smile in place and slowly raised his middle finger.

"This is how it works," I said. "As smart as you are, surely you know that. You write down where you buried Amelia Garner. A show of good faith. Then I'll take the needle away."

He looked toward the door. All bravado was gone. For one brief instant, I saw into Neil Shumway's black soul. The monster was sleeping and fear snaked around its heart.

He picked up the pen and wrote three words. He folded the paper and slid it back to me.

I didn't look at it at first. I slipped it into my briefcase, rose, then turned my back on the devil.

Chapter 35

THE SCANDAL BROKE two weeks later. The public demanded a second look at all of Phil's convictions during his litigation years. Matt Orville and the Delayed Justice Project lawyers took front and center. I realized it was the very reason Orville walked away from the Shumway case so easily. He'd found a better way to get his name in the papers. He could paint himself as a justice warrior now instead of the devil's mouthpiece.

Today, the county and state leadership wanted my office to put on a show of strength for the cameras. I stood with Sam, Jason, Howard, and Kenya in a room just off the City-County building press room waiting for the switch to flip.

My big day.

"They're ready for you." The mayor's press secretary poked her head in. Jason gave me a grim-faced nod. He'd decided to hang back, watch from the shadows.

I stepped out and took my place to the left of the podium as Kenya went to the microphone.

"Thank you, ladies and gentlemen," she said. "I'll keep my comments brief then open it up to some questions. Understand that there is an ongoing investigation on several matters, so I'm limited to what I can discuss.

"First, I'd like to thank Governor Wendell for entrusting me with this honor of serving as acting county prosecutor for the remainder of Mr. Halsey's term until a special election can be held. I promise to serve the constituents of Maumee County to the best of my abilities. I hope to prove myself worthy to the voters and to this incredible team behind me.

"As of this morning, Neil Shumway has been charged and has confessed to the cold case murders of Jennifer Lyons in Kalamazoo and Amelia Garner in Tiffin. I hope you understand I'm not at liberty to discuss the specifics of his plea bargain at this time. But I want to make it clear that this monster will never be in a position to kill again. I have my team to thank for that, in no small part to Mara Brent who valiantly led the prosecution team in the Denise Silvers case. I owe her a personal debt of thanks for that. I am immensely grateful to have her on my team as we go forward. She was also instrumental in securing information from Shumway on the location of Amelia Garner's remains. I cannot convey how important that was for her family. She can finally be laid to rest.

"I would also like to assure the citizens of Maumee County that our office will fully cooperate with the Attorney General's investigation concerning Mr. Halsey's alleged misdeeds. The hallmark of my tenure as your prosecuting attorney will be transparency. Now, we have a lot of work to do and I know the rebuilding of trust won't be easy. But I'm committed to it. I'll answer any questions that I can."

There were many. Kenya fielded them smoothly, managing to stick to her talking points and avoid any real discussion of Phil's conduct or the circumstances surrounding his suicide.

After a few minutes, the rest of the team and I retreated back to the anteroom, leaving Kenya the spotlight.

"I've got to head back to Columbus," Jason said. He had a light hand on my arm. "I'll check in later this evening."

"I'm fine," I said. "I'm going to pick Will up from school and we're going to order in from Papa Leoni's."

Jason smiled. "He'll love that."

There was an awkward moment between us. It would have been natural for Jason to lean in and kiss me on the cheek. We weren't there yet. I wasn't sure if we ever would be again. I had hard decisions to make. Now that I was supposed to have time to come up for air, I found it was still tough to breathe where he was concerned.

"I'll talk to you later," I said. "Will's going to want to fill you in on his science project. His teacher convinced him to try telling the iceberg's story. He's been learning about glacier formation."

Jason's smile broadened. "I can't wait to hear it." He cast a glance toward Sam, shook hands with Howard, then slipped out a side door.

Sam came to my side. "I'm never gonna not think it's garbage they gave the gig to Kenya over you," he said.

I tucked a hair behind my ear. "What makes you think I wasn't asked?" I said, smiling.

He tilted his head to the side. "Does Kenya know?"

I put a finger to my lips. "It's not my style, Sam. I never wanted to be a politician. I've got more of my dad's DNA in me than my mom's. I like it that way just fine. I belong in front of a jury, not a bank of microphones. Plus, Kenya's inherited a mess from Phil. Her job won't be easy."

Sam held the door for me and we walked out in the hall together.

"Yeah," he said. "I guess we're alike in that. Never had any inclination to go for command. Never even took the sergeant's test."

"Well," I said. "Color me glad. You do good work, Detective Cruz."

He paused for a moment as he held the door to the street open. We headed out the staff door which led into an alley. Far less likely to encounter a stray reporter or two. "Thirty-seven," he said, his expression turning grave. "That bastard has confessed to assaulting thirty-seven women. Three murders."

A chill went through me. I'd taken Neil Shumway's final statement three days ago. His fate was sealed. He would serve three consecutive life sentences for the murders of Amelia Garner, Jennifer Lyons, and Rachel Shields, a victim in Orlando that hadn't even made it on the task force's radar. But he would avoid the death penalty. It was still up in the air whether he'd do his time in the Ohio prison system or somewhere else.

It was enough. It had to be. I hoped someday Denise Silvers and the other victims could find some peace. They could never have the lives they lived before Shumway hurt them.

But he would pay. And with his confession, the lengthy appeal he threatened faded away. He was going to die in prison, even if it was slow.

Blaine Pharmaceuticals had moved to distance themselves from him, but Shumway's drug racket might have rippling effects. If he'd used his enterprise to extort his way out of any other criminal charges, it would come to light. I'd make sure of it.

"We did all right," I said to Sam.

"You did," he said. "Mara, everyone on the task force knows who's really responsible for bringing that bastard down. They won't forget."

I smiled. "Thanks."

"Come on," he said. "Let me buy you a drink. I'm off duty and we could both use it."

We'd reached my car. "Raincheck. I meant what I said to Jason. I want to spend the rest of the day with my main man."

Sam nodded. "I'm probably way out of line to say this. But … Jason's an idiot. I hope he realizes what it is he's lost."

His words took me by surprise and for an instant, I felt tears spring to my eyes. "I'll see you around, Cruz," I said.

"Yeah," he said, dropping his chin. "Yeah."

Sam reached around me and opened my car door. I waved back at him as I slipped inside and pressed the ignition.

Twenty minutes later, I sat in the school drop-off line as three hundred grade-schoolers poured out the double doors of Grantham Elementary. Will walked alone, head down. But when he saw my car, his face lit into a lopsided grin that melted me.

"Hey, kiddo," I said, leaning over to open the passenger door. He dumped his backpack in the backseat and clicked his seatbelt.

"They smell," he said. "Did you know icebergs have a particular scent? I looked it up. Majesty Cruises has an Alaskan itinerary. We can go to Prince William Sound. There's a ship leaving the first day of Spring Break. It's six hundred per person, all-inclusive. That's after the election. Under your contract you get twenty paid vacation days next year. I've already talked to Mrs. Milton about missing days for me. She said I can earn extra credit if I present my findings on glaciers to the class when we get back."

I turned onto Hyatt Road. "Six hundred a person," I said. "I don't know if Dad can get the time off. If he wins, you know he's going to have to live in Washington D.C. a lot of the time."

Will went silent. I know he knew all of this. I also knew this latest plan of his was a test. He was asking me a hard question I didn't yet know how to answer. Were Jason and I staying together?

"Maybe," I answered. I knew Will was perceptive enough to know I meant for all of it.

"You don't have to get me a Christmas or a birthday present," he said. "I just want this. We can do Dallas and Dealey Plaza some other time."

Those same stinging tears came to my eyes that started with Sam Cruz's comment. I turned down our gravel driveway and headed into the woods. As I pulled into the garage I made a decision. It wasn't a complete one. But it was for now.

"My trial is over," I said. "You know it was a big one. And you know how important it was."

"Neil Shumway," he said. "I read the news. I'm glad you made him go to jail. I hope he never gets out."

"He never will," I said. "Promise."

Will nodded.

"So," I smiled. I still didn't know what to do about Jason. But I knew what to do for Will. "We're going to see Alaska and smelly icebergs, huh?"

My son's face lit up. He slid across the seat and threw his arms around me. I kissed the top of his head and pulled my son close. My heart melted as he sunk into the embrace. As he hugged me back, I knew I would face any monster the world could throw at me for him.

Up Next for Mara Brent...

Mara's office is thrown into turmoil when she learns, Phil Halsey may have withheld critical evidence during the county's biggest trial. The notorious King brothers perpetrated a heinous, religiously motivated murder spree in northwest Ohio. Now, they may be set free. It's up to Mara to make sure that never happens.

Click to Order!

As Jason's election approaches, his choices could rip Mara's family apart for good. Don't miss **Price of Justice**, Book 2 in the Mara Brent Legal Thriller Series!

https://www.robinjamesbooks.com/poj/

Newsletter Sign Up

Sign up to get notified about Robin James's latest book releases, discounts, and author news. You'll also get *Crown of Thorne* an exclusive FREE ebook bonus prologue to the Cass Leary Legal Thriller Series just for joining.

Click to Sign Up

https://www.robinjamesbooks.com/marabrentsignup/

About the Author

Robin James is an attorney and former law professor. She's worked on a wide range of civil, criminal and family law cases in her twenty-year legal career. She also spent over a decade as supervising attorney for a Michigan legal clinic assisting thousands of people who could not otherwise afford access to justice.

Robin now lives on a lake in southern Michigan with her husband, two children, and one lazy dog. Her favorite, pure Michigan writing spot is stretched out on the back of a pontoon watching the faster boats go by.

Sign up for Robin James's Legal Thriller Newsletter to get all the latest updates on her new releases and get a free digital bonus scene from Burden of Truth featuring Cass Leary's last day in Chicago. http://www. robinjamesbooks.com/newsletter/

Also by Robin James

Cass Leary Legal Thriller Series

Burden of Truth

Silent Witness

Devil's Bargain

Stolen Justice

Blood Evidence

Imminent Harm

With more to come...

Mara Brent Legal Thriller Series

Time of Justice

Price of Justice

With more to come...

Made in United States
Orlando, FL
31 December 2021

12704885R00193